AN OFFER HE
COULDN'T REFUSE

"It's not too late to make amends," the case officer said at last. "Here's what we're going to do: You're going to show me around. I want to see the dumb agents, cut-outs, drop points, the entire menu. Is that understood?"

Jalak stared at Santoul. "You're not going to cut me off?"

Santoul shook his head. "No. But I expect to see some changes: Lose the beard, the glasses, the stoop. I want a new and improved Jalak or word goes straight to the Dazyldesk."

"I understand. And I want to—"

"No, don't thank me yet, professor. You've still gotta earn this one. We want intell on movements through the flashpoint. And you"— he raised a thick forefinger—"are going to help me recruit the talent who'll gather it."

By James Luceno
Published by Ballantine Books:

RIO PASIÓN

RAINCHASER

A FEARFUL SYMMETRY

ILLEGAL ALIEN

ILLEGAL ALIEN

James Luceno

A Del Rey Book

BALLANTINE BOOKS • NEW YORK

A Del Rey Book
Published by Ballantine Books

Copyright © 1990 by James Luceno

Library of Congress Catalog Card Number: 89-91540

ISBN 0-345-36254-3

Manufactured in the United States of America

First Edition: April 1990

Cover Art by Barclay Shaw

For Brian Daley, partner
in travels, travails,
tomfoolery.

PART ONE

—UPSIDE

PART ONE

—UPSIDE

ONE—

PRACTICALLY EVERYONE REMY RAN INTO lately knew the joke: *What do you do when you find yourself in a quandary?*—the final word compressed so that it came out sounding like NCorp's Dazyldesk tag for the planet and its downside indigs.

"You grab yourself two handfuls of pelt and enjoy the ride!"

Remy, emerging from torpor on the *Chakra* with tingling palms and sinuses plugged from the residual effects of the aromatic tutorials, had heard the joke from a medtech in biostat decomp. The guy's I.D. badge read KRAUS, ELLAR—a broad-shouldered vet with a loose, friendly style, who kept referring to himself as Tiger.

"So I tell myself: Tiger, one more jump and you're gone, okay. No more starslinging, that's clear. Dhone, Ralii, Enddra, Burst . . . I know the sector like I know my own genome. What's left to see besides? I've run with the coats, the 'berries, the slopes. Three tours in the war and Tiger's still retscanning biostat displays. I'm dazzled, I'm fucking screen weary." A lopsided nod had motioned Remy off the padded bench. "No, it's back to home system for this redundancy. Already got my aps in for work in the 'tats."

3

Remy hadn't bothered to ask which orbital habitat, but Tiger told him anyway. "Triple M'd suit me. Even Golden Arches or AmWay. I've got family there, two half brothers."

"I'm from Citi," Remy had told him.

"Figured you for a spacer. So you know Triple M."

"Used to visit about once a year before the new regs. It's a tight wheel. You'd get by."

"The way I see it," Tiger said. "So what's your de-bark dest, Santoul?"

Kwandri, Remy told him, and that's when Tiger had volunteered the joke.

"The fucking *coats*," he laughed.

The planet was listed in the registry files as Q'aantre—which apparently meant "chosen land"—but some deskbound umbilicaled processor in Semiotics had started calling it Kwandri and the name stuck.

Six months of force-fed input had familiarized Remy with Kwandri's cultural basics (just as the aromatic tu-torials had prepared his nose to handle the indig's ol-factory idiom), but he still couldn't get used to having his testicles cupped where a simple handshake would have sufficed.

"You will be a worthy addition to the rite," an effete specimen of the planet's upper class was telling him now, one furred hand lingering at Remy's groin.

The lingua franca scarcely did justice to the ritual greeting. *Your testicles are swelled with anticipation* would have been a more accurate translation. But what with the greeting normally reserved for the middle months of "Red Years" and *Tegganon* a standard-year off, Remy had to ask himself if Norak Baj didn't have more than etiquette in mind.

Densign, the Terran mission's envoy, had made the introductions before slipping off to resume a purposeful orbit through the crowded hall.

"A son for your household," Remy returned, weighing Baj's heavy scrotum in his right hand. The Kwandri's oblique eyes widened with delight. It was the rare Terran who was familiar with *Tegganon*, let alone conversant with the subtleties of ritual exchange.

TechSciDiv had warned Remy about hands-on contact. The Kwandri could pass info to one another through secretions as well as exhalations, but Baj's trousers muffled whatever his glands might have been saying.

"Q'aantre is pleased to welcome all representatives from Earth," he told Remy, steering him by the elbow toward a quieter spot beneath the thickly curtained windows along the west wall.

The indigs were somewhat myopic and hard of hearing by human standards. Remy had once heard them referred to as "the little bigfoot," but he didn't understand the reference.

At just under six feet, Baj was tall and gangly for a Kwandri, his fine coat reddish brown where it peeked from the elastic cuffs of loose-fitting trousers and blousy sleeves, but dark honey blond where swept back in oiled waves from an almost flat, flesh-toned face.

Red Year of the *Lulle*, Remy ventured, summoning a mental image of the indigenous lynxlike creature. Kwandrian births of that particular year were generally of an apolitical type. His eyes had immediately been drawn to the distinguishing blond streaks; such markings, especially if artificially applied, told much about Ser Norak Baj.

A precis would have helped, but the Dazyldesk operations chief had insisted on sending Remy down cold. Better to bring in someone who knew nothing than someone who knew too much.

"I presume you're with the mission legation, Mr. Santoul?" the Kwandri continued in a louder voice. The hall was rapidly filling with fashionably late arrivals, offworlders for the most part, their names and titles announced over a primitive PA system of amp-driven speakers.

"I'm with DisneyCorp," Remy said in the same loud tone. "Artifact and Icon Exchange." The first time he had used the cover there was some trace of hesitation in his voice, but that was absent now.

"Then I'm doubly honored. I knew your predecessor—Ms. Canu." Baj moved from trader's tongue to high Kwandrian to add, "She was a perfume of astonishing clarity. Aggressive yet pleasingly transparent. A bath in a cool mountain stream."

Tiger had told him to expect such appraisals. *The coats don't see well, but they can sniff you out across the room and taste you like a wine.*

"So I've heard," Remy said.

"We were all so sorry to learn of her transfer to . . ."

A heady redolence of enthusiasm momentarily eclipsed the hall's olfactory leitmotif of prosaic scents. But beneath Baj's deliberately projected exhalation, Remy detected suspicion. The tutorials had trained his nose to sculpture the exhalations into human-recognizable scents and their attendant qualitative components. And just now Baj smelled of patent leather and old rugs.

"To Enddra," Remy completed. It was fact, but he tongued the release of a reinforcing oral mist nevertheless. Truth unassisted could rarely be counted on to convince.

The Kwandri's suggestion of a nose twitched. "To Enddra, of course." He adopted a conspiratorial look and began to tug back the right sleeve of his garment. "She made a gift of this shortly before she left."

Remy glanced at the bracelet the Kwandri wore high up on his forearm. "Swatch," he said with feigned professional interest, aware that Baj was continuing to test him. "Earth, early 1990s. Korean assembly, glass crystal set in a plastic housing. Battery-powered."

Baj smiled, wrinkling the skin around narrow eyes. "Correct on all counts."

"It's customary to wear it on the wrist."

"Oh, my," Baj said, blushing, blunt fingers already working at the watch's Velcro band. "These pointers are supposed to turn, I believe. Unfortunately, the thing lacks a battery."

Remy was about to say that he would see what he could do about procuring one, when Densign reappeared, his first orbit complete.

"And how is Mr. Santoul comporting himself, Ser Baj? Nothing untoward in his emanations, I trust?"

The Kwandri stiffened perceptibly. "I think the Terran Consortium has finally seen fit to send us an educated Earther, Mr. Densign."

Remy concealed a smile.

"Yes, well I'm sure you're right about that," Densign said, gravely voiced and mimicking Baj's canted posture.

He was a long-faced, stoop-shouldered man of about sixty, with heavy jowls, a bulbous nose, and pronounced sacks under close-set eyes. His hair was black and wiry, brushed straight back from a hairline distinguished by twin scoops of forehead flesh. Envoy to Xella before the war, a founding member of the Orbital Club . . . Remy could picture him relaxing under two milligrams of Halflife at the club's on-station franchise, a hired hand for company in the baths. Rumor had it there was Dick Nixon donor-clone in Densign's ancestry.

Baj had his wide animal mouth arranged in a grin. "I was just lamenting the fact that so few Terran trade products reach us." He shrugged. "Of course one hears stories this is about to change. But who can say, given the Grand Assembly's current infatuation with Xella."

Remy didn't need his reeducated nose to tell him that Baj was baiting the envoy. Densign cleared his throat with ambassadorial vigor.

"Naturally, the Consortium would like to see trade

relations improved between Terra and Kwandri.'' He gestured with a manicured hand to Remy. "That's one of the prime reasons DisneyCorp was invited downside, Ser Baj."

Remy heard it coming.

"*One* of the prime reasons? Then there are secondary purposes?"

Densign's head seemed about to disappear down the round collar of his formal tunic. "I only meant to suggest that artifact exchange might speed the process some."

The envoy's response triggered a confusing array of aromas from Baj: irritation, optimism, eagerness— coffee and vanilla extract, peaches and tomatoes, along with several more elusive scents.

"There is certainly a place for DisneyCorp's resources, Mr. Densign—as we both know. It concerns some, however, that the Consortium has placed Q'aantre in a position where in order to be awarded this priceless orbital tower, it must at the same time accept to heart the political ideology of the culture that perfected it." Baj summoned a sigh. "Perhaps we are destined to remain planet-bound after all."

"Extraplanetary travel is the right of all worlds," Densign insisted, stating mission policy, "not a privilege for Terra, Xella, or any other planetary system to grant."

"And yet your two great systems possess what amounts to complete control of the technologies. *And* you have seen fit to strip the Raliish of that right in the wake of their defeat."

Densign's face, jowls quivering, was growing ruddier by the moment. Remy wished he could take him aside and give him a whiff of the provocative scents Baj was emitting.

"If Kwandri is suddenly so eager for space, Ser Baj, perhaps the Assembly should be persuaded to contract with one of the private corps."

"And barter what? some would ask. This precious wormhole the Inner Arm League had deigned to consider part of our celestial territory?"

"Exactly that, yes. This alone should convince you of the importance we place on self-determination."

"Self-determination!" Baj snorted, the three waxy nostrils of his nub of nose flared. "Yes, I suppose you could have swept down on us as conquerors rather than far-flung brethren. But perhaps you've forgotten what it's like to be confronted with the sudden realization that your race is but a primitive, inconsequential member of this would-be fraternity of worlds." The Kwandri regarded the two Earthmen curiously. "Perhaps you have never known."

Densign relaxed his scowl. "Contact was a gradual process for us. But your planet is far from inconsequential," he was quick to add. "Cosmicization is the destiny of all worlds."

Baj studied the hairless palms of his five-fingered hands. "Ah, yes, the evolutionary goal," he said quietly. "Cosmic consciousness, the planetary mind. That most important element of the cultural view we are asked to embrace in exchange for the tower. So at odds with the quaint traditional values Q'aantre perpetuates." He looked up from his hands. "Again, Mr. Densign, it strikes some that Terra's aim is a self-serving one indeed. Xella makes no such demands on us."

"The Xell'em are superstitious bas—" Densign began, but stopped himself.

Baj's grin returned. "Yes, they are like us in that respect. Ripe, I suspect, for conversion."

Remy decided that hanging around listening to Baj and Densign debate Kwandri's future wasn't going to get him anywhere, so he excused himself and set off trailing a servant shouldering a drink tray.

The burnished-metal service bar in the hall's domed antechamber was doing a brisk business in offworld liqueurs, but Remy was after a sweet mug of the local brew. He'd sampled the beer on debarking days ago and hadn't been able to slake his thirst for the stuff since. Thick and amber-colored, it was served warm and topped with pungent spice, as was only fitting on a perpetually chilled world.

Several Kwandri Assembly members sought to place themselves in his path as he jinked through the crowd, but he was successful in avoiding direct contact and returning greetings without arresting forward motion. Moments later he was treating himself to a long pull from an embossed tankard, while his blue eyes scanned the room.

The Consortium was well represented by Densign's mission staff and a score of high-profile Terrans speaking for various private corps and special interest groups. There was a scattering of singletons as well, rogue spacers by the look of them, the sons and daughters of wealthy families who fled the orbital habitats when Earth Force had moved in to quash the rebellion.

Remy tipped the tankard to his lips in a silent toast.

Enddrese, sinister-looking in robes and headgear of prewar Xell'em design, comprised the offworlder majority. Like the Kwandri and the dozen odd sentient lifeforms who inhabited the inner curve of the Arm, they were humanoid in aspect and in character, swarthy endomorphic bipeds with unreadable eyes and rotten dispositions.

Subscribing to the NCorp line, Remy accepted that every planetary race chosen to ascend evolution's ladder to self-awareness and cosmicization was predetermined to assume the form for a time; that every creature spit from an ocean or dropped from a tree eventually arrived at an upright two-legged stance.

But if the proper physical form for evolvement had been found, the proper mindset most often had not. For while this very *sameness* had made communications and information exchange such a straightforward affair at

the onset of galactic expansion, it had likewise made
warfare a simple matter in the end. The Consortium,
however—firmly convinced that its victorious emer-
gence from the war constituted proof of what lay in
store for the right-thinking—had undertaken a crusade
to correct that oft-encountered psychic imbalance. And
so NCorp had been conceived, initially to implement
the Consortium's policies and to counter the plans of
all those who would stand in the way of planetary
wholeness and conversion.

But with war's end the intel corp had fallen on hard
times, and there was even talk about phasing out NCorp
entirely. Several thousand operatives had already been
reassigned, and Remy figured it was only a matter of
time before similar notification surfaced on his own
screen. He hoped that wouldn't happen until he had had
a chance to tip the scales in his own favor.

Remy wasn't sure just what was expected of him on
Kwandri, but the jump costs alone made the operation
a high-priority concern. Then there were the additional
costs of the olfactory and tactile tutorials . . . It was a
willingness to undergo periodic neural rewiring that had
kept Remy out in the field gathering HUMINT while
most of his peers were umbilicaled to consoles back at
Center with neat rows of cyberports dimpling their
heads; but the buccal and pore modifications were about
as far as Remy cared to go with implants.

He wasn't, however, the only spy in the room. And
even now a raven-haired Xell'em female was assessing
him over the rim of an upraised wine goblet.

Remy favored her with the friendly nod he'd been
using all evening, and followed it up with a Kwandrian
gesture of salutation before edging back into the crowd.
Odors in the thick of things were cloying, floral—save
for the occasional whiff of offworlder moodscents—but
devoid of data in any case. Where Remy's nose picked
up traces of genuine Kwandri emanations they were of
a lighthearted, socially acceptable sort.

He paused once to drain the last of the beer, and in so doing spotted what looked to be the best seat in the house: a circumferential balcony some fifty feet above the hall's polished floor.

But first, another drink.

One of the taller beings in the room, it took him only seconds to relocate the Kwandri with the drink tray. He began to work his way past a dozen or more food tables and arrived finally at the foot of a sweeping marble staircase, only to find that the servant had already moved on. In his place stood a group of Kwandri females, who were waiting for the elevator to return from the balcony. The five appeared to be in some sort of huddle, an illusion maintained by the wedge of heel bone that lent a forward cant to Kwandrian carriage. The slimmest among them—a girl of seventeen or so—watched Remy approach and exhaled something that brought the entire group around.

There was less somatotype diversity among the Kwandri than some of the other Inner Arm dwellers, and the typical young adult female was long-legged, high-breasted, and narrow-hipped.

Remy fashioned a flat triangle with his hands and brought the backs of his extended fingers to his lips. Giggling, the females returned the greeting, delicate hands at mouths to stifle private exhalations. The one nearest touched a forefinger to her upper lip, then motioned to Remy. He considered for a moment that he had neglected some detail crucial to the ritual exchange, but soon understood that the girl was merely commenting on the ridge of beer foam adorning his upper lip.

The five were dressed alike in woolen shawls and shapeless long-sleeved gowns cinched by narrow belts; outfits designed to be practical and unappealing, as dictated by tradition, which restricted the wearing of bright clothing or jewelry to the three months preceding *Tegganon*. Answering to restraints of a biological nature, the Kwandri female's coat was dun-colored—save during estrus, when it took on a red sheen—whereas the male's could run what someone back at Center called "the Crayola gamut." It was somewhat coarse as well, and sparse across the whole of her ventral side—*enticingly* sparse, to hear Tiger tell it.

"I hope he's still here at *Tegganon*," the slim one said as Remy was licking the foam from his lip.

The fucking coats, Remy could hear Tiger laugh. *You grab yourself two handfuls of pelt and enjoy the ride.*

Back in the main room, the crowd was beginning to congregate around the hall's central arch—a sign that Ambassador Xu had arrived. The Xell'em were known for their entrances. They'd certainly put on a show during the war, Remy reminded himself. Laying waste to Raliish cities with little of the fanfare that attended their social and political events. He had had frequent dealings with their operatives then—NCorp and the Manifest's intel networks allied for a time—but peace had since made them competitors.

Musicians and dancers led the line as the legation filed in, playing to Kwandri's dearth of visual and auditory exotica. Percussion and wind instruments conspired in riotous concert, while Xell'em youths wearing brass bells and finger cymbals gyrated in gauzy costumes. Behind, marched a phalanx of soldiers outfitted in antique armor; a resplendent retinue of fifty or more masked maidens and stately attendants; and last, the hover litter bearing the ambassador himself, a cruel-visaged male of indeterminate age, his gilded torso configured into a twisted cross-legged posture.

Remy watched in childlike fascination. As the crowd parted to afford the Xell'em space, the air grew loud with an overwhelming array of intoxicating exhalations. Remy felt himself begin to respond to the offworlders' display; to experience the sights and sounds the way the Kwandri were experiencing them. The loss of control was unnerving at first, but he found that regulated breathing could successfully dampen the olfactory impact.

TechSci had equipped him with filter implants to safeguard against sensory overload, but the chief of station on the Kwandri wheel had suggested he see just how much he could withstand before bringing them into play.

The extravaganza was nothing more than the opposite face of the operation NCorp has set in motion by inserting DisneyCorp reps downside, taking advantage of a sudden back-to-basics movement that was sweeping the local group. Traders in Terrana, as Earth artifacts were called, were making fortunes on dozens of worlds by selling off bits of the planet's preexpansionist past. Genuine artifacts of that time had even become a basis for currency in places.

NCorp hoped to further Terra's chances with the Grand Assembly by bartering period pieces for Kwandrian hearts and minds. Xella hoped to hold on to its influence with costume and pageantry.

At the heart of it, though, Terrans and Xell'em—despite the latter's penchant for dermal design and cranial deformation—were not all that different. Both cultures tended to be as acquisitive as they were inquisitive, and both, in their consolidation efforts among the worlds of the local group, claimed to be guided by truth. But where the Consortium recognized one unifying cosmic principle, the Manifest—much like Earth's ancient Maya lords—saw a plethora of gods and demiurges. A few historians had advanced the view that the Xell'em actually *were* Earth's Maya. But Remy had enough trouble comprehending trends of the past hundred years to bother much with those that had shaped the previous two thousand.

By now the Xell'em had spiraled their dazzling parade to the center of the floor, and Xu and his near-chinless wife were preparing to address the crowd.

Remy, stalled not far from the elevators, spied the

beer tray bobbing nearby and began to angle toward it while the ambassador was unfolding himself atop the hover litter. But no sooner had the Xell'em eased out of his contortion and uttered his first words than the hall was rocked by the concussive reports of three separate explosions.

Remy ducked along with everyone else in the immediate area, but surfaced grinning as he watched the ambassador's cleverly orchestrated spectacle deteriorate into chaos. The Xell'em presented quite a picture, crouched on his bit of baroque while a hundred Kwandri ran crazed circles around him, laying down a miasma of unadulterated dread.

"She is saying that she likes you better with the face comb," Baj said uncertainly, using the lingua franca term for mustache. "But I'm not sure I understand. You didn't have one earlier this evening."

Remy accented his bow to the Kwandri teen with a long-distance smile, one hand behind his back concealing a skewer of roasted meat and tuber. "From the beer," he explained.

"The *yika*?"

Remy turned to face him, toothing the last piece of meat from the stick. "I had a tankard inside. Left some foam on my lip. Here," he added, touching himself.

"Ah, of course," Baj said with a slight laugh.

They were standing halfway up the ramplike stairway that fronted the hall, Remy trying to stomp some warmth into his feet, Baj at ease in his natural coat and blousy homespun. Densign and a few of his staffers were several steps below, wrapped in warmcloaks emblazoned with the mission's pyramidal logo. Most of the offworlder contingents had moved back inside, including the Xell'em, who were trying hard to pick up where they'd left off.

The Kwandri were easily sidetracked when it came to bombs.

Remy licked grease from his fingertips and tucked his hands under his arms. "Damn, it got cold. Shoulda grabbed my jacket."

"Nature played a cruel trick by turning you into the world naked, Remy," Baj said. "But speaking of jackets . . . Ms. Canu once showed me a holo-image of something called a bomber jacket. Do you happen to own one of those yourself?"

Remy snorted. "You and I could retire, Norak. You're talking museum piece."

"Just a thought."

Baj had more to say, but was scarcely into his thought when two uniformed police interrupted him. Remy watched Baj descend the stairs to rendezvous with a stocky male, who had Special Investigations written all over him. SPECVES agents were said to be masters of deadly scents and secretions. A pair of Xell'em advisers accompanied the Kwandri officer, shaved and deformed heads encased in quilted thermal bonnets.

A block west of the Grand Assembly hall the towering iron gates of the Xell'em embassy had been blown clear off their hinges. When Remy and a hundred others from the panicked hall had arrived on the scene, the police were already cordoning off the street; not that there was much to see or smell, save for twisted metal and a security booth that had seen better days, and a lingering odor of angry discontent.

Floodlights illuminated the area now—huge, electrically powered things, sweeping tight arcs across nearby alleyways and rooftops. Kwandri's night was the blackest of any world. Even so, entire families of curious Kwandri were hanging out of upper-floor apartment windows, and scores of vendors had scurried in from the Old City to set up food and drink stalls on the broad sidewalks.

"Someone has a keen sense of timing," Remy said as Densign approached. "Just when things were getting interesting inside.'' He blew into his hands and cupped them to his face.

The envoy grunted something unintelligible. ''The Xell'em will demand a full accounting. I pity the group responsible.''

Kwandri had recently enacted legislation calling for harsh punishments for terrorist acts. Few on the Grand Assembly wanted to see the promise of extraplanetary travel jeopardized.

The Terran mission, as well as banks belonging to both camps, had all seen their share of protests and pyrotechnic, stinkbomb displays of discontent. Small wonder the Consortium was reluctant to construct an embassy downside, Remy thought.

''Conversion's rarely won without a cost,'' he commented, quoting NCorp's Dazyldesk chief.

Densign, head lowered and shoulders hunched beneath the warmcloak, scowled at him. Remy ignored the look, motioning with his chin toward Baj and the Special Investigations team. ''What's he do? Baj, I mean. I didn't get a chance to ask.''

Densign glanced over his shoulder. ''Interior Ministry. A low-level functionary, but family money has kept him well connected if not especially well placed.''

Baj returned with the SPECVES officer, who introduced himself as Lieutenant Els Matut. Baj explained that the bombs were believed to have been relatively simple devices.

''But the triggering mechanisms were of offworld design,'' Matut said leadingly. ''They bear similarity to certain Terran-made devices.''

Densign looked uncomfortable.

''I'll bet you had help with that one,'' Remy said.

Matut directed a look at his Xell'em advisers, who had remained at the foot of the staircase. ''Tracing the origin of the mechanisms could prove difficult.''

Densign said, ''The mission will of course do all it can to facilitate the search.''

Matut offered a crisp nod. "The perpetrators will be apprehended and questioned. They'll tell us what we need to know."

Remy's nose burned. Baj's concern smelled of ash and urine; the lieutenant's determination carried the olfactory sting of fried electrical circuitry.

TWO—

"Now I recognize the face," the Kwandri station chief told Remy after the cabin hatch had chirped a sequence of secure tones. She continued to appraise him from behind a slab of matte-black desktop, long legs crossed underneath, one softboot-encased foot tapping the carpet. "The opticals we received made you look Arabic. What was the donor-clone name?"

"Beatty," Remy said, suspecting she just wanted to hear him announce it. "Warren. Film actor, turn of the twentieth."

"You're DiNA-pure?"

Remy shook his head. "Last I heard there were two pure living on TransAm. I've got three generations of parentals behind me." He paused to show her a roguish grin. "Though I'm told I retained all the good parts."

The station chief nodded, but didn't smile back. "That's right, your family were spacers, weren't they." She ran a fingertip along the cheap, neck-breaking desktop screen. "Citi, it shows here. And on your ring if I'm not mistaken."

Remy caressed the ring's raised symbol—a glass ramp modeled after the crown of a landmark Earth skyscraper. "At the end."

19

He recalled what the liaison officer aboard the *Chakra* had offered about the station chief. *Name's Audjo Ishida. Army brat, born in Singapore and raised on half-dozen in-system bases. Transferred to the Kwandri wheel eleven months ago and not very happy about it. Trying hard to make a name for herself. Degrees in systems analysis and motivational psych. Act cyborg, you'll get along.*

Audjo Ishida was narrowing her dark eyes at the screen. Attractive dark eyes, Remy decided. Nicely proportioned if unremarkable features; a lamp-tanned face of planes and hollows, with Occidental eyes and glossed lips. She wore her black hair short and straight in what would once have been termed a boyish cut. The liaison man claimed that she wasn't as glacial as she pretended to be, but Remy didn't see that it was any of his concern. Although it was interesting to note they shared the same taste in earrings.

Ishida motioned him to a bench seat. "Relax, Santoul," she said, glancing up briefly.

Remy set his attaché down and adjusted the height of the seat to accommodate his long legs. He'd chosen an outfit of twentieth-century design for the appointment—pleated trousers and a tight-fitting satin jacket from the DisneyCorp wardrobe File Integration Division had assembled—but contagion control had confiscated the clothes and issued him a jumpsuit that was an inch short in the sleeves and way too tight in the crotch. The narrow bench seat made matters worse.

"A moment more," Ishida said, raising a hand.

He rested his left ankle on his right knee and did what he could to stretch the synthetic fabric of the jumpsuit. Somewhere a seam gave, and Ishida looked up at the popping sound.

"Do you always fidget so much, Santoul?"

"The jumpsuit," he explained sheepishly, plucking it away from his chest. "Gave me one off the kids' rack."

The station chief's gaze returned to the desktop, searching for what Remy couldn't imagine. Maybe she was behind in her work, he thought, or monitoring her estrogen levels. Or maybe it was her habit to call up an operative's dossier only after she'd formed a first impression. Why else would she have made a point of bringing up his ancestry? It wasn't anything he could alter; besides, he felt that he had overcome most of the donor-clone's proclivities, grown into his own person, as it were. This far from home you didn't meet many people who recognized the Warren Beatty in him. Or cared, if they did.

"An impressive résumé," Ishida said. "You've done well these past four years. Making up for past mistakes, is that it?"

She didn't mention the *Ambii'th* Incident directly, but she might as well have. "Aren't we all," Remy told her.

He slipped a cherry-flavored stim-wafer into his mouth and sucked on it while he took in the office. That it was inner rim told him just how NCorp rated on the wheel. You could languish in here watching the tugs or the shaft elevators, or you could do as the station chief had: move in some personal items, requisition a couple of potted plants, turn your back to the cabin's narrow rectangle of viewport. Maybe sit daydreaming about a reassignment downside or a transfer to some office on the outer rim where DisneyCorp, Golden Arches, and the other star corps played.

NCorp execs had enjoyed that privilege during the war; now it was enough to be awarded office space in a wheel and receive the occasional invite to embassy functions.

He let out a slow, cleansing breath as the stim-wafer went to work on his frazzled nervous system. He was still a bit lagged from biostat, and his sinuses were raw from exposure to Kwandri's scent-laden air. Ishida had had him shuttled up from the surface six hours ago, but he and a handful of Densign's staffers had been whisked off by contagion control for four hours worth of med-scans and ultrasonic bombardment. It was one of those things field agents were supposed to get used to, but for Remy the experience always summoned memories of the distrust and outright paranoia that prevailed in the orbital habitats before the rebellion.

"This what I can expect every time I come up the well?" Remy asked at the stim-wafer's prompting.

Ishida stared at him for a moment, then blanked the screen with a verbal command. "What's that, San-toul?"

"CC. I'm prepped for more viruses than I can name and they keep me chambered for four hours. Hasn't anyone down there been apprised of my antigen pro-file?"

Ishida snorted, leaning back, folding her arms under her small breasts. "I won't even entertain that. First of all we don't want you singled out on the wheel or pla-netside. But more important, we're dealing with biota from one of this sector's least understood worlds." She shook her head. "I shouldn't have to explain this to a spacer. Of course, if it's going to be an issue . . ."

"Who said anything about an issue," Remy said, laughing to diffuse things. "Assign me a few couriers, I won't even mention it again."

"No couriers on this one."

Remy shrugged. "Then I guess I can live with the delay if you can."

"Damn right you'll live with it." Ishida swiveled her chair left, then right. "Tell me about the Xell'em re-ception. I understand you made contact."

"Densign pushed me on a file-fiddler with the Inte-rior Ministry, name of Baj."

"Is that Res Baj?"

"Norak Baj," Remy said. "Secondborn." Only four first names being possible on Kwandri for males and

females alike: Res, Norak, Els, and Ayyum, corre-
sponding to first, second, third and fourthborn.

"Anything there?"

"I don't think so. He's had his forelock laser-combed
and confesses to an interest in Terrana. But he's tight
with Special Investigations. A Lieutenant Els Matut."

"What about the explosive device?"

"Low-impact damage to the embassy real estate and
one helluva stench. The Xell'em have SPECVES
convinced the dispersion earmarks match our N-14 det-
onator profiles."

"They're suggesting we're supplying the dissidents?"

"Stands to reason we'd try to falsify popular support.
Anyway, Xella's been hit harder than we have downside." Gingerly, Remy touched his nose. "By the way,
they're following me around."

"Who is?"

"SPECVES. The hotel suite's online."

"Do you need a workaround?"

"Not yet. The DisneyCorp cover's holding."

Ishida paused to consider this. "I'd be interested to
hear your assessment of the situation, Santoul. Do you
think we can succeed in our efforts?"

"Win over the Grand Assembly? Sure we can.
They're already taken with us—the indigs you meet in
the streets. The Xell'em might have been first to insert
themselves, but most of the Kwandri don't seem to enjoy having them around. Except when they put on one
of their sound and lights. They've isolated themselves.
They've got nothing to offer. They don't interact with
the local merchants. The streets reek of discontent. You
hear whispered fears of secret alliances between the
Manifest and the Grand Assembly. The Kwandri got rid
of their aristocracy a century ago. They don't want to
see it return in a new form."

Ishida's expression had changed; her round eyes held

a hint of approval. "Very astute, Santoul. I'm impressed."

"Yeah, well, I still don't know what I'm doing here, do I."

The station chief was suddenly all business again. "You've been briefed on Kwandri's strategic importance?"

"Some," Remy said, "if by that you mean the wormhole."

"And what's your reaction to our handling of the matter?"

"My *reaction*?"

"For example, do you feel that Kwandri has a right to the wormhole as the League suggests, or should we simply use this system as we please?"

Remy thought about it and laughed.

"There's something funny, Santoul?"

"In a way. I mean, first we tell them there's a black hole out at the edge of Dazyl's wind—a hole that allows ships to jump to a star system Kwandri's native scopes weren't even sophisticated enough to pinpoint ten years ago. Same time we assure them the hole is *their* hole, that we're perfectly willing to pay for the right to use it." Remy sniffled. "The Consortium'll even throw in an orbital tower. Did anyone back at Center actually believe they'd say 'Sorry, not interested.'?"

"No one thought that," Ishida said flatly. "But you still haven't told me how you *feel*. It doesn't disturb you that we've gifted them with a thousand years of progress in less than a decade? That we've moved them preindustrial to stellar overnight?"

Remy ran a hand over his mouth, realizing all at once that he was being fluttered, vetted. He began to wonder where the detectors were concealed. In the holoportraits on the desk, perhaps, or inside the flowerpots.

"Why should it disturb me? Extraplanetary contact has helped unify the planet. I'd rather have them accept our interpretation of progress than Xella's."

"But perhaps you think it's time we relaxed our efforts some—to allow Kwandri time to sort things out. As the product of several generations of spacers, I imagine you have strong feelings about cultural freedoms."

The seat, Remy decided. The bench seat itself was the device. "What chance does Kwandri have with the Xell'em ensconced on the surface? We should *increase* our efforts if anything. Flood Kwandri with the best we have to offer. Look what happened on the habitats when Earth relaxed control. We grew a systemful of debased ideologies."

The station chief shook her head and smiled. "You're very clever, Santoul."

"I'll tell my teachers you said so." He smiled back, holding her gaze. Ishida broke it off and stood up, bringing her hands to her thighs in a downward wiping motion.

"There's more at stake here than the Consortium's interests in influencing Grand Assembly policy," she began. "For the past eleven standard-months, the Xell'em have been making frequent use of the wormhole. We've only been able to monitor the destinations of a few of their ships, but there's reason to believe that Xella is moving armaments into former Raliish-controlled sectors."

Remy arched an eyebrow. "What's the traffic like at the egress?"

"Significant. But no incidents yet. Xella could be preparing to move against the Burst and Daleth systems."

"That's fuzzy logic," Remy said. "They know we wouldn't sit still for that. Center must be misreading it."

Ishida threw him an ice-cold look. "Are you presuming to know NCorp's assessment?"

Remy accepted the rebuke, deciding it wasn't worth an argument. Even if the story was a fabrication, an-

other of Center's attempts to keep itself alive with false
alerts, he had no way of knowing. News in the outer
reaches traveled by rumor, and people like Ishida were
paid to exercise careful control over the facts.

"So Xella's picking up where Ralii left off, is that
it?" he asked.

Ishida offered a tight-lipped nod. "We can't allow
those systems to fall—not when they're so close to accepting Consortium creed."

Remy was ahead of her. "But the Consortium wants
proof before it presents its case to the League. Troop
strengths, destinations, shipping manifests."

"We had all of that until about four months ago.
Then the flow began to weaken. What intel we continue
to receive is suspect."

"Then someone's gotten to our agents," Remy said,
thinking out loud. "What about the downside case officer—is there a problem?"

Ishida was quiet for a moment. "That remains to be
seen." Remy waited for her to finish. "There's an
NCorp person on-station I want you to see before you
go back down the well. His name is Dakou, Phajol
Dakou."

Warren Beatty, in white ruffled shirt and blue trousers, piloted the two-wheeled, surface-effect vehicle
through a tight curve of asphalt roadway, past pastel-
colored stucco homes and sweeping lawns of emerald
grass. He had just been fucked by several women and
was about to engage in an emotional showdown with
the one he professed to love.

The woman of his past.

Remy was familiar with the flickdisk, although not
the dimensionalized version running in Dakou's office.
One of his grandfather's favorites, he had viewed it several times as a teen and had recently sat through it again
as part of the DisneyCorp cover training. Flicks were
venerated for what they had contributed to the early

formation of group mind; a major step on the path to cosmicization.

Watching *Shampoo* now made Remy wonder if he had entirely rid himself of the donor's persona. Jasna was the one in Remy's past; on Dhone at last report, where the *Ambii'th* horror had its start. Remy had opted for a more active form of penance.

"A motorcycle," Dakou said in disbelief.

"Monoxide machine," Remy said. "Ancient history."

Dakou deactivated the player. "I hope you don't mind. I sent a runner up to DisneyCorp's library as soon as Audjo informed me you'd be dropping by."

"No, it's great, uh, quite a surprise." The Beatty in Remy talking.

"You do bear a striking resemblance. Except around the eyes, I think."

Phajol Dakou's high brown forehead was deeply furrowed, even when his thin face was at ease; a web of laugh lines surrounding deep-set eyes, an upward turn to the corners of his mouth. He was from Dow-'Bishi habitat by way of Juba, an African micronation that had since been engulfed by Sahil.

"My mother's side," Remy told him.

"There are more in the library." Dakou glanced at the memo screen on his desk. "One entitled *Heaven Can Wait*, another called *Reds*—a political thriller, I believe." He gestured to the player. "I thought this one was some sort of product advertisement."

Remy made a mental note to inform Ishida that all Beatty features should be excluded from DisneyCorp's downside film consignments. The last thing he needed was to find himself the overnight star of Kwandri's burgeoning Terrana-infatuated underground. Unless that was part of NCorp's plan.

Another inner-rim cabinspace, Dakou's office was a step up from the station chief's, spacious and somewhat better situated, with a view that encompassed several orbital toruses operated by offworlder concerns and private corps.

The tall African's official title was diplomatic counsel, but in this Dakou wore a trio of hats. As the person whose function it was to assist Earthers in adjusting to alien cultures he worked for the mission. MediCare paid him to allay fears of terrorist reprisal attacks, treat addictions to exotic drugs, or therapy language difficulties or exophobias about hosting luncheons, interfacing with servants, conducting the business of day-to-day living. When running neurometric evaluations, he answered solely to Center.

"I suppose we should get down to business," Dakou said. A verbal numeric called up a holo where Warren Beatty's motorcycle had negotiated the curve moments before. Remy found himself looking into the face of a man who had been away from home far too long.

"His name is Simon Jalak," Dakou explained, coming across the room akimbo. "Professor Simon Jalak. NCorp's man on Kwandri."

"Recently fluttered, I hope."

Dakou laughed. "Last month. Routine reevaluation."

"Here or downside?"

"Downside. I doubt contagion control would let the beard through."

Remy nodded. But it wasn't only Jalak's full beard that troubled him; it was the shoulder-length hair and the worried, almost feral eyes behind thick glasses.

"Glasses," Remy said, shaking his head in wonder.

"He refused elective microsurgery."

"Man's a frequent flier. More of this back-to-basics spread."

"He did his best to dazzle the detectors, but there's only so much one can do to alter urine, blood, hair, and hormone workups." Data bars took shape alongside the primary holo-field as the counsel spoke.

"What's this one?" Remy asked, motioning to an obviously elevated reading.

"Serotonin level. But we expected that. Epiphenomenon associated with the chemosensory training and olfactory tutorials. Your own biochem would undoubtedly reveal similar elevations." Dakou paused. "While we're on the subject—"

"No complaints—except here," Remy said, pinching the bridge of his nose.

"What about the palms?"

Remy flexed his hands. "Everything I touch downside starts them tingling. But I haven't had a chance to put the tactile-training to the test."

"I'll prescribe something to lessen the sensation."

"Don't bother. Just tell me about Jalak."

Dakou tapped out a note to himself. "He's quite well known in culturist circles. Ethnobotanist, linguist, epigrapher. Did extensive fieldwork on Dhone."

Remy stiffened at mention of the planet. Was the counsel trying to flutter him now? He masked his concern and pressed on. "How long with the corp?"

"Four years—all of it on Kwandri. Center's responsible for his being here."

"Recruited?"

Dakou shook his head. "Jalak initiated the approach on Dhone. Kwandri was still under stringent entry regulations. He wanted in in the worst way."

"He cut a deal."

"NCorp already had a small network of agents in place. Jalak was told he could do all the ethno-fieldwork he wanted, provided he was willing to run the program and recruit local talent. Which he did, with excellent results."

"Until a couple of months ago."

Dakou cracked his knuckles. "It goes further back than that. The test results show a gradual but steady deterioration." He called up additional datagraphs and color-enhanced brain scans. "The upper graph is a biorhythmic projection, the lower an actuality collation. Notice how the downward trends of the middle and lower ones coincide.''

Remy studied the moving lines of the holo. "What's the middle?''

"Testosterone levels.'' Dakou indicated the brain scans. "The fluctuations are reflected here, in the dorsal thalamus. We also discovered changes in the limbic chemosensory pathways and the amygdala.''

Remy scratched at his thick hair. "So what are you saying—the man needs a macfuck? If that's all it is, shuttle down some software. I'm sure the wheel's equipped to cater to all tastes.''

Dakou made a side to side motion with his head. "That's not the problem. Jalak has never placed much importance on sexuality—his own, that is. The man spent seven years on Dhone without so much as *seeing* another Earther. He's an outsider, here or wherever it is that captures his attention. No, I think the biochem changes reflect something more basic at work. Jalak is in some sense *becoming* a Kwandri.''

"He's gone indig.''

"A deliberate transition, essential for the fieldwork.'' The counsel regarded Remy. "You've been briefed on the *Tegganon* ritual?''

"Universal estrus,'' Remy said. "Mating once every two standard-years. Unless, I hear, you're willing to do or endure a substantial amount of soft tissue trauma.''

"Every two years if you're one of the fortunate ones,'' Dakou amended.

"But you said Jalak is asexual.''

"Correct. But he's been downside long enough to have experienced two *Tegganons* firsthand. Who knows how far he's gone. These physical and biochemical changes—the hormone levels, the long hair, the sudden myopia—they could be the result of, well, intimate contact. There's a lot about Kwandri sexuality that we simply don't understand.''

"Maybe that Jalak doesn't even understand."

"Or hasn't told us." Dakou paused. "His accounting reports have grown more and more creative. Center's willing to stand for only so much."

Remy thought things through. "Our friend has forgotten under whose good graces he was installed here." He looked up at Dakou. "I'll have a talk with him, see if I can't learn why he's gone floppy on us. Can I threaten him with deportation, or is that just going to send him running?"

"By all means threaten him. I'm certain that he's decided to make Kwandri his life's work. Expulsion from paradise may be the shock needed to bring him back online. You might also point out that Xell'em control of the Grand Assembly would amount to the same end for him. It isn't likely they'll tolerate his presence—especially if an account of his past affiliations should surface."

They discussed options; then spent another hour sharing a flask of brandy and comparing notes on places and stations they had in common. Remy felt a kinship with the counsel, who for all his hard edges was still a fine drinking partner.

"Hey, Santoul," Dakou said as Remy was palming the cabin's hatch release sensor. "What's the difference between a flashpoint jump and sex on Kwandri?"

Remy tried to recall if he'd already heard it. "I'm coming up blank."

Dakou grinned. "In a jump you get to use a hole."

THREE—

Simon Jalak FELT THE BLOOD DRAIN FROM his face as the vein-reader issued a short verification tone. The NCorp man from Department Five removed his right hand from the reader screen and folded himself into a high-backed chair inadequately suited to his size.

"Any problems, Professor?" the man asked.

"No, no, of course not," Jalak managed, staring fixedly at the archaic device's data display. "I just, that is, just . . . give me a moment please."

Jalak didn't dare raise a hand, but he could feel beads of perspiration squeezing from his brow. An icy runnel coursed down the left side of his face, just in front of his ear, working its way through the tight coils of his beard.

Below a computer-generated portrait overlaid with the legend, D-5, C-NC-S, R-18, the screen displayed the name SANTOUL, REMY. There was more, but Jalak was having difficulty reading past the Department Five designation. And what purpose would it serve now to know the operative's personal history, his birthplace and war record.

Cautiously, Jalak raised his gray eyes, fearful of what would greet them from across the room. But Santoul wasn't even looking at him; he had taken a wooden carving from the shelf and was turning it about in his large hands. Almost appreciatively, Jalak thought.

And indeed there was something calm and composed about Santoul. The handsome face—cherubic, Jalak wanted to say—under an undisciplined thatch of brown hair. The wide mouth, even teeth, athletic physique. Eyes a deeper blue than Q'aantre's crystalline sky, matched in shade by a single cabochon earring and a choker of Enddrese burial beads from Dhone, of all worlds. The suit was two-piece, an iridescent woolen loom-weave appropriate for a DisneyCorp rep.

The cover I.D. was what had gotten Santoul through the front door fifteen minutes earlier; but then there were few Jalak would refuse entry to his home.

He continued to marvel at the man. And yet the truth behind the calm exterior was pulsing from the reader screen: Department Five. Penetration, Counterinsurgency, Political Assassination.

"You've come to kill me," Jalak said softly.

Santoul carefully replaced the statue and turned to him. "Kill you, Professor?"

Jalak's bony hands fluttered in spite of his best efforts to keep them still. "Please, Santoul, don't game me."

"Remy, Professor."

Jalak said nothing.

"This room," the operative began, leaving something unsaid.

"It's secure."

Santoul grinned and popped a cherry-colored stim-wafer into his mouth. "Then let's have a talk. You can start by telling me what you think you've done to warrant termination, and I'll tell you whether you're right or wrong. How's that sound?"

Jalak worked his jaw. "I asked you not to safeload it. We both know why you've come."

Santoul curled his fingertips in a beckoning motion.

Jalak sighed resignedly. "Your people are convinced

they're no longer getting a proper return on their investment. The current has slowed, the well's run dry . . . God knows what clichés are in vogue back at Center. But I'll tell you something, Santoul: It's not my fault. It's the Xell'em. It's this damn Special Investigations squad they persuaded the Assembly to create. My agents are frightened—and with good cause. There have been seven arrests this past month alone. Seven, Santoul. Do you have any idea what that means?" Jalak snorted, gesturing dismissively. "No, of course you wouldn't. You see only what Center tells you to see."

Santoul's fingers formed a steeple, which he bounced against his lower lip. "Tell me about the embassy bomb. Was that your work?"

Jalak shook his head. "Locals. A noninterventionist group opposed to all offworlder influence. A request was made for fuses. I put the parties in touch using a once-removed agent as go-between."

"And it took SPECVES all of about fifteen minutes to determine those triggers were Titan-manufactured."

"I was assured they came with a long history. They were carried down aboard an Enddrese shuttle. There's small chance of rebound."

Santoul fell silent.

"I'm not a complete fool," Jalak said, "no matter what you think."

Santoul shrugged. "Let me make sure I understand you: You're denying that you've allowed things to get a bit . . . disorganized down here."

Jalak swallowed hard—audibly.

"Professor?"

"I . . . I won't deny I've been somewhat remiss in my duties."

"Somewhat remiss."

"It's just . . ."

"Talk to me, Simon," Santoul said. "Convince me I should go back up the well and tell Ishida that everything's been worked out. That Simon Jalak recalls the terms of the contract he signed with NCorp and has promised to increase the output of the network.'' The operative paused to let his words sink in. "Look, Professor, maybe you figure you're done with Kwandri. You'd like a transfer, back to Dhone or something.''

Jalak's jaw dropped. "You can't! My work's here!''

Santoul's face turned hard. "And what d'you think's going to become of your work when Kwandri has itself a Xell'em-backed regime? You think they're going to let you hang around to conduct your interviews? They're going to award you citizen status while you're filing away your observations, publishing your esoteric articles?''

Color returned to Jalak's face with a vengeance. Santoul extracted a mirror from the breast pocket of his jacket and tossed it across the desk.

"Take a look at yourself, Professor. Your hair, those ridiculous glasses . . . Your vision's failing, you want to grow a coat, is that it? Tell me you're not in over your head.''

Jalak reached for the rectangle of alloy but stayed his hand at the last moment. He knew perfectly well what he looked like; knew perfectly well what he was trying to accomplish.

"You don't understand,'' he said, shaking his head. "This world, these people . . . They're extraordinary, Santoul. And we're eroding their culture—Terra, Xella, all of us. The League should never have decided in favor of contact.''

"The Kwandri aren't your children, Professor,'' Santoul said in a minatory tone. "They're your *study*. You wouldn't even be here if contact had been voted down. Besides, it's too late to reverse things. All we can do now is contain the damage the Xell'em have done.''

Jalak showed him a pitying look. "Hasn't it ever occurred to you that our own methods are equally destructive? You're operating under DisneyCorp cover, Santoul—Remy. You've obviously been briefed on their methods. We saturate worlds with media presentations and consumer trinkets to bring them into the fold. And well the Consortium might gain another member, but no one stops to think about what's been lost in the process.''

''You're talking blasphemy, Professor.''

Jalak laughed. ''That doesn't concern me, Remy. Terra's worldview is merely one of many, and I've seen the damage the imposition of that view can do. I can't bear to sit still and allow it to happen here.''

Santoul rubbed his jaw. ''You're downloading a new program all of a sudden, Professor. Right in front of my eyes.''

Jalak brought his fingers to his mouth.

''I mean, first you tell me your agents are in hiding because of SPECVES. Now I hear you preaching this cultural relativism crap, and—I'll be straight up, Professor—I've got to ask myself if Simon Jalak hasn't been sabotaging his own network.''

Jalak felt his throat dry up. ''Nothing I've told you will come as any surprise to your superiors, Santoul. NCorp knows why I agreed to terms. Someone had to map this culture before it deteriorated beyond recognition. But Center asks too much of me. I'm a scientist, not an espionage specialist. It gnawed at me each time I had to ask someone to be my nose and fingertips at one gathering or the next.''

''Nose and fingertips,'' Santoul said, laughing to himself. ''That's great. You're even talking like an indig.''

''I won't permit that word—''

''You've been following the program, Jalak,'' Santoul said. ''And my guess is there's no shortage of volunteers.'' He leaned forward in the chair and gestured to the room's outer wall. ''For every Kwandri waving a Xell'em flag, there are ten waving fists, Professor. You want to do this planet a favor?—then get your network back online.''

Jalak ran a hand through his matted hair. "I know all this. It's just . . . well, I've simply retroed things temporarily. I haven't been pushing for information. I listen to rumors. That's what I send up the well."

The operative's gaze turned harder still. "You asked for four thousand last month, six the month before. You're twenty-three over budget for the period. And you're telling me you've shut things down?" Remy shook his head in a mournful fashion. "Maybe you should be terminated."

Jalak began to lower his head, but instantly felt Santoul's hand take him by the hair, forcing his face up. "Don't make it tough on yourself," the operative seethed, his sweet-scented breath brushing Jalak's cheek.

Santoul relaxed his grip and Jalak fell back in the chair, heart pounding.

"You think you're the first one to pull this? You think Center doesn't know when one of their people is scamming funds? Hell, the corp expects that. But stop time-sharing that genetically boosted brain of yours. You want more, you better make damn certain you transmit more. Even if it's junk, it's got to be acceptable junk.

"NCorp's in financial trouble. We could all be reassigned tomorrow and your problems would be over. But you've gotta play the game until that happens. We all do."

The operative ceased his pacing to regard Jalak for a long moment. "What is it, you've got yourself a drug dependency? I know it isn't sexual, 'cause I had a look at your medcharts before I came down."

Jalak felt nauseated. "It's nothing like that. I've been helping a few families see to medical costs. You can't imagine how deeply these people have been affected by contact."

Santoul laughed. "You're a regular saint."

"Hardly a saint. I'm human, Santoul. Perhaps you're

too young to remember when that counted for something.''

Back in motion once more, Santoul was preoccupied with his own thoughts. He came to a halt beside the desk.

''It's not too late to make amends,'' he said at last, perching himself on the desk edge. ''Here's what we're going to do: You're going to show me around—the resident culturist escorting the DisneyCorp rep through the city. It's a natural alliance. I want to see exactly how you worked things—dumb agents, cut-out teams, drop points, the entire menu. Is that understood?''

Jalak stared at Santoul. ''You're not going to cut me off?''

Santoul shook his head. ''No. But I expect to see some changes. I want you to lose the beard, the glasses, the stoop. The next time Dakou vets you, the results better show a new and improved Jalak or word goes straight to the Dazyldesk.''

''I understand. And I want to—''

''No, don't thank me yet, Professor,'' Santoul interrupted. ''You've still gotta earn this one. NCorp wants intel on Xell'em movements through the flashpoint. And you,'' he raised a thick forefinger, ''are going to help me recruit the talent we need to gather it.''

FOUR—

WALKING LIKAT'S COBBLESTONE STREETS the next morning, Remy was forced to rethink his earlier evaluation of Jalak's physical condition. The culturist was even fonder of the local beer than he was, and Remy had to wonder whether the drink, the *yika*, wasn't addictive. An unrecognized addiction might go a long way toward explaining how the Earther had gone from serious academic to nascent Kwandri in less than a year.

Jalak was quaffing a warmed, spice-topped tankard now, pausing every so often to continue his account of the changes visited on Kwandri's principal population centers since contact.

They were seated side by side on tall wooden stools at a crowded watering hole at the fringe of Likat's sprawling market area. A triangular banner affixed to the roof of the stall announced that homebrew was available, as distinct from the commercial brand normally offered in the city's shops and restaurants. A group of young males was gathered at the entrance, inhaling the offworlders.

"This entire area," Jalak was saying, "from the river all the way to the Monument used to be forest land. But as soon as word spread about aliens and the technological wonders their ships were ferrying down, Li-kat began to burst at the seams. Half the farmers in the land dropped their hoes and pickaxes, packed up their families, and moved here expecting to see all their dreams fulfilled.''

Jalak's outfit consisted of layer upon layer of shirts and vests, in contrast to Remy's all-weather suit. Just Jalak playing Kwandri, but it bothered Remy. There was nothing worse an operative could do than seek to resemble the locals. The man had been too long without proper supervision.

''Instead, they learned that their planet had been visited by a very discriminating breed of aliens, who, while they might be willing to impart a bit of technological wizardry here and there, were certainly not going to refashion the whole world overnight.''

Jalak interrupted his monologue to drink. ''Q'aantre suddenly found itself more *occupied* than adopted. The people hear about this war taking place in some unimaginably distant sector of space, but the only glimpse they have of it comes in the form of battle troops sent downside for a week or two of biostat decomp.

''Then just as suddenly this unseen war ends and the Xell'em arrive. Only they aren't quite so reluctant to involve themselves in upgrading Q'aantre's standard of life—particularly if in exchange the Grand Assembly is willing to grant what amounts to exclusive rights to the wormhole.''

Jalak hammered the tankard on the countertop in a traditional gesture of thanks and appreciation. The female behind the counter smiled as she accepted the Earther's payment and praise, bringing the backs of triangulated hands to her mouth in salute.

Remy followed Jalak outside, the group of young males parting, then forming up behind to shadow them down the market corridor. Piglike dogs lay sprawled in geometric patches of light. Merchants touched one another in wordless greeting, wafting a dizzying catalogue of scents into the chilled morning air.

Kwandri had been described to Remy as an Earthlike world, but Tiger held a different opinion. *You grew up in the fucking Himalayas it's Earth-tolerable,* the med-tech had said. *Otherwise plan on shittin' ice cubes.*

Sunscreen drops protected Remy's eyes from Dazyl's UV intensity; the planet's slightly lower-than-standard gravity added an uncharacteristic bounce to his step. The tail SPECVES had assigned to him—and who had been with him from the moment he left the hotel—maintained a respectful distance.

"It wasn't long before the Consortium decided that technological magnanimity was the key after all," Jalak resumed. "Regardless of what impact that decision might have on the indigenous culture. So Earth began to match Xella gift for gift, innovation for innovation, promise for promise."

And Likat had grown and grown until it had spread itself clear across the river and up into the surrounding, now denuded hills.

"Down came the trees and to hell went the traditions. The Grand Assembly's primary concern was how best to maintain a balance between the Manifest and the Consortium—to profit from both without alienating either." The professor laughed in a self-amused way. "Which brings us to the present mess we've fashioned."

Remy left the statement unchallenged; experience had taught him there was more to be gained by listening to people than arguing with them. The more Jalak talked, the more relaxed he became, and that's all Remy was after for the time being. It wouldn't do to have the culturist fighting him every step of the way.

He had woken with the thought, shivering in the hotel suite the Interior Ministry reserved for visiting DisneyCorp personnel, Dazyl suffusing the rooms with a misty orange glow. After a breakfast of bread and fried tubers, he had ridden an electric coach crosstown and collected Jalak from his native-style stone cottage near the river.

The professor looked as though he'd been up all night, but Remy was certain he detected an attitude of healthy resignation in Jalak's rheumy eyes. Healthy because Remy was in no mood to repeat the hardhanded performance he had given the previous afternoon.

"It's Dazyl's intensity that accounts for this near molecular examination of the near environment," Jalak said as they emerged from the open market onto a broad street of shops and scent-stands.

Remy recalled the detail of the statue he had examined in Jalak's office, and began to note like motifs on doorways and cornices.

Downtown, the recent history of Kwandri was more clearly etched than anywhere in the city, for it was here that the indigenous and the offworld had collided head-on: beast-drawn carts, trikes, and steam-driven trucks vied for space with electric cars and maglev trollies; preformed structures of ferrocrete and plasteel rose next to iron-girder construction and ramshackle wooden dwellings; Kwandri who made their living trading in forged plateware and hammered utensils engaged in daily shouting matches with those who now dealt in mass-produced plastics and ceramics. And this, Remy knew, was only the tip of the offworlder's iceberg . . .

Jalak said, "This harsh sky, the essentially colorless trees and grasses that dominate these habitable latitudes, the silence of the precontact landscape, the very constraints nature has placed on Q'aantre vision and sexuality . . . Where else but under such conditions might one expect smell and touch to take precedence over sight and sound."

Jalak stopped at an odor-controlled crosswalk.

Smells, tastes, and tactile exchanges *were* Kwandri's colors and songs, the culturist explained. There were dozens of words to describe the fragrance of a night-

blooming rose or the ocean at low tide. And in the few
instances of Kwandrian psychosis he had recorded, de-
rangement always followed an olfactory course. Sub-
jects reported an ability to exhale or emanate scents that
defied objective verification.

SPECVES agents were said to be adept at this; and
of course the shamans of the hill tribes employed the
same talents in prognostication.

"If you're still here at *Tegganon*," Jalak said, "you'll
see just how important smell and touch are."

The briefing Remy received hadn't amounted to much
more than a description of the mating ritual lifted from
Simon Jalak's own comptexts. The professor maintained that he was the sole offworlder who had ever
been permitted to remain downside during the rite; but
Remy had only to recall Tiger's and Dakou's jokes to
question the assertion.

"And despite what you may have been told, *Tegganon* does not occur every two standard-years. When my
informants first furnished me with the years of the six
previous rituals, I assumed there was some calendric
regularity or periodicity. But I've since learned that the
determinations are much more subtle. They seem to
involve a universal physiological alteration whose true
prompt—if indeed one exists at all—has yet to be identified."

"But it is a kind of estrus," Remy said.

"Among females who have birthed fewer than four
children, yes."

"And the males?"

"The males are universally affected."

"And no sexual contact in between?"

Jalak shook his head, introspective for a moment.

Remy took a look around the street. The gender split
gave all appearances of being equal. "But with some
of the females exempted from estrus . . . It must be
one hell of a male scramble come *Tegganon*."

"*Tegganon* wreaks havoc with marriage vows," Jalak said. "It's a chaotic time."

Remy tried to picture it.

"Of course, there's no guarantee of conception. Like the ritual itself, the process seems to be governed by inherent constraints, possibly linked to ecological determinants. These are conveyed by a complex system of scent and smart-secretion signals.

"The population remains stabilized because only a small percentage of the eligible females are successfully impregnated." Jalak swept his arm through a broad arc. "In case you haven't noticed, Santoul, hospitable territory is at a premium."

Remy shivered inside the all-weather fabric of his suit. "I've noticed," he said.

Jalak set off again, Remy alongside in a matching stride; behind them, a dozen young males hurried to keep up.

"I worry about *Tegganon* most of all," Jalak said out of the corner of his mouth. "Who can predict what impact our continued presence will have. Xell'em or Terran, it makes little difference. Each culture in its own fashion promotes an acquisitiveness and sensuality unknown to the Q'aantre. Color, fashion, and music have always been associated with the mystical side of Q'aantre religion. Now we're bringing all that into the open."

"Inherent constraints, Professor," Remy said, thinking he was making a point. "No matter how much the Kwandri want it, they can't have it. Anyway, suppose it *is* all a wipe, every female on the planet becomes pregnant. We'll do what we did back home: build 'em habitats, or find them another world."

Jalak muttered something to himself, then said, "An NCorp response if I ever heard one."

Lunch was thick slabs of fire-grilled meat, eaten without benefit of utensils in a restaurant of brightly lit back rooms with butcher-block tables. Afterward, the two Earthers gradually right-angled their way out of the commercial center, made a loop around the Monument, and headed back down to the river, through the rutted streets that mazed the industrial sector.

Ultimately Jalak directed Remy to a wooden bench in a small kiosked plaza, where a stand of native fir had somehow survived the ax.

"The overturned trash container by the engraver's was a cue," Remy said. They had passed the thing half an hour ago after giving their SPECVES tail the slip.

Jalak nodded while he was checking the digital display of a pocketwatch.

"What's the procedure?"

"If the can's upright, there's no contact," Jalak told him. "We use several other locations as well. I generally compose a list for the month and leave it at a dead drop near the new station. Coded, of course. Anyone reading it would think they found a shopping list. Live drops are always assigned to days following trash collection."

"When most of the containers are empty."

"Precisely."

"So your agent left you a positive signal. Now what?"

Jalak checked the watch again. "He should be along anytime."

Remy glanced in both directions down the dirt track that wound through the plaza. "He'll see you've got company. What's the wave-off sign in case you're being followed?"

From the pocket of his sweater Jalak produced a coin-sized disk that might have contained cologne or an aerosol narcotic. Remy guessed that it was an obsolete version of the oral and dermal misters his body could trigger with tongue-to-tooth pressure.

"One whiff and he knows to pass on the drop."

"And suppose I was a Kwandri?"

"Only my agents are familiar with the scent. Anyone else would simply think I was indulging in drug-taking or poor eating habits."

Remy was pleased. For all the professor's failings, he operated a well-run network. It was just a matter of coming up with new incentives for Jalak's agents—which could mean money, drugs, or even Swatch wristwatches.

He rested his head against the uppermost slat of the bench and took a deep breath of Kwandri's spiced air. Dazyl was long past midheaven but the air had retained the warmth of noon. The temperature was a good fifteen degrees higher than when he left the hotel suite.

A Kwandri couple entered the park from the street, sniffing openly as they passed by the bench. There were other strollers about, some with news-slates, others on a late lunch. On the river side of the plaza was a small playground filled with young children on recess from school. Remy kept thinking that the place reminded him of somewhere, but he couldn't locate the source of the memory.

"Here he comes," Jalak said suddenly.

Remy observed a long-legged Kwandri approach the bench from the direction of the Monument. The rhythmical grace to his forward-leaning drag-step gait recalled vid-images of black youths on urban Earth streets, sauntering to the beat of broadcast music or some interior tune.

This would be "Glans," Remy thought, one of Jalak's principal contacts with the underground. A woodworker by trade, Glans frequently dealt in black market icons and was a habitué of the cult clubs and cin-dens along the river strip, where most of DisneyCorp's goods ended up.

The Kwandri's real name was unknown—Glans was already in place when Jalak had assumed the network—but included in the file dossier Remy had perused the previous evening was a list of the payments he had already received: a pair of ersatz Ray-Ban Wayfarer sunglasses, a necklace of U.S. coins and subway tokens, a Seiko digital watch, a Cher action figure, a plastic model of the *Millennium Falcon*.

"What's he waiting for?" Remy asked.

"Patience," Jalak said. "He's being cautious. He's never smelled me with anyone before. He's not sure what to do."

Remy looked away, hoping Glans would read it as a cue to follow through. "Damnit, Jalak, I thought you had him trained."

Jalak looked peeved. "There's no need to turn away. Give him a chance, Remy. He can barely make us out from that distance."

Remy realized that his nonchalant pose couldn't have been more studied. Glans passed in front of the bench without breaking stride and continued on down the dirt path. Jalak was quiet, save for the sniffing sounds he was making.

"Tell me what you smell?" he asked after a moment.

Remy inhaled as though someone were holding a bouquet under his nose. "Coriander and peppercorns," he said, drawing on the olfactory tutorials. "A baseline of sweetness, like spun sugar, but undermined by vegetal rot. Wet leaves from hardwood trees. Tannic acid and mold."

Jalak voiced a sound of disapproval. "That's your nose talking. If this is what Center considers olfactory training, why didn't they send down a sniffer and save themselves the bother?"

Remy laughed. "You asked what I smelled, Professor, not what I *felt*."

"Let's have it then."

Remy took another whiff. The Kwandri's acidulated exhalations were somewhat dispersed by now, so he had to content himself with trace odors. "He's nervous," Remy said at last. "There's a hint of anxiety, but nothing he can't handle."

"And?"

Remy shut his eyes in concentration.

"Don't *think* it to death," Jalak cautioned. "Look to your memories."

"I'm, uh, I'm remembering the first time I lied to my parents. Told them I was going to class when I was really headed for rec deck. Two friends did the same thing, and we all got caught."

"Not bad," Jalak said, "for a novice. Now you have to let those memories dismantle themselves into their basic emotive components. Once you've learned to recognize those, the hard data will begin to assemble itself."

Remy quirked a grin at Jalak. "No need to waldo me, Professor. What was Glans telling us?"

"His nervousness probably had more to do with your presence than anything else. He had no important information to impart, but he wants to make a live drop—tomorrow night, at our usual place."

"Which is where?"

"A scent theater not far from my home. A 'cin-den,' as they're termed."

Remy showed him a puzzled frown. "You're telling me you can pick out a single scent in a place like that."

Jalak shook his head. "For close quarters we employ an actual brush pass."

"So something tangible's exchanged—a comp chip, what?"

The culturist smiled tolerantly. "Fluids, Remy. Bodily fluids."

Before development of the tutorials and the Drexler implants that facilitated on-site analysis of olfactory binding proteins, NCorp had had to rely on robotic sniffers and a wide spectrum of agent-deployed absorbant materials. These had to be shuttled up the well, treated with heat, and desorbed of aromacules, which were then irradiated, subjected to gas chromatograph-mass spectrometry, and finally broken down into constituent elements.

Remy, with his retrained nose and implanted nano-analyzers, was all three in one. But even these didn't guarantee full comprehension of Kwandri syntax and scent-idioms. He was like one who had learned a language from print media but had yet to hear it spoken. And while he could successfully decipher the inherent meaning of an individual odor, the combinations—the idioms and *slang*—baffled him.

"A chef bends over a pot of stew and identifies the dozen different spices you've teaspooned into the pot. But it takes the connoisseur to fashion a description of the dish that captures the overall flavor. Wine tasters do the same thing when they anthropomorphize the grape with adjectives like *arrogant* or *bold*."

So said Jalak, at any rate, as he walked Remy back to the hotel. They would stop at scent-stands or on street corners to decipher smells as Kwandri urbanites went about their business. Nearly everyone gawked and sniffed, but no one was particularly guarded about exhalations or emanations. Kwandri reactions to offworlders weren't all that varied, and as for the offworlders themselves, well *they* certainly weren't conversant with the olfactory idiom.

"The range of scents a Q'aantre can deposit is almost unlimited," Jalak explained. "Scents have colors, shades, nuances, volume, duration . . . There are those which can arouse trust or distrust, interest or sympathy. Those by which one can attract attention or lose oneself in a crowd."

But scents weren't the only way the indigs passed information to one another, Jalak went on, turning to an explanation of the brush passes he employed with some of his network agents. No, it seemed that in addition to the data to be gleaned from coughs, sneezes, whispers, wheezes, and farts, there was just as much to be learned from certain varieties of pats on the back, handshakes, or testicle squeezes in the communal baths.

"Saliva, mucus, blood, tears, and sweat—although there's little of that here . . . They all contain biochemical signals which can be rendered accessible to the trained operative," Jalak added with professorial authority.

Remy didn't want to ask about Kwandri analogs of semen and vaginal secretions.

The professor was regarding him slyly. "I'm sure you've heard stories about the chemical debriefings NCorp's first operatives here had to endure."

"Actually, I haven't—"

"I sometimes think the Q'aantre have more in common with insects than with true anthropoids."

Remy remembered an ant farm in a touring zoo that had once played Citi habitat.

"Personal inclination and creativity have a lot to do with it," Jalak mused. "But it's rare to encounter the creative aroma in public settings." He inhaled discreetly. "Here, for example, you find yourself bombarded with prosaic odors—colored, of course, by whiffs of surprise or curiosity elicited by our presence. But I doubt anyone pays these much mind—or much *nose*, as the Q'aantre say. Think about it in visual terms, and try to imagine just how many optical signals we dismiss during the course of our everyday lives."

Remy's own nose bore this out. But he seemed to detect something else in the air—a scent not unlike the tannic anxiousness Glans had deposited in the park.

"Yes, I've been aware of it for several blocks now," Jalak admitted. "From the time we reached the Monument. Tart yet somewhat curdled. Definitely unidirectional. I suggest we've been walking right into it."

Remy's nose had been working overtime since the park. He encouraged his eyes to do a bit of intelligence gathering, and recognized the intersection from the previous night, when he had left the suite to reconnoiter

the hotel grounds and adjacent buildings. He was surprised to find they had come so far from the river in
what seemed so short a time. Olfactory preoccupation,
he decided. Unlike sight and sound, scents had a way
of triggering deep-seated memories. Active participation,
olfactory dialogue, became an introspective experience;
and with that came a sense of timelessness.

The shift from smell to sight was momentarily jar-
ring. It was as though someone had shaken him from
an afternoon dream. But his eyes immediately told him
what his nose couldn't. The reasons for the astringent
emanations were standing across the intersection and
on nearby corners in the form of SPECVES plain-
clothesmen.

Remy was suddenly alert to the sound of distant
chanting—angry chanting at that—which in Kwandrian
fashion took on a kind of barking quality.

"Around the corner," Jalak said, pointing. "A demonstration of some sort."

Remy pivoted through a quick circle to get his bearings. The hotel and the Interior Ministry were directly
in front of them, perhaps three blocks away; but his
evening recon hadn't taken him in the direction Jalak
was indicating.

"What's down there?" he asked.

"Stores, shops," Jalak said, shaking his head. Then
his eyes widened. "The Xell'em bank!"

Colliding with Kwandri who were hurrying from the
scene, the two Earthers rounded the corner in time to
see a sizable mob of coveralled protesters position itself
directly in front of the bank. Fists were being raised in
cadence with the chant, but the mob was also targeting
the ferrocrete building with a collective scent cloud that
reeked of spoiled eggs and tooth decay.

No translations were necessary for the several
Xell'em who were gazing down from upper-floor windows with pinched nostrils and hands pressed to
mouths.

"Is this yours?" Remy shouted in Jalak's ear, encouraged for a moment that the culturist's subagents had organized a monster rally.

Jalak denied involvement. "Could be the same group that attacked the embassy," he proposed. "Or perhaps the bombing merely incited further demonstration."

Remy thought the latter more likely. And as long as things remained anti-Xell'em he could afford to be pleased. By the sight of the dissidents, if not the nauseating smell of effluvia they had conjured. He wanted to add his own voice to the guttural chant, and would have done so had the police not chosen that moment to arrive.

"It might be prudent to secure a spot of shelter," Jalak advised nasally as uniforms began to pour from the open doors of official vehicles. "This could turn ugly."

Shopkeepers on both sides of the street were already lowering security grates and hustling passersby inside. The police were grouping behind ballistic shields at either end of the block. Remy caught a glimpse of riot batons and stunguns.

"Prudent's the operative word," he said louder than necessary, since the energy the protesters had been directing into the chant was not being funneled into a search for cover.

Kwandri were edging along the buildings in an effort to circumvent the closing cordons. The police were donning transpirator masks. Jalak was already halfway across the street, making for an unshuttered storefront. He shouted to Remy over his shoulder. "This way, *hurry*."

Remy started off on his left foot. Behind him he heard the growl of a powerful engine and the strident squeal of hydraulic brakes. Suddenly there was a monster squatting in the intersection—an enormous, fanged demon painted in more colors than Likat displayed from one end to the other.

Piloted by two Kwandri, the creature was equipped with all-terrain treads, huge fans behind the eyes, and what looked to be a muzzle where its Terran-proportioned nose should have been. Up top rode two Xell'em military officers and a couple of SPECVES lieutenants outfitted in bodysuits and anticontaminant masks.

"It unleashes a riot-scent!" Jalak said, back at Remy's side all at once and tugging at the shiny sleeve of his jacket. "They want an excuse to break open a few heads."

Some things never changed, Remy thought, recalling the tactics Earth Force had used against the habitats during the rebellion.

"Come on, man!"

The wind when it reached them carried a stench of pig dung, petrochemicals, lamp oil, and burning rubber. Remy watched as the crowd fissioned. Panic took up where fear left off. The protesters scattered in all directions, encountering blocked doorways and unscalable walls when they weren't brought face-to-face with foul-tempered police units in visored helmets.

It was doubtful anyone felt the sting of the shock batons, but their appearance alone was enough to fuel a greater frenzy. With nowhere to hide, many of the dissidents simply dropped to their knees and brayed at the blinding sky. Others attempted a kind of crazed counteroffensive, assailing the cordons with the same fists and scents they had waved and wafted moments before.

Remy saw dozens go down, felled and drubbed by batons and rifle butts. Kwandri of both sexes stumbled past him, faces smashed, clothing torn, coats matted with blood and street grime. Jalak was spread-eagled against a brick wall, eyes glazed behind his glasses, screaming sound bite invectives borrowed from a dozen tongues.

Remy was closing on him when he spotted the boy.

The scent cannon was trundling up the street and he couldn't imagine how the kid had gotten himself caught up in things. But there he was: twelve years old at the outside, paralyzed with fear, and apparently oblivious to the festooned monstrosity that was bearing down on him.

An innocent, as most victims turned out to be.

The Kwandri drivers had no intention of crushing demonstrators undertread, but they were a moment too late in swerving the vehicle up onto the sidewalk. The boy was struck broadside and launched fifteen feet down the street.

By the time Remy reached him a small crowd had gathered around, but no one was going to the boy's aid. Two police stood among the silent, odoriferous circle, their confederates busy herding demonstrators toward waiting trucks. Some had removed their helmets and masks to avail themselves of a breath of riot gas, an aromatic incentive.

The boy's crumpled form moaned and exhaled a scent for succor that got to Remy where he once lived.

He was already pushing his way through the circle when he heard Jalak's voice crying, ''No, Remy, don't! You mustn't!''

FIVE—

"AND YOU'RE SURE THERE'S NOTHING else I can get you?" Remy asked, relying on the translator-assist to ease him through the intricacies of Kwandrian speech. "A dessert or something? Maybe you'd like to have a couple of friends over?"

Smiling broadly, the youth shook his head and went about eagerly fingering morsels of meat and sweet bread into his mouth.

His name was Els Nanff, the third offspring of the Nanff clan. And he lay propped on pillows in the suite's master bedroom, arms, legs, and hip dressed in bandages; an assortment of breakfast goodies piled on a tray in front of him. The vid set was running a comedy Remy had asked DisneyCorp to include among its downlink transmissions.

It was one of Kwandri's manifold peculiarities that the rendering of aid to an injured party was tantamount to assuming all responsibilities for the treatment and continued good health of said individual. Until such time as the courts decreed the obligation satisfactorily completed. This was especially so when the injured was a minor. And indeed when Remy had pushed his way

through the previous afternoon's circle of onlookers he
was in effect making a choice to *adopt* Els Nanff.

Medtechs at Likat's Terran-run clinic had seen to the
bandages, casts, and such, but local law prohibited them
from supplying additional care. So Remy had decided
to have Nanff brought to the hotel.

There were planets where such an arrangement would
be looked upon with suspicion, and others where it
wouldn't merit a glance; but on Kwandri the possibility
of sexual overtones wasn't even addressed. Homosexu-
ality wasn't unknown, but save for the occasional flirtation, the libidinal drive was reserved for *Tegganon* and
the months preceding it.

Remy wasn't bothered by the arrangement in any
case. The boy would have ended up a cripple if someone hadn't seen to his care.

Now if only one life could balance one hundred thousand deaths, he mused, thinking about the *Ambii'th*. It
was hard to know just how these things were measured.
The creed maintained that the lives of individuals or
whole species were of small consequence where cosmicization was at issue. The evolution and perpetuation
of group mind. But then here was someone like Simon
Jalak hanging it on a girder for Kwandri and a doomed
mindset. And here was Remy Santoul nursemaiding an
XT teenager. Back to basics. Like some contagious re-
trovirus.

As for Nanff's recuperating in the hotel, well, the
suite had more room than Remy required, anyway. Far
more than he'd had growing up in Citi, where the standard bedroom was coffin-size and the baths and kitch-
ens were communal affairs.

The same was true of living conditions on most of
the Consortium's outer stations and the wheels of the
private corps. It was only downside that Remy could
avail himself of the space and physical pleasures indigs
throughout the Arm took for granted.

The shower, for example. The suite was equipped

with a water unit as opposed to an ultrasonic, and how he had luxuriated under its heated liquid flow these past few days. The feeling was difficult to convey to wheelies. As difficult as trying to describe the textures and tastes of Kwandri's foods to people who subsisted on engineered foodstuffs; the feel of the breeze to people who knew only recirculated air. Not that Remy thought of himself as one to go native. But there was no denying the appeal . . .

He told Nanff to call out if he needed anything, and pulled the door to the master bedroom closed. Positioned by the window in the adjoining room was the transceiver he had assembled at first light from components ingeniously contained in his luggage.

For ordinary transmissions—like keying in the request for the comedy flickdisk—he made use of the DisneyCorp MW dish. But Audjo Ishida had instructed him to employ the burst transmitter for all sensitive communiqués. While the Xell'em might monitor the bursts, it was safe to assume that any signals they scanned would remain hopelessly scrambled.

Remy checked his watch. The message he had recorded earlier couldn't be transmitted for another forty-five minutes.

In the meantime, he huffed his way through a series of tone-maintenance exercises. The Earth Force regimen was required of him, and included meditation, aura cleansing, and chakra balancing techniques. A monitoring device sent the results upside.

He ran a check of his implants; rubbed TechSci's pore-trainer lotion into his palms. He submitted himself to stress analysis, and fed specimens of tears, blood, hair, and urine into the device's scanner ports.

With a minute or two left, he activated playback mode on the transceiver and called the prerecorded message onscreen.

I've made contact with our downside rep, he watched himself say after reciting Ishida's code, *and we have*

*reviewed all recent transactions. Some damage has been
done, but I'm satisfied that the basic structure is sound
and merits continued investment.*

*Our competitors have made a strong showing, but the
streets are full of surprises. For the moment I have high
confidence and soon expect to reopen an old channel.
The following are required: one pair acid-washed blue-
jeans, one pair Calvin Klein men's briefs, one Lamy
pen, one Nissan Thermos, one Mr. T collectible—either
action figure or simulated gold chain set.*

Remy paused the playback and thought for a moment, then composed himself for the visual pickups and
voice-commanded record mode.

"Addendum to six-slash-nought-nought-niner: Phajol Dakou, Eyes/Ears Only." Remy smiled for the
camera.

"Hey, Dakou," he asked, "what's the difference between a Kwandri and a Neanderthal?" He gave the
counsel a few seconds. "The Kwandri's the one with
the blue balls."

Baj and two of his underlings from the Ministry of
the Interior arrived with lunch, which consisted of various starch and complex carbohydrate dishes, served by
three giggling female room attendants dressed in Old
Kwandri costume.

"And how do you like your rooms?" Baj asked in
trader's tongue, sniffing around the place while his colleagues were sitting down to the meal.

"It's more elaborate than I'm accustomed to," Remy
said, watching him from the front door.

Baj waved a hand. "You flatter us. I'm sure this is
the very least that DisneyCorp affords you." He finally
got around to opening the master bedroom door, gently
closing it after he'd had a peek inside.

"Then it's true," he said, eyes as wide as they could
get. "And here I was telling everyone they must have
the story wrong."

Remy had joined Ayyum Dali and Ayyum Legguum at the table. "I guess that all depends on the story."

"Why, simply that you rescued this country boy from misfortune. That you saw to his treatment at the Terran Clinic and had him brought here."

"That much is true," Remy said, spooning up some sort of tuber gruel.

Baj discarded his cloak and sat down, patting his bleached forelock into place. "But whatever do you mean to do with him—after his wounds heal, I mean?"

Remy savored the taste of the porridge. "He wants to go up the well. Says he wants to visit the wheel."

Baj and the two Ayyums stared at him, aghast.

"You don't propose . . . Surely, you can't be considering . . ."

"Well, why not?" Remy said. "The Xell'em have some of your people working out near the wormhole. It's about time DisneyCorp showed you how we live upside."

"B-but only Assembly members have been permitted to visit the Xell'em station." Baj gestured to the bedroom. "He's just a poor country boy!"

Remy laughed at the falsetto notes that punctuated the Kwandri's objection. "You're suggesting we choose someone more deserving . . . Someone like yourself, maybe."

The coat around Baj's eyes prickled. "I wasn't suggesting myself. But of course I would be most honored. Just tell me what I need to do."

Remy rubbed his jaw, taking in the electroplated nuts and bolts that adorned Baj's blouse. The Kwandri were fond of wearing hardware. "I suppose you could always get yourself hit by a scent-cannon, Norak."

The three indigs studied their plates in silence.

"A most regrettable occurrence," Baj said at last. "The entire incident. First the embassy gates, now this. Likat hasn't found itself so divided in a century of *Tegganon*."

"Could mean you'll have to make a choice, Norak."

The Kwandri snorted through his nub of nose. "Suddenly you sound like Densign, Remy. Heaven forbid that we should receive from two sources. Or perhaps I should say, that we serve two masters."

Later, the four of them sat around the holo, viewing icons available for exchange from DisneyCorp's updated catalogue. The company was revered because of its founder's early contributions to cryogenics, animatronics, and role-modeling; and along with its extensive library of film art and music, DisneyCorp offered thousands of artifacts from the planet's preexpansionist period.

Late twentieth century was very big just then: Buchsbaum tables, Starck three-legged chairs, Tizio lamps, Ward Bennett furniture, Memphis Group pieces, Day of the Dead figurines, Braun kitchenware, Ollie North and Ronnie Reagan photo-mannequins, Hindu masks, Roy Hamilton ceramics, greeting cards, animal-shaped place mats, Gucci tote bags, Rolex watches, 7-Eleven coffee mugs, Katharine Hamnet underwear, Chanel T-shirts, Cabbage Patch dolls, Transformer toys, Nautilus equipment, Nike Aquasox, amulet bags of Woodstock soil, electric razors that left stubble, Concorde souvenirs, and bath towels.

The furred Kwandri, however, showed a preference for steam irons and epilators; cordless pet-grooming vacuums, Dustbusters, rechargeable mustache trimmers, and toilet seat covers; reflecting suntan mats, Krazy Glue ultrasonic massagers, and electric toothbrushes.

Baj was already familiar with most of the items in the catalogue, but he saved his requests for the end.

Remy hadn't planned on cornering him earlier on, and felt bad about what had gone down at the table. But he was trained to regard everyone as a potential agent. Forcing individuals to take a stand wasn't ideal for cultivating friendships, but the approach worked best for rough cuts.

"I must admit I like everything you've showed us," Baj was saying, "but I'm particularly interested in items four-one-nine and five-three-eight. Is historical data available?"

Remy called the former back to the holo, commanding the device to turn it about in the beam. "Pez Dispenser," he read from the display screen.

"Ah, yes, a religious artifact, is it not? Ms. Canu told me about an orally ingested sacrament of some sort."

"No, you're thinking of something else."

"Then this 'Pez' wasn't a sacrament?" Ayyum Dali asked.

"A candy," Remy told him. "An ingot of artificially colored pseudocitric confection."

"And are these ingots still available?"

Remy checked, scrolling data on the screen. "Ersatz only."

Baj conferred with his associates for a moment. "Yes, we'd like one hundred units to award when the Grand Assembly reconvenes."

Remy entered the order.

"And what about five-three-eight?"

A wafer-thin, yellow disk filled the holo-field, marked on one side with eyespots and an upward curve of mouth. "Smiley Face," Remy read. "Peace symbol associated with mid-twentieth–century geopolitical conflicts. Adapted for use by some of the NeAsian prototype habitats to symbolize their independence from Earth."

"Perfect," Baj said, "absolutely perfect." The two Ayyums were nodding along with him; one of them emanating an olfactory nimbus of cloying, nectarous odors.

"Ayyum Dali," Baj said in a scolding voice. "Don't scent with your glands full."

Remy studied the three Kwandri as he leaned back into his chair. "Which meaning appeals to you—the face as a symbol of peace or of independence?"

Baj looked at him nonplussed. "Why, neither, Remy. For the Q'aantre such a smile could symbolize one thing and one thing only—the *Tegganon.*"

"The boy's father wants a whiff of you," Jalak told Remy later, outside the cin-den. "Tomorrow, about noon."

"Where?"

The culturist gazed at the river and pointed north. "There. After a hundred miles of foul road."

"I'll see about a car," Remy said.

"That would be wise. I'll accompany you," Jalak added after a moment.

"Afraid I'll get lost?"

Jalak frowned. "That's the last thing I'd expect of you. But you won't find anything like Likat out there, Remy. We'll be journeying into Old Q'aantre."

"Sounds interesting."

Jalak's shoulders heaved under his poncholike garment as he turned to face the theater. "Probably not as interesting as you're going to find this place."

The building, like most of those along the river, was two stories of precisely fitted stone that had a slightly pink cast to it. The windows were wood-framed and double-glazed, large on the lower floor and little more than vertical slits above. Remy ventured that the wind could be vicious when the hills across the river were snowcapped. Just now the air at day's end was chilled but calm.

Jalak led the way inside after a stop at the ticket booth to purchase two seats. Those Kwandri on line were mostly young males, dressed in the same loose style affected by Glans and many of the youths Remy had observed around town. A few offworlders were present, several Enddrese and one of the unaffiliated Earthers Remy recalled from the reception—a tall woman in jackboots with two synthcrys-encrusted cyberports glinting from her shaved skull. She seemed to want to pretend that she was the only human around, so Remy left her alone.

Jalak had called the place a cin-den, but Remy knew better than to expect too much from the clientele. Theaters like this one catered to the softcore, the floppies; and while the stretch along the river could be considered a Terrana strip, the entertainments here, offworld though they might be, had received Grand Assembly sanction. The kids who frequented them were just doing what Baj and dozens like him did in the privacy of their own homes.

The hardcore, the undergrounders, gathered elsewhere, in places denied to Jalak. The culturist wouldn't even acknowledge their existence, but Remy could sense them: deeper, darker, too dangerous to surface above Likat's cobbled avenues and perfumed boulevards.

Glans was here, though, and that constituted a start.

The concentrated commingling of a myriad exhalations assaulted Remy as he followed Jalak through a set of swinging doors and down into the theater. The only light in the room was that given off by a large rear-projection flatscreen outfitted with a special lens that compensated for Kwandrian myopia. Holos and dimensionalized vids were lost on them, a fact that restricted their interest to primitive twentieth-century works.

No one seemed to be questioning Jalak and Remy's tour guide and newcomer partnership. Remy watched the SPECVES tail take a seat in the back row.

Onscreen was a laserdisk version of a Formative Era musical espionage allegory. The plot concerned the desperate but comical efforts of several ocean-vessel stowaways to infiltrate one of their number into an opera company, which by extension symbolized the USA.

Remy had trouble making sense of it, and he initially thought that the mixed scents buffeting him—odors of cumin and new-mown grass, aged paper and ocean spray, boiled eggs and cotton sheets—were an indication of like confusion.

"Scent-conjurers," Jalak said into Remy's ear, above honking noises in the film's original soundtrack.

Remy's eyes followed the culturist's finger to the front of the theater, where a trio of Kwandri were seated at what looked like an old pipe organ. On closer inspection the organ resembled a redolence device of the sort used in aroma therapy salons in the habitats.

"Subtitles!" Remy said, in sudden realization.

Jalak nodded, one hand reaching for a beard that was no longer there. "Most of them don't understand the words or the onscreen actions, but a good team of scent-conjurers can summon appropriate responses with artificially produced aromas."

"Like piano soundtracks for silents."

"Somewhat, yes. But the scents are more than accompaniment or background. They *are* the dialogue."

Remy got a strong whiff of nose-tickling pollen admixed with ozone. A smell of oft-used storage lockers, a hint of methane. Onscreen a dozen people were trying to cram themselves into a small cabinspace aboard the ocean vessel. The audience was howling, acting out the scene in interpretive pantomime. Aliens and movies, Remy thought. Like love and marriage.

"Glans is here," Jalak said quietly.

They were standing at the back of the theater, but off to one side; so Remy had a clear view of the trendily attired youth as he made his entrance and stood akimbo at the head of the center aisle.

Glans glanced at Jalak, then began to saunter off in the opposite direction, his right hand trailing along the low wall directly behind the uppermost row of seats.

Remy watched him turn the corner into the far aisle and sidestep into a sparsely occupied midsection row. Glans threw his wedgelike feet over the forward chair and tipped his head back in a bored fashion.

"All right," Jalak said, "let's get on with it."

The SPECVES agent was thoroughly engrossed in the film. "Go," Remy told him.

The culturist walked in Glans's tracks, right hand trailing the wall. Remy assumed they were making for the empty seats on either side of the Kwandri agent; but just short of the aisle Jalak about-faced. Remy caught up with him in the lobby.

"What was all that about?"

Jalak, eyes closed and arms at his sides, was leaning against the rear wall, flexing his hands, as though exercising them.

"It sometimes takes a moment," Jalak said, breathing hard.

Laughter filtered in from the theater. "Glans left an infosmear on the wall. Your hand absorbed it."

Jalak nodded, eyelids tight. "He has information about the embassy bombing."

"Why the hell didn't he pass that at the bench?" Remy seethed.

"Because he didn't have it then."

Remy made an exasperated sound. "I want details, Jalak."

"I'm not Q'aantre, Remy," the professor returned in a pained voice. "We need a face-to-face. I can use the aromatic to signal him," he added, patting the pouch pocket of his trousers.

"Then do it, for chrissake."

The safehouse NCorp had set up for payment exchanges and emergency situations was located in a residential district a few blocks from the river strip. The lower floor was given over to Jalak's library and office, where he conducted cultural research interviews with Kwandri informants. The culturist was well known to his neighbors in the area, who thought little of the constant comings and goings through the tall glass-paneled front doors. Subagents, however, made use of the corridor door that linked the safehouse to an adjacent five-story, multiple-dwelling unit.

The house had been under surveillance some time

ago, Jalak explained, but Special Investigations had satisfied itself that nothing untoward was going on.

The two Earthers were waiting to remote the Kwandri through the side door.

"I stopped to have something to eat," Glans announced as he entered, in full control. Remy could smell the cockiness clear across the room. "I'll give you what I have, but I want something extra for it."

Jalak felt Remy studying him from behind the curtains and looked away.

Remy stepped out and ordered the Kwandri to the couch. Glans threw Jalak a panicked glance.

"Sit down," Remy repeated.

The professor nodded reassuringly and Glans warily perched himself on the far arm of the couch. Remy put on his working face.

"Simon tells me you're a woodworker, 'Glans.' "

Glans looked to Jalak before answering. "Yes." The reply was tentative; the Kwandri's self-possession gone.

"And where does a furniture maker learn about acts of terrorism?"

The Kwandri's fine brown coat bristled above the collar of his Enddrese jacket. "You're not in any trouble," Jalak said. He showed Remy a hard-edged look. "There's no need to frighten him."

Remy showed them his palms. "I'm not trying to frighten anyone. But I want assurance the data came from a reliable source." He regarded the youth. "Maybe Glans was there when the embassy was bombed. Maybe he overheard something in a conversation. Which is it, Glans?"

"Someone in the wood shop was talking," the Kwandri began on a reticent note. "He knows two of the ones involved in the bombing—Norak and Els Fas. He himself isn't a sympathizer. He would never participate in such things." Glans looked imploringly at Jalak. "Please, I don't want to reveal his name."

"That's all right, we don't want the name."

"Then . . . you'll pay me and I can leave?"

Remy adopted an expression of surprise. "Pay you? For *two* names, Glans? How many terrorists are there— twenty? Thirty? Fifty?"

"I—"

"And these two siblings—Norak and Els—are they just anti-Xell'em, or have they been involved in demonstrations against the Terran mission as well?"

Glans wore a helpless expression. "But Maestro Jalak has never asked— That is, he pays me—"

"I know what he's paid you," Remy said. "And I know he's been helping you with your wardrobe. But things have changed. If you want to keep yourself in Terrana, you're going to have to do better than two names."

Glans said, "I'll try, I promise."

Remy sniffed fear, confusion, a willingness to please. "Good. In that case I want to add a little something to your reward—a gesture of my appreciation."

Glans's eyes widened at sight of the Mr. T gold-plated chains. Remy let the jewelry dangle from one hand. "Go on, take it. I know you won't disappoint me."

Glans leaned over and slipped the necklace from Remy's finger. "I don't know how to reply."

"Hey, it happens," Remy told him.

The Kwandri looked about uneasily. "I should be getting home."

"Yes, go home, Glans," Jalak said with undisguised regret. "Just be careful. And remember to mark your dead drops. It's important we remain in touch."

Glans's nod was an earnest one. He was halfway to the door before Remy said, "There is one more thing . . ." The Kwandri blanched. "At the cin-den tonight. I couldn't help notice you seemed disinterested."

Glans shuffled in place. "I've seen that one before."

Remy raised his chin. "That would explain it." He waited until Glans was through his turn. "I suppose that's about as exciting as it gets in Likat, huh? A vid, a pair of UV glasses, a gold-plated chain . . .''

The youth was staring at him, nostrils flared.

Remy raised himself to his full height. ''Where's a Kwandri go for real excitement, Glans—the new kind of excitement?''

It was Jalak's turn to wear the puzzled frown. ''What are you asking of him?''

Remy narrowed his eyes. ''Glans knows what I'm talking about.''

The Kwandri met his gaze with a sudden aggressiveness. ''Is that what you want?''

''For now.''

Glans mulled it over. ''Meet me at the theater tomorrow night. Wait until the show has ended.'' He made a smirking sound. ''The 'new excitement' doesn't get going before midnight.''

SIX —

"**I** JUST THOUGHT YOU WERE A BIT HARD on the boy," Jalak said when they were about fifty miles outside of Likat. The four-seater methanol burner was courtesy of DisneyCorp and the culturist was driving.

"Plan on my being just as hard on the rest of your subs," Remy told him. "Remember your training, Professor: It's the politically motivated agent you've got to watch out for. The rest you reward when they've been good and scold when they haven't. You learn what they run on and you use that to insure a strong return. You get nowhere trying to make them like you. I'll tell you again: They're not your children."

"No," Jalak said flatly, "we just treat them that way."

Remy glared at him, then turned away to face the passenger-side window. He knew that Jalak wasn't to blame for the foul mood; it was just the damned openness and desolation of the landscape. They hadn't left the city environs when the agoraphobia settled on him like bad weather, and he couldn't shake loose the irritability that went along with it.

He had reconned comparable downside scapes on Daleth and Raliish moons and experienced the same

sense of imminent panic. The result of too many years
spent in Earth Force starships and orbital habitats; a
spacer's cross. Odd to think he found more comfort in
crowded cities, but there you were.

Nanff's village was called Tsegg Tsirran, which meant
"place of the high wall." *Old Q'aantre*, Jalak kept saying, as if the cursed plateau they were traversing wasn't
old enough. Els was back in the suite, vidmerized when
Remy had left him, the envy of the hotel and half the
Interior Ministry to hear Baj tell it. Everyone in Likat
yearned for a Craftmatic adjustable bed, a Rubik's
Cube, a set of Leggos, and a trip up the well.

"And why does one have to be careful with the
politically motivated agent?" Jalak asked, breaking a
five-minute silence.

"What?" Remy said.

"You said you had to watch out for them—the political ones."

"Because they've got their own agenda—no matter
what they promise you. You take your time to cultivate
and nourish a network and the next thing you know
you're being ordered offworld by the same ones you
helped set up in positions of power."

"Is that NCorp's aim on Q'aantre—to ascend certain
individuals to positions of power?"

Remy scowled. "You're making too much of this,
Professor. Center just wants the Xell'em out of here."

The two Earthers fell silent once more.

Dazyl burned through gray clouds hugging the edge
of the plateau and a wind came up to stir the bunch
grass. A chain of saw-toothed, snowcapped mountains
appeared on the horizon and Remy began to understand
why the village had been so named.

Tsegg Tsirran had a few buildings that could be considered modern by precontact standards—a bank, a
consumer outlet, a communications center—but most of
the village was earthen in texture, in composition and
smell. The kind of treeless, windswept place kids ev-

erywhere were wont to abandon for the thrills of urban life. Word of the Earthers' visit had imparted a festive mood to the unpaved main street, where several dozen Kwandri were turned out in resplendent homespun garb.

Most, however, were naked. Clothing was New Kwandri.

Remy and Jalak made their way from the car to a decoratively awninged platform erected in the central square. Dark-coated children with outstretched hands asked for vid players and fax machines. Odd-looking domesticated animals growled but kept their distance.

Adult Kwandri were lined up on both sides of a woven trailer two hundred feet in length, leaning in on wedged feet, exhaling gustative welcome scents of cinnamon, baked bread, and mother's milk. The males cupped their genitalia with one hand, waved with the other. The females kissed the backs of their fingertips and bowed their heads. Some hid their breasts.

"I am Els Nanff," the old one on the wooden throne announced as Remy and Jalak approached. Remy watched the culturist for cues, determined not to shake testicles unless he had to.

The elder Els was a shaman and healer of some reputation among the tribes of the plateau.

"This is Res Santoul," Jalak said, indicating Remy with his right hand. "The offworlder who came to the aid of your thirdborn."

Silver-coated Els studied his son's benefactor more with his nose than his oblique eyes. Remy considered toothing a dermal fragrance but decided to go with whatever his body was emitting on its own.

"Els is being well cared for?" the shaman asked.

Jalak did the translating. Remy likewise relied on him to convey his promise that Els would continue to be cared for until his bones knit.

"And does the Terran wish to honor the *bal*?"

The *supplemental*, Jalak had called it. The pledge Remy had made to carry out Els's wish to go up the well. Remy reaffirmed the pledge now. He couldn't follow Jalak's High Kwandri translation of "up the well," but faces were soon beginning to tilt skyward.

Els sniffed thoughtfully. "And Res Santoul will also see to my thirdborn's return?"

Like the station was just another place on the plateau, Remy told himself. Hell, maybe it was. "Yes," he said, "I will oversee his safe return to Tsegg Tsirran as well." Even if that meant another damned trip through agoraphobia.

The statement brought a rise out of the crowd and all at once Remy found himself at the center of a deluge of spiced emanations. His head swam with chords of ozone and rain-dampened earth, of leather and musk, olive wood and feathers.

The elder Els offered a toothless smile and conjured a floral scent-storm for the crowd. Odors reminiscent of hyacinth, violet, carnation, and sweet pea that put Remy in mind of the fragrances Jasna, his ex, wore. He squeezed back a sneeze and a painful memory.

"Well, well," Jalak said, nodding as he looked over his inside shoulder at Remy, "it looks like you finally made yourself some downside friends."

"What happened to your car?" Glans asked as he slid into the passenger seat hours later. He was on time and there was no hint of the combativeness that had surfaced the previous evening. Remy didn't want him to feel too at ease, so he added an edge to his response, eyes fixed forward, gloved hands gripped on the controls.

"A rock jumped out in front of it," he said, around a dissolving peppermint stim-wafer.

"A rock?" the Kwandri said.

Remy eyed him askance. "That's right. Now, which way are we going?"

Sullen, Glans flipped a bleached forefinger toward the windscreen. "Straight to the shuttleport."

Remy commanded the car out into traffic, enabling the contracollision system when they had attained the center lane. Vehicular traffic was light, but there were plenty of pedestrians to worry about, most of them shuffling preoccupied from darkening cin-dens along the strip.

The rock had actually jumped in front of Jalak, who had the wheel when they rammed into it. Standing in the chill mist of the plateau afterward, the two Earthers agreed that given the copious amounts of *yika* they had consumed in Tsegg Tsirran and the score of bottomless crevasses that lay between there and Likat, a crumpled front end was the least of what could have transpired. It had seemed the shaman's purpose to so sate them on foodstuffs and exhalations they would be forced to spend the night; but in the end the nonstop drinking only caused them to forget to engage the vehicle's contracollision system.

With the midnight rendezvous in mind, Remy had managed to fit in two hours of dreamless sleep back at the hotel. Not near enough to clear the haze from his peripheral vision or mute the ring in his ears; but the car was equipped to compensate for the former, and Glans had little to say after the initial exchange.

Rain slick on the inner city streets was snow out by the shuttleport. Nothing the car couldn't handle. Glans instructed Remy to turn left toward the cargo hangars, then left again as they neared the turnoff for Pov Tam, a small prefab settlement that had grown up with the landing zone itself.

Remy had killed a couple hours here a week earlier, wandering around while an unexplained warning pulse in shuttle control had comptechs at the port arguing it out with the wheel mainframe. The place wasn't much more than a hexagon of inwardly aligned ultratech buildings and blackmart stalls catering to cargo movers, space tramps, and transients. But Pov Tam's purportedly off-limits status naturally encouraged visits from the more courageous and experimental of Kwandri's citizenry.

All in all it was the perfect setting for underground action, so Remy wasn't too surprised to see couples stepping from chauffeur-driven cars and hurrying off through the flurries toward one garishly plasticized doorway or another.

Glans directed him to a parking zone in back of a small semicylindrical hangar. They walked down a narrow ramp that led to a card-only portal and entered a dank and fetid-smelling holding area.

Queued up at a pneumatic entry pillared by two imposing examples of transgenic Enddrese musculature were thirty or more Kwandri, fenced behind a shifting curtain of laser fanlight. A cyan scrawl of plasma-script above the door identified the place as the Club Terrana.

"I can get us in," Glans said, loud enough to be heard over frenzied, high-register horns and a heart-throbbing bass. Remy stepped aside to let him take charge. Glans displayed for the queue as he sauntered by.

"What's your drive?" the hirsute of the two Enddrese asked in tradespeak, with a slab of callused hand raised to Remy's chest. Glans was already standing proudly at the hatch, his admittance secure.

"I was dropped from the *Chakra*," Remy told him in fluent Enddrese. "Holing for Ralii on the *Anglo*."

"You sorry fuck," the XT said, grinning. "Guess you deserve a good laugh." The hand that had been splayed at Remy's midsection slapped an inset reader on the wall and the heavy quilted hatch slid aside.

Four wide steps led down into something lifted from Earth's preexpansionist past: a seemingly boundless room of deafening music and incoherent light. Off to one side, backed by a wallscreen of explosive, kaleidoscopic color, was a low stage featuring a trio of scantily clad Kwandri females in outsize cages, convulsing their way through a bizarre interpretation of suggestive, synchronized dance. On the floor below, Kwandri females in bell-bottomed pants and miniskirts were mimicking the dancers' stiff movements, while groups of males clapped off-time from booths, tables, and couches.

Remy's nose grappled with musky and perfumed aromas; odors of burning paper, smoldering tobacco, whiskey, urine, and chemical disinfectants. No one was smoking, though, or drinking, or engaging in any activity that could account for the heady redolence of sex in the air.

Glans was smiling, tapping his foot. "You said you wanted to see the real thing."

Remy gave him a dubious look and made straight for a seat at the bar—a circle of stainless steel, centered around a thick column adorned at intervals with half a dozen heads-up monitors. Crudely filmed and self-indulgently edited twentieth-century music vidvertisements were running on some of these; others displayed similarly aged adverts for sports cars, cigarettes, beer, and sundry consumer goods.

Atop the bar, ninety degrees from Remy's stool, a young Earth woman who had spent too many years in the atrophying effects of null-gee was playing air guitar. The high heel she kicked in Remy's direction nearly took out his left eye. Most of the ensuing laughter came from offworlders.

"You lose eye, you make love like Kwandri," a female indig told Remy as she skillfully positioned herself between him and a bemused Glans. She was attractive if a bit overweight, with widely spaced eyes and a wavy coat the color of ferrocrete. "You buy Kitti drink?" she continued in pidgin, canted in that crazy Kwandri posture, stroking his shoulder.

"Kitty?!"

"Kitti, Kitti," she said, accenting the second syllable. "You buy drink, Kitti be nice-nice with tall Terran?"

"Nice-nice?!"

She bobbed her head, eyes mere slits when she smiled. The rotund Earther polishing the selector knobs on the bar's drinkmaster was also smiling. "Two champain," she told him.

"What about me?" Glans asked, shouldering into the conversation.

Kitti sniffed in his direction and issued a scent of disapproval. "Kitti no drink with boy." She followed it up with a phrase of rapid-fire Kwandri that brought a look of outrage to Glans's face; but the bartender intervened before Jalak's agent could respond.

"Why don't you two take it down there?" the big man suggested. "So the Earther and I can merge words." He eyeballed Remy's synthsilk jumpsuit and vented jacket as the two Kwandri moved off in argument. Remy put a hand over his ringed finger. "Haven't seen you here before, have I?" he asked.

"First time," Remy said. "Only been downside for a few weeks."

"You're on a ship, then?"

"The wheel. I'm with DisneyCorp."

The man tucked in triple chins in feigned surprise. "The one night I don't wear my clean shirt. So how's the trade in icons . . ."

"Remy, Remy Santoul."

"Vegas."

Remy shook the proffered hand—the first thing he felt safe touching since entering the bar. Vegas's bulk was real enough, but everything else about him—from the lightning bolt hairline to the triple chins and extra digits—had been altered at one time or another. "Business is," Remy said.

"Yeah, I suppose. Had a guy in here, what, maybe three weeks ago, said he had a photo-mannequin of Ayatollah Khomeini he wanted to sell. Looked ersatz to me, told him so."

"You did the right thing. They're not bringing what

they used to. You see a Ronnie Reagan, you grab it though.''

Vegas was quiet for a moment. "You're from BASF, my guess. Citi maybe.''

"Right the second time.'' Remy showed the Citi ring.

"Never miss an accent.''

"And you're Fabríca.''

Vegas smiled. "Always good to meet another spacer. So what can I have the bar fix you?''

"You're saying you have valid goods in there?'' Remy asked, gesturing to the drinkmaster.

Vegas looked puzzled, then laughed and motioned to the tables and dance floor. "They don't come here to drink. Just act it out, you know. Get loose, drink 'champain.' Just like in the cin-dens.''

"I'll have a brandy, in that case.'' Remy tuned in to the music while Vegas's back was turned, realizing only then that what he'd taken for a kind of frantic march was simply an old standard the Club Terrana veejay was running at twice normal speed.

"To Sol,'' Vegas said, lifting a snifter of his own. "And to warmer worlds.''

"*Nazdorovye.*'' Remy raised his glass and sipped at the amber liquid. "So who's chief programmer for this little bit of heaven?''

Vegas knocked back the drink and ran a hand across his full mouth. "You want the rumor or the story everyone's supposed to believe?''

"Give me both and the next round's on me.''

"Ready. The accepted truth's that Golden Arches went online with some honchos in the Grand Assembly—some kind of probe to see if a franchise'll run here. There's talk about expanding the shuttleport, putting up hotels, casinos, making Kwandri a downside stop for tour ships out to Burst and Daleth.'' Vegas put his elbows on the bar and adopted a conspiratorial tone of voice. "'Course that spin's got a lot to do with what the Xell'em have planned for the place.''

Remy swirled his drink. "And the rumor?"

Vegas's voice became lower still. "NCorp funds." He pronounced it *encore*.

"NCorp? Why would they want to open a bar?"

Vegas looked around. "It's not the *bar*, Santoul, it's what the bar does, you understand? Go ahead, glance around, you see what Terrana does to the coats. They keep craving the music, the colors, Xella gets dumped, right? But what do I care? My credits come at the end of every month. Hell, Santoul, you're in the business, you see what goes on."

Remy held the big man's gaze. "What business?"

"Disney, Santoul. Your corp does the same thing."

Remy shook his head. "Vegas, I assure you our exchanges are undertaken with the full consent of the governing body. Years of research go into determining—"

"Yeah, yeah. But it calculates the same, doesn't it?"

Remy motioned to the stage. "We'd never condone this . . . travesty."

Vegas snorted. "You're a case, Santoul. So we dazzle them with some sound and light, waft in some aromas to get them high, encourage them to take their clothes off. The coats still can't act on anything."

"What do you mean, they can't 'act' on anything."

"Just what I'm saying: We can saturate this place with musk, dope, and flesh and it just can't go nowhere."

Remy kept his theatrical bewilderment in place.

Vegas laughed, shaking his huge head. "Santoul, I like you. And when Vegas likes someone, it means they're in for a special treat. So how about it: you game for a special treat?"

Remy hesitated. "Special treats have a way of costing more than I can afford," he began, reaching for his credit card. But his hand never made it to his pocket.

"Tonight's on the house, how's that?"

Remy slowly exhaled. "Well, sure, Vegas," he said. "I'm game."

* * *

The offworlders-only back room turned out to be a comfortably appointed lounge with a mobile drinkmaster and an inhouse holo system. The room was unoccupied when Vegas led Remy in, but the holo was activated, offering a close-up of one of the Kwandri dancers onstage.

It was only after Remy had stated his preference for the live view that Vegas had called up a much wilder scene, presumably remoted from elsewhere in the club. Infield now were two naked Kwandri females and one rather diminutive male, engaged in what was less a simulation of copulation than a pathetic misinterpretation of it.

"Life in the VIK room," Vegas said, leaning into the holo-field with an enormous grin on his face.

Remy figured the male was the Very Important Kwandri in question, although that wasn't necessarily substantiated by the would-be carnal activities taking place on the large bed.

The orgy room itself was red-lit and equipped with its own flatscreen; theirs, however, was running a fuck vid that had to have been disked on Dhone—one of the few places in the Arm where humanoids coupled with such graphic abandon. The human male in the field and the Kwandri spread-eagled on the bed were presently in like positions, as were the females bending over them. Except that where mutual arousal was blantantly obvious in the flatscreen vid, it was conspicuously absent on the bed. In fact, the trio's urgent gropings and wild gyrations bore no more resemblance to human sexuality than the clipped contortions of the caged females out front bore to expressive dance.

Still, for all his sudden disquietude, Remy couldn't take his eyes away. Simon Jalak's words came back to him; the culturist's concerns about the impact of Earth's exported culture on the Kwandri's hithertofore biorhythmically regulated sensuality. Jalak either didn't know about places like the Club Terrana, or chose to ignore them.

"Santoul," Vegas said leadingly. "How many Kwandri females does it take to change the flux rods in a jump transformer?"

Remy wasn't sure he wanted to know.

"Five," Vegas continued, undaunted. "One to insert each of the four rods, and the fifth to wipe them off and put them back where they belong!"

Remy let him laugh for a moment. "I don't under—"

"Sure you do! The whole planet's got a performance problem, see? Outside of Teg'non, when they all get nuts, so to speak. I mean, look at them, will you? The poor coats wanna be just like us but it doesn't run. They wanna fuck at the drop of a suitflap but they can't."

Remy watched the trio in the cone-shaped field change positions and try again. At the bar he had at least sensed something *heartfelt* about the dancing and merrymaking, but this . . . this was a perversion.

"Jeez, haven't they heard of aphrodisiacs?" Remy asked.

Vegas shook his head. "They don't work. People have tried, believe me."

"What about direct stim?"

The bartender laughed. "You're out of synch, Santoul. The coats don't want dermatrodes, they want action. The meat. Shit, the whole Arm's sick of direct stim."

"I know," Remy said, cutting Vegas off. "Back to basics."

The Kwandri male was on his stomach now, facing the optical pickup in the room, his partners raking taloned fingers through his rear coat. Ash-blond and slender, he had soulful, downward-turning eyes, widely spaced in an almost triangular face. His pink belly looked freshly depilated.

"Who is he?" Remy asked finally.

Vegas leaned back into a couch barely large enough to contain him. "Hey, spacer, I'm not really supposed to reveal names. But what the hell," he hastened to add, "you'll probably run into him next time Disney-Corp's invited to one of those Assembly dos."

Vegas crossed his hands on his paunch and belched. "Name's Morli. Liaison chief with the Ministry of ExtraPlanetary Affairs. Assembly member. Comes in here maybe twice a week, strictly back-room stuff."

Remy was all ears. "What makes you think he's with the ministry?"

"I know the guy, is why. He's into Terrana. I put him in touch with a guy who had a legit Bug Zapper. I hear Morli's got it on display in the front room of his house. But he's not like some of the flashier coats who walk in here—not like the one you came in with."

Remy didn't ask for Glans's real tag; the fewer names you knew the better for all concerned. "You keep doing favors for the right people, you'll end up with your own invite, Vegas."

"Could be, Captain, could be," Vegas said. "But I'll tell you one thing: This Morli's got the goods on Xell'em futures downside. I hear it, he's even been up to their station."

"What, the flashpoint station?"

"Am I the CEO of valid?"

Remy glanced at the figures in the field. "What about the women? Always the same ones?"

"Not a chance. Morli might be an ineffectual little fuck but he's not brain-damaged. The girls work the house."

"But I thought they couldn't—"

"No, they can't. But like I say, they wanna be just like us. That Kitti'd talk you into buying her 'champain' all night and tell you her life story if you'd let her. Be the first to marry herself a Terran mate. 'Sides, who knows what'll happen after a year or so of music, movies, and amp-ed light? Maybe they'll start feeling the urge out of season, open up a bit."

Vegas laughed. "Coupla space marines come in here a month back, start talking about organizing things, set up a fixed price and start numbering the females like they do on Dhone."

Remy ran a hand down his face; when he looked up, the bartender had a thick finger on the holo's selector button. "What d'you say we jump around, see what's cooking in some of the other rooms?"

"Other rooms?" Remy started to say when the first of the warning hooters sounded.

Vegas cursed and tapped the selector button until the field showed a view of the club's front door from the vantage of the bar. The two Earthers watched as an unseen directed-energy weapon vaporized the door seal.

"Piss in my goddamned neural helmet!" Vegas said, propelling himself to his feet. "A raid, a goddamned raid! And I just paid those fuckers off," he added, turning to Remy.

The front room was pure pandemonium now as police in full riot gear began to file through what was left of the entrance. Behind them came plainclothes officers and several Xell'em.

"SPECVES," Remy said.

"And then some," Vegas amended.

Remy followed him out into the dimly lit corridor where dishabille was the order of the moment. Kwandri of both genders were slipping into whatever articles of clothing were nearest as they rushed madly for windows, stairways, and exits. Concern for Glans made Remy turn for the bar, but Vegas restrained him.

"Not that way," he shouted. "There's a better way out."

By the time Remy spun around, the big bartender was twenty feet down the hallway, several Kwandri lying dazed in his wake. Must have spent a small fortune on bodywork, Remy thought, hurrying to catch up. Whoever had done the overhaul had outfitted Vegas with more than enough muscle to carry the load.

Remy put his long legs into it, and was just streaking through the first corridor intersection when he collided with the Xell'em.

They met head-on and went down together, victims of momentum, hands held to sore skulls as they looked up to glare at each other from opposite walls of the corridor. A dozen fleeing, barefoot Kwandri hurdled their outstretched legs and went keystoning around a far corner.

The XT male was sizing Remy up. Given their relative positions, Remy thought he might have five inches and six kilos on the guy, but what the Xell'em lacked in height he made up for in shoulders and filed teeth. And when the Xell'em pulverized a small piece of the plaster wall with a lightning fast chopping motion of his left hand, Remy realized that the combat modifications weren't limited to his mouth.

The Xell'em sprung himself into a crouch and Remy kipped in response, kicking him two-footed in the face. The XT fell back against the wall, but the blood he smeared from under a nose commentators were fond of terming *Romanesque* only prompted a second, staggering display of agility.

That Remy barely saw the punches coming was what saved him from anticipating the pain they inflicted. He slid out from under the rain with consciousness intact and got in a spin kick that connected with artificially hardened body muscle before the Xell'em had him wrapped up in a forward-facing bear hug and was slamming his elongated cranium into Remy's chin.

When the XT tired of that, he opened his jaws and began to withdraw his head for a carotid strike. That's when Remy decided to tongue one of the oral mists.

Credit for the repellent spray had to go to the wetware junkie back at Center who thought it might prove effective in tight quarters, and so it did. Triggering the fetor simultaneously dammed Remy's olfactory pathways, but the Xell'em inhaled more than a good lungful and was now writhing on the floor, coughing fitfully.

Remy aimed a solid toekick at a tattooed cheekbone for good measure.

Vegas appeared, scowling and waving a hand in front of his face. "What a stench," he said. The words were muffled by his fingers. "Don't they teach you Disney reps about the pucker factor? You suck in your gut or it'll turn to mush and run right outta you."

Remy indicated his unconscious opponent. "It's this one. Something about the Xell'em diet, I guess."

Vegas regarded the XT and shrugged. "Well, now's no time for foreplay. Correct for attitude, son, the club's closed for the season . . ."

Three minutes of confusing twists and turns and Vegas had them outside in the snow.

"I gotta remember to start tying my goddamned jacket around my waist," Remy commented, shivering.

Vegas said. "And I've gotta start looking for a new gig."

Patrol wagons with Mars lights were roaring toward the rear of the hangar along the main drive. Remy spied a solitary limo lost in the darkness not fifty yards from Vegas's emergency exit. Interior light spilled from an opened rear door, and it was Morli he saw clambering inside, naked as he'd been in the VIK room only fifteen minutes before.

Remy nearly forgot about the cold air and the snow collecting on his head and shoulders as he watched the vehicle steal silently from the scene. Thinking how he'd just secured himself an agent.

SEVEN—

"R*es Santoul,*" Morli *said.* "T*hen* you're also firstborn."

"My given name's Remy," the NCorp operative said, "but I am firstborn."

"Ah, *Remy.* The one from DisneyCorp. Yes, Norak has told me about you."

Norak Baj was standing off to one side, the perfect host, pleased that the introduction had gone so well.

"It's true, Remy. I've been telling Res what an improvement you are over your predecessor, Ms. Canu. Not that I mean to belittle her efforts," Baj was quick to add. "She obviously meant well. It was simply that she lacked a certain understanding of Q'aantre ways."

"I only met the woman on two occasions," Morli said, "so of course I'm in no position to comment. But I do sense that what Norak tells me is correct—you are indeed possessed of uncommon *messegg*—what we call intuitive kinship." He sniffed ever so slightly in Remy's direction. "Is this something DisneyCorp has seen to, or do you come by it naturally . . . Remy?"

"I'm willing to split the credit," Remy told him.

Baj and Morli laughed. "A most politic response."

One of Densign's mission staffers ambled over to introduce herself. Remy made use of the interruption to converse privately with Baj.

"How'd you like the bomber jacket?" he asked quietly through a fixed smile.

"I was left absolutely scentless," the Kwandri said in a like tone.

"Sorry it had to be ersatz. I told you, we could both retire on what a genuine commands."

Baj waved a hand. "The jacket was more than I dared hope, believe me."

The Kwandri probably would have been the first to deny it, but Remy was convinced it was the jacket that had secured the invitation to Baj's formal dinner. Just now Baj was sporting Slinky bracelets, and a red aluminum ant-trap pendant hanging from a large-linked choker of chrome chain.

A little over a standard-week had gone by since the raid on the Club Terrana. Remy had spent most of that time ferreting out background data on his new quarry, Res Morli.

Red Year of the *Bontom*, he had correctly surmised. Baj's polar opposite, zodiacally and politically.

Vegas was on target about much of it: Morli was a member of the Grand Assembly, was well placed in the Ministry of ExtraPlanetary Affairs, and was indeed shuttled up to the Xell'em wormhole station on a regular basis.

It struck Remy initially that Morli was perhaps too well situated if anything; and it seemed possible that the Xell'em were grooming him for some more lofty position than liaison chief. The more Remy asked around, however, the more he became convinced that Morli simply regarded the Xell'em as the only game in town. Densign, after all, hadn't extended any invitations to visit Terra's torus; and it was obvious that construction of the proposed orbital tower might never commence.

Glans—through the same woodwork shop contact

who had furnished the names of two of the terrorists—
had verified Morli's single status and his fondness for
Terrana.

The young agent, along with several dozen club
goers, had spent two nights in jail as a result of the
raid. The charges brought against them had more to do
with violating Pov Tam's off-limits restrictions than violating any statutes of public decency. But SPECVES
had interviewed and photographed all of them, and
while Glans seemed to be taking the whole matter in
stride, Remy was forced to consider him dirtied.

The data on Morli, though, had been corroborated
and was firm enough to include in the précis Remy had
compiled. He had finally flashed all the material upside
to Ishida—along with a lengthy recruitment assessment
that emphasized Morli's sexual proclivities—and almost
immediately received operational approval to make an
approach.

The arrival of the invitation to Baj's dinner party
couldn't have been better timed.

The house itself was a spacious, imposing structure
of turrets, grand stairways, and massive fireplaces. The
main room where Remy and some sixty others were
gathered was electrically lit by chandeliers and wall
sconce fixtures. There were perhaps a dozen others
chatting and exchanging scents in the step-down den.
Each of Baj's Kwandri guests had received a Pez Dispenser and a pocket diet-dessert spray at the door, including young Els Nanff, Remy's personal guest, whom
he had last seen limping off with Baj's secondborn son.

Baj had been careful to invite an equal number of
Terrans and Xell'em. Among the latter group, Remy
had spotted a broad-shouldered bodyguard with a dis-
colored cheek. The man recognized Remy as well—
although Remy's own minor bruises from the corridor
encounter had long since healed.

He was the ugliest member of Ambassador and Madame Xu's retinue, but had been paired for the occasion

with a statuesque woman in a strapless, backless gown, stiletto heels, and long black gloves, whose visible alterations were confined to ears and chin. Remy thought she might be one of the most handsome women he had ever seen—of the Xell'em or any other planetary race— and even now he had his eye out for her.

"Karine," Morli said suddenly.

Remy turned around and found himself alone with the Kwandri, Baj and Densign's staffer having walked off together. "I'm sorry, Res, I didn't—"

"Karine Mareer," Morli completed. "The woman you were admiring. She processes travel applications for the embassy." He smiled. "It's not unusual to see fifty people lined up at her office door—by sunrise, mind you. Although I suspect half that number have no intentions whatever of requesting visitor permits to Xell'em station."

"I can appreciate that," Remy started to say as a new scent filled the room and a bell chimed in the foyer.

"That would be our call to dinner, Remy," Morli said, inhaling and offering his arm. "Shall we?"

Remy shrugged without showing it and linked arms with the shorter being. "Delighted," he said, grinning.

Glass and glazed ceramic dinnerware covered a T-shaped arrangement of intricately carved wooden tables. Baj's guests of honor—Grand Assembly members and ministry officials—occupied tall-backed chairs along the crossbar, while Terrans and Xell'em, intersperced with Kwandri and a few Enddrese, sat facing one another along the length of the leg, log fires crackling in cavernous stone fireplaces at their backs. Place settings were equipped with Terran-made translingual devices capable of rendering dozens of languages and dialects into Inner Arm tradespeak.

Remy was seated halfway down the leg, flanked on the left by Ayyum Legguum and on the right by a mission staffer. Densign was closer to the head of the table, where Baj and Morli had adjacent seats. Nanff and the other youngsters had a room to themselves near the kitchen, where Baj kept the prize of his Terrana collection: a terribly battered Wurlitzer jukebox. The vinyl disks it had once played were no longer available, so Baj had decorated the ancient round-topped thing as a shrine to Moki Jo, the Kwandri goddess of the home.

Opposite Remy across a six-foot expanse of embroidered cloth topped with candle-heated tureens and crystal decanters sat Xu's undersecretary—a woman whose facial tattoos, receding chin, and severely elongated skull embodied the very ideal of Xell'em transmogrification. To her immediate right was Baj's second subordinate, Ayyum Dali; and much farther right, almost at the foot of the table were the bruised bodyguard and the XT beauty Morli had identified as Karine Mareer.

Baj stood up to give a short welcome speech that was long on hope and optimism for Kwandri's future, and after a brief series of sniffing and sipping rituals, the dinner got under way.

Remy made polite conversation with Legguum and the staffer while course after spice-laden course was expertly set down and effortlessly swept away. He put the number of servants at thirty-two before losing count.

The feast had just reached the dessert stage when the modified voice of the Xell'em ambassador issued through the room's score of translingual annunciators. Xu was rising in place when Remy turned to look.

"Wishing neither to dissipate nor disturb the ambrosial redolence of this gathering," he began, "I would like to take this occasion to comment on the rash of incidents that have recently been directed against Xella's downside presence on this wondrous world."

Despite Xu's use of the high-formal introduction, Remy could feel discomfort uncoil itself through the room.

"I certainly don't mean to suggest that these incidents have been undertaken with either the knowledge or sanction of anyone in this room—and I'm aware that

Terran concerns have also suffered at the hands of these terrorists—but I do find myself perplexed at their occurrence. So perplexed that I am of a mind to entertain explanations from anyone present.'' He paused. ''Why is this such? And what exactly are the demands of this group, so few in number and yet so powerful in influence?''

Xu looked around for a moment. ''Can no one answer me?'' It was plain that the Kwandri weren't going to touch it, so everyone turned to the natural second choice: the Terran envoy. Remy craned his neck around Legguum's head to catch sight of Densign's reluctant rise.

''Ambassador Xu,'' he said, head lowered and jowls already quivering, ''I take you at your word that you don't wish to disturb the aromatic bouquet of the moment, but I'm afraid that's precisely what you've done.''

Densign showing Xu two could play, Remy thought.

''You conceal the piquant nature of your inquiries in perfumes and incense, but their acerbic exhalations come through. Now let me just say this about that—''

''Permit me to interrupt, Mr. Densign,'' Xu said calmly, showing his hands. ''Perhaps I was too all-embracing in my solicitation a moment ago. Both of us are but spokespersons for the policies of our homeworld governments. But I don't seek to turn this evening into a debate. I'm asking for responses of a personal sort—from an impartial quarter.''

Xu's epicanthic eyes scanned the table. ''Perhaps the representative from DisneyCorp has some insight to offer.''

It took Remy a moment to grasp that everyone was staring at him. Densign looked pale. Baj, Morli, and several other Kwandri were smiling. The Xell'em undersecretary had her arms folded beneath her serpent-patterned bosom.

''Yes, please, Mr. Santoul,'' one of the Grand

Assembly members enthused. "We're most interested to learn what you have to say."

Remy opened his mouth and closed it. He blew out his breath and cleared his throat. The mission staffer urged him to stand up.

"I, uh . . . " Ayyum Legguum elbowed him in the thigh, presumably as a demonstration of encouragement.

"Frankly," Remy said, "I'm not as shocked by these incidents as Ambassador Xu professes to be. Now I know some of you are surprised to hear me say this, and I suppose Mr. Densign probably has his hands over his ears by now"—which he in fact did—"but the truth is these bombings and demonstrations have less to do with the Xell'em than they have to do with the Xell'em *presence*."

Remy stole a downward glance at the undersecretary and immediately regretted it; the woman's crossed eyes launched a preemptive first strike that silenced him for several seconds.

"What I, uh, mean to suggest is that Q'aantre is using offworlder concerns as stages on which to act out its own rightfully incited inner turmoil. I feel confident about suggesting this because my own world suffered through millennia of similar travails."

People were leaning forward, rapt.

"At one time we actually thought it was wrong for white to intermarry with people of color. We took slaves, we denied women their rights, we even wore coats made of animal pelts. We thought it was perverse that those of the same sex should create homes and families. We distrusted our neighbors and fought wars over religion, territory, and economic needs.

"Ultimately it took near self-destruction to unify our manifold peoples, but even then we hadn't put all our problems to rest. When we spread out into local space, the old order of things began to reassert itself in the habitats. And again we went to war with one another.

Fortunately, Earth Force prevailed and corrected the matter.

"But this is bound to occur when a world people finally dispenses with its cherished notions of heavenly salvation and begins to accept responsibility for its own destiny. When it is finally forced to make an ethical decision about what it seeks to be, and what face it wishes to display to other worlds."

Remy was way over into autopilot now, spewing forth what NCorp's engrammers neurowired into him at least once a year.

"I see Q'aantre poised at this same juncture. Extraplanetary contact has brought unity and the worlds of the Inner Arm have brought technological wonders. But Q'aantre has yet to decide which way it wants to go. Q'aantre has yet to decide whether to dispense with the traditions that have guided it from infancy to adulthood; it has yet to struggle with issues of religion and equality and, yes, even sexuality and reproduction.

"So in response to your question, Ambassador Xu, the emanations you inhale from angry crowds, the bombs you hear exploding outside the gates of your banks and offices are not really meant for Xell'em noses or ears. They are for other Q'aantre to breathe and hear. They are the signs of a world coming to grips with self-determination. The signs of a world about to be reborn."

The cheering startled him. The Kwandri were up on their feet applauding wildly; the dining room filling up with saporous scents and buttery aromas. Remy smelled apples and peaches and amaranth and lily; he smelled baby's breath and sugar and myrrh.

The Xell'em sat frozen in their seats, and Densign wore a look of absolute despair. But Morli . . . Morli was ecstatic. Morli was inspired, astonished, and most of all, Morli was *convinced*.

And Remy knew by the Kwandri's expression that he had him.

PART TWO

—DOWNSIDE

EIGHT—

Morli marched along Likat's broad sidewalks exhaling anonymity and ignoring caution scents at intersections, just another preoccupied citizen in coveralls and poncho hurrying home from work after too long a day. No one inhaling him, save for the closest of his friends, would be able to identify him as Ser Res Morli, Director of Liaison with the Ministry of ExtraPlanetary Affairs, let alone sense that his belly was depilated and that underneath the street clothes of a laborer he was wearing Terran-made bikini briefs. Nor would anyone perceive the *secrets* that were stewing in his secretions: the names and departure dates of Xell'em ships, the hard data on flashpoint transits and shipping manifestos, the assessments of troop strength and combat capabilities, the minutes of the latest Grand Assembly meeting.

The sudden wealth of offworlder goods he received in exchange had certainly done wonders for his standing among certain Consortium-leaning members of the Assembly, but the designer briefs, monogrammed bath towels, celebrity makeup sponges, high-tech kitchenware, and low-impact workout vids had never provided the real impetus for his flirtation with covert intelligence gathering. And it disturbed him some to think that Remy still considered their relationship one of simple give and take, when in fact there were far nobler causes being served.

The principal thing that had drawn him to the tall, brown-haired Terran who looked every bit a vid-star himself was the impromptu speech he had delivered the night of Baj's dinner extravaganza. How moved Morli had been by the words and sounds of Remy's voice— words that somehow seemed meant for him alone, in answer to the torment that had raged within him since Q'aantre's early years of postcontact visitation. Then there had been many talks and discussions the two of them had engaged in since, long into the night on occasion, when Remy had spoken of his past and his distant homeworld.

That Remy had been born and raised on a station not unlike the ones that orbited Q'aantre was nothing less than inconceivable. And that he spent most of his life in similar stations and ships . . . well, it constituted a realm of experience that was perhaps generations removed from Q'aantre reality. On his most recent visit to Xell'em station, Morli had tried to imagine a life lived entirely in space; but he had only succeeded in arousing in himself a deeper sense of homesickness. Q'aantre appeared so fragile and insignificant against the deathly cold backdrop of the void, and he had experienced a moment of panic standing by the viewport of the Xell'em shuttle, a strong yearning to plant his feet firmly in the dark soil of his homeworld and remain there, forever . . .

During those long nights of discussion, however, Remy seemed disinclined to address the issues he raised in response to Ambassador Xu's challenge—the Xell'em's transparent attempts at inflaming an already dangerous situation. It was as though Remy refused to permit politics to intrude on their friendship. But with some continued encouragement in that direction, he had finally urged Remy's own secret to the surface and the Terran had told all.

Up until that point, Remy was something of an enigma; at times an unsavory combination of contradictory scents. Here was a man strong in *messegg*, a man who had taken one of Q'aantre's own into his life, and yet there hung about him a bitter odor of deceit.

Not unlike the chaffing emanation Morli was himself issuing now, as he quickened his pace into Q'aantre's night.

But with Remy's admission, how clear the air had become; how rich and fragrant. Even now he could summon scent memories of Remy's change from ambivalence and self-doubt to relief.

Remy revealed that it had long been his desire to be stationed on Q'aantre. But in exchange for the transfer DisneyCorp ultimately granted him, he had been ordered to function as a kind of spy as well. The reasoning was complex, as things that had their origin on Earth often were.

It seemed that the Consortium—to whom DisneyCorp in turn answered—was convinced that the Xell'em were plotting to utilize Q'aantre as a staging area for military operations they were conducting in star systems at the far end of Dazyl's wormhole. Without hard evidence of this, the Consortium was reluctant to confront the Manifest or the local group League; and equally reluctant to approach the Grand Assembly, fearing that concern might be misconstrued as manipulation.

Even with proof of a Xell'em plot, the Consortium pledged itself to a policy of nonintervention, which could only be amended by direct request from the Grand Assembly. If and when that occurred the Consortium would lend its support in deposing the Xell'em regime; but only with the understanding that that support would not entitle Terra to insert itself in Xella's stead. Q'aantre was and would always remain the sole arbiter of its destiny.

Remy had been instructed to gather intelligence that would assist Earth's ruling body in mounting its case.

You can't imagine how difficult it is to be living a lie day after day, Remy had said. *You don't know what it feels like to have to walk around like some kind of transmitter, eyes and ears alert for signals of one sort or another.*

Morli admitted at the time that it was difficult indeed for him to imagine himself a walking receiver attuned to sight and sound; but he had no problem sympathizing with what it felt like to be living a lie. He had only to think of the sweet but forbidden activities that lay at the center of his nocturnal being . . .

He wasn't ready to discuss that part of himself with Remy, though he often wondered what the Terran's reaction might be. It was Remy who said that Q'aantre and its people were poised at a turning point—one that could very well bring sweeping change. But what would he make of a Q'aantre addicted to *lust*—there was no other word for it—one whose life had begun to revolve around the quest for sexual gratification? A quest that had yet to lead in any direction but *down*.

He shuddered at the memory of his narrow escape from the Club Terrana.

He had, however, offered to be Remy's nose on Q'aantre, if not his eyes and ears. Remy plainly didn't want him involved, but he had forced him to consider the logic of it. Where could one find a more suitable candidate? He had access to places Remy was denied; why, he was even a regular guest of Xell'em station!

All this was more than a month behind him. And in the intervening weeks he and Remy had worked out the most intriguing method for exchanging information—*trafficking* in information, Remy called it.

First they had combed the city—separately, of course—for places where one might leave an unobtrusive message: chalk marks on a utility pole, or a garbage drum overturned; a drawn drape, or a door or window left ajar at a prearranged time. Then they had searched out less traveled spots where he could leave a specific whiff in the air to indicate how things were going, or if he was presently in possession of intelligence worthy of exchange. It had taken days to familiarize Remy with the emanations and scents, but he had proved to be a surprisingly quick study.

The routine of passing scents in these isolated spots—which Remy termed *dead drops*—was safeguarded from olfactory surveillance by Special Investigations by a series of hand cues and wave-off signals. But the really important exchanges were carried out in crowded places where activity alone was safeguard enough.

These were the "live drops," where he would deposit gathered data in a secretion that had no analog in human biophysiology. Remy hadn't explained just how he was able to translate the encoded secretions. Morli assumed that DisneyCorp was directly involved in the process.

Remy had encouraged him to find agents of his own to handle, and he had done so, both downside and on Xell'em station, where a few Q'aantre technicians were undergoing training. So now there were people that reported to him before he reported to Remy, who then reported to DisneyCorp, which itself answered to the Consortium . . . He pictured it as a grand pyramid of some sort, similar to the one that adorned the Terran mission flag and the warmcloaks of Envoy Densign and his staffers. Though he sometimes asked himself just who sat at the pyramid's apex . . .

Servicing the drops had necessitated changes in his quotidian routines, which hadn't left him much time to indulge his nocturnal interests. The covert activities had also put an end to the evenings of discussion he and Remy had enjoyed, although they continued to meet every so often in the safehouse—an office, really, belonging to a Terran culturist named Jalak.

Morli had known Jalak on a casual basis, but was

now—to insure the security of the meets—one of the
professor's cultural informants as well. He never knew
what examples of Terrana remuneration Remy would be
bringing to these meetings; and only rarely had he entered a specific request.

Morli caught sight of Remy now as the two of them
were approaching the live drop from different directions. He was a bit behind schedule, but he didn't suppose it mattered much. He rubbed his right shoulder to
indicate that he wasn't being followed and stepped up
to the food stall to order a *yika*. While the woman behind the counter turned her attention to the keg spout
and spice shakers, he casually ran his hand along the
underside of the stool.

The emanations and "smart secretions" remained
viable for only a short period of time. Anyone inadvertently coming across them could process the data, but
make little sense of it. Morli employed a kind of scent-
code, which Remy had termed *shortnose*.

He drank the warm brew in a single swallow, laid a
few chips on the counter, and exited the stall, pretending not to notice Remy, who stood nearby seemingly
engrossed in a newscreen display.

He was especially eager to be on his way. Across the
river a new club had opened, and the talk was that the
house girls had only recently arrived from Masik, a city
known far and wide for the sheer wantonness of its
Tegganon.

His thoughts turned briefly to the data he had just
deposited, wondering whether any of it would be of use
to the Consortium's intelligence specialists.

He had yet to come across any evidence that even
hinted at a Xell'em military operation aimed at some
remote star system, but then who was he to judge.

It perplexed him somewhat that both Xella and Terra
had taken such an interest in inconsequential Q'aantre
to begin with. The comings and goings of their ships
through the wormhole were of no concern to anyone

downside, and what, besides, could Q'aantre's allegiance to one side or the other possibly mean to the balance of power among the worlds of the Inner Arm?

It was a question to which even Remy couldn't supply an answer. Probably not one worth considering.

Remy ceased his incessant pacing to work some of the tightness out of his joints. He extended his arms over his head; he dangled them at his sides; he crossed them over his chest. When he hugged himself, his spine issued a cackle of worrisome cracks. He shrugged his shoulders and touched his fingertips to his distended nostrils.

"Got yourself a virus," the tech said in response to Remy's sniffle. "I'll bring along an antigen booster next time I come down."

Remy tried to rub the irritation from his eyes as he turned to the man at the dubber controls. "I don't think it's a virus, but thanks just the same."

"Your call." The man shrugged.

The filthy room was about the same size as the one behind the bar in the Club Terrana, but the similarity ended there. Except for the shimmering holo-field and the strident motions of the four figures captured within it.

The warehouse dive had risen from the ashes of the Terrana, and the tech cameraman was courtesy of NCorp by way of Audjo Ishida. He was thirty, give or take, intense, and muscular, which said something about how many downside assignments he had drawn lately. "Detlef," he said when he'd practically crushed Remy's hand two hours before. *Det.*

"Humpin' in the holo," Det said now.

Remy tugged his eyes open as he regarded the cone of light. Four Kwandri—two males and two females—on a floormat in an even dirtier storeroom downstairs, trying their best to emulate four onscreen Enddrese. Trying their best to make it work.

Det shook his head, thick wire-black hair, not a strand out of place. "Man, I almost feel sorry for them. Ever happen to you, Santoul?"

"What's that?"

"The fatal curl. You know, not being able to get it up."

"Find me someone it hasn't happened to," Remy said, disinterested.

"Happened to me during the war a coupla times. You see much action yourself?"

"My share, if you're talking about combat."

"That, too," Det said. "Anyhow, my unit was first to be dropped on Burst Prime, and lemme tell you, Santoul, we had our pick of everything downside. Half the planet cheering us as liberators, the other half scared shitless we were on a termination run." He paused to reflect. "So I meet probably the best-looking leg I've ever seen, and nothing. I'm yelling 'Stand up, you prick!' And this sorry soldier thinks I'm talking to him, so he gets up and jumps to attention. Meanwhile, I'm looking down at myself and cursing my luck."

Remy waited to make sure Det was finished. "The brain's the sexual organ, Marine. Talk to yourself next time instead of shouting at your hose."

"Yeah, well, it was enough to hook me on direct stim for the next few months. Bypass the meat, you know."

Remy felt a shiver pass through him, a residual effect of the intel he had absorbed at the beer stall. His insides always seemed to itch afterward, long after his doctored body chemistry had completed the translations.

The sound of Det's voice was getting to him, just as Morli's exhalations and secretions were. Odors of camphor and wicker, chlorophyll and wood smoke, gangrene and stairwells. All straightforward enough on the surface; and yet each was attached to memories he hadn't necessarily wished stirred. He dreamed in smells now, instead of sights and sounds. Crazed mixtures of odors, alchemical nightmares.

Absorbents coursed through his bloodstream like irradiated particles, plugging up his nose, swelling his joints . . . Worst of all, opening doors he had locked for good reason.

It was Jasna who kept coming to mind lately, his lover for too little or too much time depending on who was telling it. He didn't like to think of her on Dhone, punishing herself. He wanted to see her again; to talk over the memories.

And there he was thinking about her again.

He returned his attention to the holo—not because he wanted to but because it seemed his only route back to the present.

Det was closing the camera remote on the action, centering a familiar face in the 3-D field. Remy felt aversion run through him.

He hadn't expected Morli to show up at the club. After the Kwandri had deposited his live drop of ship tags and dests he must have made directly for the warehouse—arriving just before Remy had.

Morli's appearance only pointed up how quickly commo spread through Kwandri's underground network. In search of recruitment potential, Remy and Det had been instructed to commit to disk a selection of faces from the new club's hardcore clientele, and now it seemed Morli's face would be included among them.

Well, it never hurt to have backup evidence. The raw data.

But he didn't want to see it come to that with Morli. All month long he had been playing strictly by the rules—circumspect in his approach, methodical during the cultivation phase, diligent about nourishing the relationship—and the result had been one of those classic cases where the agent is convinced that *he* recruited the handler.

The Kwandri was still running high on the game, servicing the drops, running his own subs. Remy didn't foresee any problems—unless something happened to scare Morli off.

"We've had about enough of these four," Det said. "I've got plenty of head shots. What d'you say?"

"Go to," Remy told him, "change channels."

Det soon had another foursome in the cone, three females and a male this time. "Does get you kinda horny . . . Watching them, I mean. Makes me wanna go in there and show them how it's done."

Remy showed his disapproval. "I doubt they're ready for you, Marine."

Det nodded. "There'll come a time, though."

You grab yourself two handfuls of pelt and enjoy the ride.

Remy supposed there probably would. And although he wouldn't confess as much to the tech, the holos *were* getting to him. But Karine Mareer was the one he kept fantasizing about.

He'd seen her on three occasions since Baj's dinner party: once at a mission function; then, briefly, in the lobby of the Ministry of the Interior; and most recently at the shuttleport. She wore Xell'em overcloaks and jumpsuits as well as she had heels and strapless gown; but there was a hardness to her features he hadn't noticed that first night. No matter how soft he was imagining her—

"Say, Rem, I don't suppose you'd, uh . . ."

Det was gazing at him, low-lidded and sexy. Remy snorted. "I'd hate myself in the morning. And every morning after that."

The tech looked hurt. "No call for insults, is there?"

Remy sighed. "None intended, Det. I was thinking of someone else, is all." The frown disappeared from the tech's face. "Look, suppose you station yourself here for another hour or so, then transmit what you have upside. Come on by the hotel in the morning and we'll compose a program for tomorrow night."

Det shrugged assent and busied himself with the task

of fine-tuning a singularly offensive anatomical closeup.
Remy slipped into jacket and cap, and had a hand on
the door when the tech said, "Santoul."

Remy divined what was coming.

"Two Kwandri walk into a bar . . ."

He shut the door behind him before Det had completed the first line.

NINE—

THE KWANDRI COUPLE WAS THRASHING about in living 3-D atop the pedestal projector in Audjo Ishida's on-station office. Remy sat tight-lipped on the fluttering bench. It wasn't enough he had to endure the recording procedure; Ishida wanted him to sit through the playback as well.

Off to one side of the station chief's slab of alloy desk, Phajol Dakou was staring at the holoed figures and saying, "Yes, yes." Remy couldn't tell whether the counsel was offering an analytical appraisal or simply getting off on the couple's hapless sexplay.

He fidgeted on the bench as Ishida regarded him, sharp-eyed and rock steady.

"What's your reaction to all this?" she asked finally.

"To what I'm seeing?"

"To our methods."

"If the results are positive, the method has been expedient."

Ishida's incongruous Western eyes were iridescent. "And would you say our results thus far have been positive?"

"We have a network. We're receiving intelligence. In

my small corner of the world the results appear to be positive. Beyond that I can't say."

Ishida nodded and dabbed a forefinger against the desk screen. Her nail lacquer matched her eyes. "Do you have any complaints about your assignment?"

"Some minor somatic distress."

"Nothing else?"

"I'm seeing new places and meeting interesting people."

Dakou threw him a cautionary look.

"Do you consider these recordings an infringement of any sort?"

"Our lives should all be open to close scrutiny. Only by exposing our innermost secrets can we hope to evolve."

Ishida waited a moment. "Are you and your crippled Kwandri teenager lovers?"

"Fuck you."

The station chief's tongue was in her cheek as she leaned back into her contour chair . . .

The communiqué ordering Remy to report upside had been concealed among DisneyCorp memoranda transmitted to the suite sometime during his walk back from the warehouse club.

Remy had deciphered the message after peeking in on Els Nanff, who was sound asleep in the master bedroom. The kid had turned the room into a veritable crib of archaic Terrana—poster art and Wacky Wallwalkers decorating the walls; empty dog biscuit and cereal boxes arranged like a house of cards on the floor; stacks of Ninja Turtle comics and self-help books stacked bedside, along with an assortment of shrink-wrapped theme erasers, a Mr. Potato Head, a black plastic divination 8-ball.

Remy woke Nanff to tell him that his wish was about to be granted—they would be going upside together on the morning shuttle. The kid was awake for the rest of the night.

Like Baj, Nanff had a penchant for wearing Terran hardware, and in the morning was sporting wrist and anklets of chrome-plated pipe flange. The outfit received *ooh*s and *aah*s in the hotel lobby. It was there Remy learned about the midnight raid on the warehouse.

Phajol Dakou had supplied the details while contamination control was subjecting Nanff to a battery of ultrasonic scans.

Detlef, the NCorp dub master, had been arrested by SPECVES agents and was being held on charges of conspiracy to engage in pornography. Several Kwandri were picked up, but Morli had been spared again. That morning, he had reported to the ministry on time, if somewhat shaken.

Det had wiped his recordings before SPECVES confiscated them; the holos running in the station chief's office now were examples of some of Det's earlier work.

"And how is Mr. Santoul's health?" Ishida asked Dakou when the projector had been voiced off.

The counsel cracked his knuckles. After Nanff was entrusted to the capable hands of a station guide, Remy had been probed, scanned, and chemically debriefed by NCorp medtechs.

"Basically sound," Dakou said. "Liver and kidney functions are excellent. Some predictable swelling of the nasal mucosa and erectile tissue. Novel readings from the forward poles of the temporal lobes—mild panic-disorder anxiety, also predictable. An upswing in metabolic rate. I would, however, recommend a refit of the buccal implants and updates of the olfactory and tactile programs."

"What about the stiffness in my shoulders?" Remy asked.

"We're working on it," Dakou said. "Present thinking is that the residues of these so-called 'smart secretions' tend to migrate to the joints.''

Remy recalled his first view of myopic, crooked Jalak, and Ishida said, ''And how is Professor Jalak doing?''

Remy managed to fight down the urge for a stimwafer. ''He's been helpful. The torpor tutorials were a good intro, but I would've drawn a blank at the live drops without Jalak's training. There's more to scent recognition than Center realizes.''

Ishida smiled tolerantly. ''I'll be certain to pass your assessment on to TechSci. But what about Jalak's attitude?''

Remy considered it. ''He's glad to be out of it. I haven't tried to dissuade him of the belief he's out from under our nose, er, our thumb. He's cleaned himself up, and he's been playing his part at the safehouse. All he ever wanted was to be left alone to conduct his studies. He probably figures he's got a good shot at that now.''

Ishida and Dakou exchanged an occult look. ''He's in for a surprise,'' the counsel said.

Ishida walked away from the desk with her arms folded. ''I want you to know we've been following this Morli case with great interest.'' She turned to face Remy. ''I'm very pleased with the way you've been handling him.''

Remy sensed a qualification hanging in the recirculated air.

''Have you learned the identity of Morli's subagents on Xell'em station?''

''I haven't asked,'' Remy said, making sure his tone conveyed what he thought of the question.

''You have a problem with that?''

''Of course I have a problem with it. I promised him his sources would be protected. I don't want to push him.''

"I'm afraid you're going to have to," Dakou interjected.

"Center has ascertained that the Xell'em are definitely using Dazyl's wormhole as a conduit for armaments to nonaligned worlds," the station chief continued. "There's a problem brewing on Burst even as we speak. This is in flagrant violation of the League Accord, and Center wants increased intelligence on all shipments leaving or transiting this sector. The Grand Assembly minutes aren't telling us all we need to know about Kwandri's position in all this. You'll have to see about infiltrating an active listener into Xella's downside embassy. Perhaps Morli himself."

Remy fell silent.

"Say what's on your mind," Ishida ordered.

"All right," Remy began, "I guess I'm surprised, is all. I mean, the intel I've absorbed doesn't indicate any buildup. I know for a fact Morli hasn't been apprised of any arms shipments."

Ishida frowned at him. "Didn't you just sit there and tell me you had no view of the overall scheme from your 'corner'? Your word, Santoul."

Remy heaved his shoulders. "That's true, but—"

"Then how could you possibly know what Center has been able to compile from sources elsewhere?"

"I don't suppose I can."

"Be damned sure you *can't*, Santoul," Ishida warned. She took a moment to calm herself, then added, "Now, NCorp wants the entire Kwandri network boostered, end of program."

Remy shook his head. "I told you, I'm against pressing Morli right now. I can't entice him any more than I've already been able to. Sure, he's happy with the things we're giving him, but he's involved because he's convinced he's doing a service for Kwandri."

"So convince him he needs to be of greater service," Ishida suggested. "Failing that you resort to raw data."

Remy understood what the station chief was getting

at. He was relieved that Det's holos hadn't fallen into
NCorp's hands. "That's not the way to handle an agent
who's been good to you," he said after a moment.
"He's scared right now. We threaten him, he's a wipe,
believe me."

Ishida put her hands flat on the desktop. "I disagree.
This is precisely the time to pressure him. He doesn't
want anyone to learn about his dirty little secret, least
of all SPECVES. Use it for leverage."

Remy turned to watch the tugs and elevators outside
the viewport.

Dakou rubbed his chin. "How should agents be han-
dled, Remy—like Els Nanff? Like children?"

Remy heard himself with Jalak and silently cursed
his outburst.

Ishida said, "We certainly don't want you to jeopard-
ize your relationship with Morli . . ."

"But you want more information."

"There *are* other enticements, Santoul." When Remy
turned back to Dakou, the counsel had a transparent
lotion dispenser pinched between his fingertips.

"Enticement," Dakou said.

Remy accepted the pokerchip-size disk and flipped it
about in his palm. The dispenser lacked drug corp des-
ignations of any sort; the lotion within was as transparent as the container itself. "Don't tell me, it's a whiff
of *enticement*, right?"

"In fact," Ishida told him.

Dakou took back the wafer and admired it at eye
level. "It's a naturally occurring aphrodisiac."

Remy laughed. "They've got the *urge*, Phajol. What
they don't have is the means."

"Yes, but this particular substance will guarantee
that."

Remy looked back and forth between the counsel and
the station chief. "Look, I don't want to spoil the party
here, but a lot of enterprising smugglers have already
dipped into this well."

"Not with this they haven't."

"And you think it'll work on Kwandri?"

"We're certain it will," Dakou said.

"Your agent won't have to wait for *Tegganon* to roll around," Ishida said. "He'll be able to fornicate to his heart's content."

Remy shook his head in an effort to erase the mental picture that was forming. He contemplated the approach instead, thinking out loud.

"So I tell him I have a special treat for him. Something to save until *Tegganon*—since I'm not supposed to know anything about his midnight activities." He glanced up at Dakou. "But how am I supposed to know if the stuff's working?"

"By watching him, just as you have been doing. You and Detlef—once we secure his release."

Remy ran a hand through his hair. "Might be a problem there. It took weeks for a new club to open after the Terrana was raided. With the warehouse closed . . . I don't know, could be months this time."

"That's already being taken care of," Ishida said, back in her chair now. "We're overseeing the funding of a new club, which will be impregnable to SPECVES penetration. It was just a matter of getting to the proper people and equipping the place with adequate monitoring devices."

"The cover owner's a man named Vegas," Dakou added. "He's savvy and reasonably certain where the funds originated, even though we've pursued a somewhat roundabout course. NCorp made use of him once or twice during the war, so we're not anticipating any negative spin." The counsel smirked. "He's wise in the ways of the galaxy."

Ishida took the dispenser from Dakou. "Mr. Densign's staffers will be carrying two dozen of these downside in diplomatic pouches. Give them to Morli and encourage him to pass some on to his subs."

"You're going to create a demand," Remy said.

"Of course we are. We'll arrange for follow-up deliveries to arrive in DisneyCorp shipments." Ishida studied Remy's face. "It's only a temporary measure, Santoul. Just to keep the information flowing."

Dakou was nodding. "The substance is in limited supply, but we calculate there's enough on hand to carry us through the remainder of the operation."

"Or at least until we see what price Kwandri's willing to pay for it," Remy said, as though trying to clear a rotten taste from his mouth.

He gave himself a week to come up with a plan he could live with. He continued, meanwhile, to service the drops, allowing Morli time to recoup from his latest close call. That his principal wasn't depositing anything, Remy took to be an indication of just how frightened he was. Jalak, then, arranged for a meet at the safehouse.

Likat was blanketed with new snow and the windows of the room upstairs from the culturist's office were frosted with ice. Morli was sipping tea when Remy entered.

"Did you and Jalak have a good interview?" he asked casually, doffing his jacket and hanging it up to dry.

"We talked about kinship," Morli said, averting Remy's gaze. The tea mug was quivering in his furred grip.

Remy positioned a chair opposite Morli's and breathed warmth into his cupped hands. "So, tell me what's been going on."

"You're referring to the drops."

Remy shrugged. "That, and things in general. You're all right?"

"Why shouldn't I be?" Morli said, finally looking up from the cup.

"Well, I don't know. The drops have been empty, so I figured you were giving your subs some time off. But there's been a, I don't know, a kind of *evasive* quality to the scents you've left.''

A slow smile split Morli's face and he barked a laugh. ''Remy, you really are the most astounding Terran.'' The smile faded and collapsed. ''But, yes, it's true, I have been evasive.''

''And why is that, Res?''

Morli set the tea aside. ''I want to put an end to this. These routines of ours, our meetings in this place, my interviews with Professor Jalak . . . It's as though my personal life has been stripped from me.'' He shook his head. ''I know it must sound terribly selfish, but my time means a great deal to me. I can't go into everything now. I have been injudicious of late.''

About getting caught with your pants down, Remy thought, summoning the phrase from some musty cell-block of his mind. He said, ''Suppose we give it a week or so and see what happens.''

''A week, a month, it won't matter. I'm sorry, Remy, but I can't be of any more help to you.''

Remy showed him an annoyed look before he stood up and paced to the center of the room. ''If you want me to return some of the gifts,'' Morli was saying when Remy whirled on him.

''You want to stop. Just like that.''

''It's not that I necessarily *want* to stop. I must, don't you understand?''

''No, I don't. I hear you telling me you have personal needs you've been neglecting. I hear you telling me you've been careless about something. But you say it isn't a matter of time, you're through.''

''Yes. Unfortunately.''

''Well, what's going to become of me in all this?'' Morli puzzled over it. ''You?''

''What am I supposed to tell my superiors?''

''Just tell them that your source of information had a change of conscience.'' The Kwandri showed his diminutive hands. ''I honestly don't see how the minutes of the Assembly meetings or the names of a few ships could matter—"

"It doesn't work that way, Res."

"What doesn't?"

"*It* doesn't." Remy turned the chair around and straddled it. "See, I could tell them just what you've told me, but it wouldn't matter. You think the information you've been gathering doesn't mean much, and maybe it doesn't, but what's important is that it means something to *them*. And as long as it does, we continue to deliver, or . . ."

"Or what, Remy?" Morli asked, distressed.

Remy cursed softly. "I'm not afraid of what they'll do to me. Hell, what can they do—terminate me? Exile me to some remote system?" He put a hand on Morli's forearm, triggering at the same time a dermal exhalation of deep concern tinged with fear. The Kwandri's nostril triad twitched in response. "They know I've been receiving information from someone well placed. I admitted that much. I didn't give them your name, but it wouldn't take long for them to get it."

Morli shot to his feet. "But you said I'd be protected!"

"They have ways, Res," Remy said in like distress. "They'll try to find out things about you—things they can use against you. And if they can't find anything, they'll arrange for SPECVES or the Grand Assembly to learn of your treachery."

"Treachery?!"

"Well, how else would you expect anyone to interpret your actions? Sure, you and I know you've been acting on Kwandri's behalf, but are the Xell'em sympathizers in the Assembly going to read it that way?" Remy forced a breath. "I never should have involved you in this." He risked a look up to watch Morli execute a short nervous dance.

"*I* was the one who asked to become involved," the

Kwandri said after a moment. "And by doing so I've endangered others as well."

"I don't know what to say, Res."

Morli sat down. "But, Remy, tell me: Would DisneyCorp really do such a thing? You said that our information has been of value to them. Doesn't that suggest that they hold us in some esteem?"

Remy allowed himself to relax. "They do, Res, there's no question."

"They've said as much?"

"More than that." Remy felt his trousers pockets. "Now, what did I do with . . . Oh, they're in my jacket," he said, getting up. Morli tracked him from the chair.

Remy fished a hand into the jacket's inner pocket and retrieved a packet containing half a dozen wafers. "They wanted you to have these—as a special gift." He dropped the packet into Morli's hand. "Though I don't suppose you'll be able to make much use of them until *Tegganon*."

"Tegganon?" Morli sniffed at the packet. "What's contained in these disks?"

Remy summoned a flush to his face. "Well," he laughed, "I'm told that it's a kind of pleasure enhancer."

The Kwandri's face fell. "An aphrodisiac, you mean."

"Of a sort. It's for, uh, assured physical arousal, you might say."

Morli swallowed audibly. *"Assured* arousal?"

"So I'm told," Remy said. "I thought you could pass it around to your subs and friends as a party favor. Who knows, maybe it'll catch on."

TEN—

REMY ASKED HIMSELF: COULD A XELL'EM woman with distended earlobes and a reshaped chin find true happiness with a tall Terran guy with arthritic joints and a perpetual squint?

It was a match that could only have been made on Kwandri.

A crowd of four hundred protesters was marching back and forth in front of the Xell'em embassy, wafting emanations through the rehung gates. Even from some distance away, Remy's nose could discern scents of angry discontent: a mix of sulfur dioxide, jalapeño peppers, tar oil, and sizzling animal fat. The odors were working on him the way hysteria works a mob.

Remy had positioned himself farther away than had been his usual practice the past two weeks, but he wasn't too far removed to observe Karine Mareer as she stepped high-heeled from the annex and began to descend the stairway that fronted the squat building. From a spot of evergreen shade just around the corner from the main gate, he watched her regard the crowd for a long moment. He had an unobstructed view of Karine's long bare legs when she swung them, knees locked, into the back seat of the waiting limo.

117

Remy was acutely aware of his heartbeat and respiration rate. He pictured himself standing there leering at her, hands thrust deep into coat pockets, shuffling in place, and turned from the fence, laughing in a manner that suggested both perplexity and self-pity. Quickly, then, he glanced left and right, concerned that someone might have sensed him. But those Kwandri within earshot or scentshot were too preoccupied with the protest to bother themselves with the unintelligible shenanigans of a stubble-faced Earther, whose sobriety and sense of decorum were obviously open to question.

No one was more puzzled by the behavior than Remy himself. The sole certainty was that he had become fixated on Karine Mareer—the way fans sometimes attached themselves to corporate idols—although he suspected the attraction arose more from an olfactory gestalt than one of visually perceived image.

Fate had favored him with precious few breaths of her—and even then her true scents lay submerged under a haze of floral-based perfumes, a dizzying Xell'em soup of rose, amaranth, and heliotrope—but on two occasions a hint of Karine's natural fragrance had emerged: in a maglift she had ridden to the fourth floor of the hotel, and later that same afternoon in the hotel's top-floor restaurant. Remy found himself utterly intoxicated. And so he had taken to strolling past the embassy each morning on his way into Likat center; on his way to inhale Morli's habit-forming intel drops . . .

The most recent shipment of aphrodisiac wafers was in the left pouch pocket of his long coat, concealed inside a half-inch-thick disk fabricated to resemble a flickdisk of *The Towering Inferno*, a late twentieth-century masterpiece of sociopolitical allegory. Remy's hand seized on the thin package now as he strode hunchbacked and sniffling into a gust of winter wind.

He glanced at his watch. The riot squad was overdue at the embassy. Likat had seen a marked increase in demonstrations against all offworlder concerns.

Routinely, Remy would have delivered the package to a secretary at the Ministry of ExtraPlanetary Affairs, who then would have unwittingly passed the wafers on to Morli; but Ishida—apparently acceding to an NCorp directive to further stimulate the Kwandri network—had earmarked the latest shipment for Simon Jalak.

The aphrodisiac had to be considered a success inasmuch as it had turned Morli and a select group of his friends and subagents into a hedonistic, libidinous clique.

Remy couldn't rid himself of the memory of the first night he had seen evidence of that success: the look on Morli's face, the near-adolescent joy on the Kwandri's triangular face as he watched his member swell and elongate out of season.

Guess Teg'non's arrived ahead of schedule, Det had smirked from the recorder controls.

At least on Club Vegas's parcel of Kwandri it had, Remy remembered thinking. Det had trained the remote on the faces of Morli's equally astonished female partners, who, to judge from the gyrating motions of their hips, must have been experiencing a wet joy of their own. Afterward—Det having hurried Vegas into the surveillance room by then—the three Terran voyeurs had obtained auditory confirmation of an oft-heard rumor about Kwandri females: They really did *purr* during orgasm.

By the following evening, Morli was deploying scents at the dead drop sites to the effect that he wanted to resume service; and three days later he was asking about the chances of Remy's procuring perhaps a few additional wafers. No mention of the successful sexplay at Club Vegas; simply that Morli thought the wafers would make ideal *Tegganon* gifts. And since he had *so many friends to see to* . . .

Remy played it according to plan: he wasn't sure how much his DisneyCorp superiors had on hand; he would have to make some discreet inquiries . . .

"Maybe if we show them upside that we can deliver like never before," he had finally suggested.

Overnight, Morli's intel output took the quantum leap.

And suddenly Remy wasn't only absorbing the names and destinations of Xell'em ships transiting the wormhole, but the names of officers and crewmembers; the content of subspace commo regarding weather fronts on distant worlds; lists of foodstuffs and dietary supplements contained in ships' stores; requested color changes to the bulkheads in the fleet commander's quarters; updates on Xella local news, hearsay, jokes, scuttlebutt.

The data could only be regarded as worthless—of even less significance than the stuff he had transmitted upside before introduction of the motion lotion. But Remy ceased to care; he had begun to realize there was something *different* about the smart secretions—something profound and almost indecently pleasurable. It got to be he could scarcely wait to absorb the live drop pickups. The rest of the day was wasted time—save for the strolls past the Xell'em embassy for a glimpse of Mareer.

Just three blocks from the embassy, Remy turned at the sound of his name and saw Norak Baj hurrying to catch up with him.

"Where *have* you been," the Kwandri said in piqued tone. "I've been leaving messages at the hotel, I've been looking for you at the mission. Envoy Densign hasn't seen you, young Nanff doesn't know where you've been going—"

"I've been busy," Remy cut him off.

"Yes, but busy *where*? We've been waiting for the tote bags and eyeglasses you promised. To say nothing of the Vita-mixers which have yet to arrive . . ." Baj stopped to regard him. "Why are you standing like that, with your head down?"

Remy tried to straighten up, but he might as well have been carrying the weight of a world on his back.

"Just a bit of stiffness." The sniffle that accompanied the excuse only caused Baj's laser-combed forelock to bristle.

"Are you feeling all right, Remy? Are you ill?"

"Hey, I'm great," he said. "Just great."

"Your eyes are as narrow as a Q'aantre infant's."

"I might have a virus."

"Yes, well, take care of yourself," Baj said, stroking Remy's arm in concern. "Is there anything I can do?"

Remy assured him again that he was fine, *great*, and promised to follow up on the DisneyCorp consignments, which were probably stacked at customs awaiting release authorization. He kept a smile in place until Baj was out of sight, then hastened to make up for lost time.

Baj hadn't been the first to notice the changes.

Els Nanff was also concerned. It had become part of the boy's morning routine to join Remy in the Earth Force regimen of exercises. But Remy hadn't meditated or balanced himself in over a week. He had discontinued the urine and blood tests as well. The monitor in the suite hadn't transmitted any med data upside in four days, but he had yet to hear word one from Ishida or Dakou. As for the physical symptoms, Remy guessed they would disappear once his body adjusted to Morli's presently hormone-laden output.

"You look like my father looks during the *Tegganon*," Els Nanff had told him.

But if Remy was changed, so then was Kwandri through his altered senses. Likat's streets were alive in a way he had never experienced, brimming with a thousand data scents and redolences; complex and wonderful in ways he had never fathomed.

Only the sight of parted drapes in a particular second-story window in the Ministry of ExtraPlanetary Affairs could eclipse the odors.

Morli's signal that he had deposited a live drop.

Following his nose, Remy raced for the *yika* stand around the corner.

Remy manipulated one of the aphrodisiac wafers through a coin roll across the backs of his fingers. Jalak, however, paid little attention to the deftness of the one-handed trick and continued to stare at him, aghast. An antique digital clock on the far wall of the study emitted a slight battery-powered hum.

"Do you mean to tell me they're . . . *mating* outside of estrus?" the culturist said at last.

"Just the lucky ones."

"The luck—but how?" Jalak gasped. "How have you done this?"

Remy gave the wafer a flip across the desk; Jalak snatched it on the first bounce. "What is it?" he asked, examining the dispenser. "There's some kind of fluid inside."

"An aphrodisiac. A drop on the tongue and a Kwandri's wet dreams come true." Remy chortled evilly.

Jalak dropped the wafer in disgust. "For intelligence?" he sneered. "I should have guessed it would come to this."

Remy rubbed his hands together in a washing motion. "Why didn't you tell me about the clubs, Jalak?"

The professor made a fatigued sound. "Because I knew you'd use them as a recruiting ground for agents." He regarded Remy with contempt. "I've never visited any of them. But I've heard the rumors."

"More than rumors, man, more than rumors."

Jalak fell silent, then said, "But aphrodisiacs aren't new to Q'aantre?" He retrieved the wafer. "What is this substance—something your TechSci people cooked up?"

"I can't help you there, Professor, can't help you there. But Dakou said it was in limited supply. Which means it's either too rich for the Dazyldesk budget or damned hard to come by. One reason the op is last ditch, the way I figure it. Center'll probably withhold resupply as soon as it has the intel it wants."

Jalak scowled. "Is that supposition designed to put me at ease? First the vids, then the Terrana. Now NCorp is tampering with something that has been kept under socio-biological restraint for millennia."

Remy's hands tapped out a beat on the arms of the chair. "Relax, Jalak. I'm telling you, it's only a temporary measure."

"And I'm telling you this entire culture revolves around the *Tegganon*. Are you prepared to assure me there'll be no permanent effect? What about population control, has Center given thought to that? Or family and clan structure? Or, or—"

"The sooner we have a clear picture of Xella's purpose on Burst the better. For everyone concerned," Remy added firmly. "Including Kwandri."

Jalak shook his head in disbelief. "This whole thing is preposterous. The Manifest has no reason to breach the Accord. No one wants another war." He growled in frustration.

"Who knows what anyone wants? You nourish, you cajole, you listen, you transmit, you just do your part. How can anyone blame you if it's false data? Maybe Center's misinterpreting the reports, but can anyone hold that against you? Even if the wrong ship gets hit, lives are lost, planets spin out of control. It's not our fault, is it, Jalak? We're just out here, all ears and noses and fingertips . . ."

Jalak was staring at him. "You're raving, Remy. By the look of you, you've absorbed more than you can handle. You're as high as an ant in a sugar bowl."

Remy ignored the remark. "Ishida wants you to bring your own network into this, Jalak. Starting now."

Jalak's initial puzzlement gave way to flushed anger. He sidehanded the wafer back across the desk into Remy's lap. "I'll have no part of it."

Remy succeeded in quieting all but his bucking legs

and feet. "Just pass a couple of wafers along to your agents and tell them to keep their nostrils opened."

Jalak was still shaking his head. "You're asking me to act against everything I hold sacred, Santoul. The sanctity, the inviolability of all cultures."

"Then we're right back where we started, Professor." Remy waited until he was sure that he had Jalak's undivided attention. "There's no menu. You follow the program or you're off-planet on the next shuttle."

"In the end it always reduces to threats, doesn't it, Santoul?"

Remy worked his jaw. "Look, Jalak, it's not like I'm asking you to pollute Likat's water supply. Just two or three agents of your chosing. Once they give it a try, they'll come through with more data than even *you* can handle."

Jalak hung his head. "You know, Remy, there used to be a word for people like us. *Pushers*," he said, looking up.

Remy made one final live drop pickup on his way back to the hotel. Onscreen in the suite was an encrypted message from Ishida ordering him to report to station the following morning.

Thoroughly buzzed from the smart secretions, Remy felt he could easily reach escape velocity without having to rely on the shuttle.

ELEVEN—

"WELL," ISHIDA SAID IN A BREEZY TONE, "you're certainly looking fit."

Remy grinned madly from the swivel armchair, his eyes blinking nonstop.

"And tell me, are you feeling as good as you look?"

"Great," Remy said through clenched teeth. "I'm just great."

Dakou said nothing; but he wore the same astonished look Baj and Jalak had worn the previous day. The station chief continued to smile; no more herself than Remy was his.

He'd managed to steal a glimpse of himself in an optical monitor after the station medtechs chemically debriefed him, and the onscreen image that greeted his narrowed eyes had shaken him clear through. He was unshaven and stoop-shouldered; his nose was swollen, his hair matted, his fingers curled. The weeks downside had begun to assume the shape of some hallucinatory experience, and something coiled at the core of Remy Santoul's being had been profoundly disturbed.

A fourth person was present in the office: a pale middle-aged woman who seemed vaguely familiar, and who had either allowed or opted for the gray streaks in

125

her long hair. She was slim in the way most station-bound personnel were, with an attractive, somewhat drawn face, which only accentuated the deep set of her large brown eyes. Remy put her at close to six feet tall.

"We've decided to alter the nature of your assignment for a time," the station chief said flatly, glancing down at her screen in a distracted way.

Alarmed, Remy sniffed at her. "We're not done with it, I hope. I mean, 'cause if it's something I did, or maybe just that Morli isn't giving us enough, I'll find the talent who will. I can do it, too. I'm only doing half a dozen pickups now, but I could go to a dozen if you want or maybe more if I—"

"Settle down," Ishida ordered.

Tight-lipped, Remy turned to the viewport, while his feet tapped and he labored internally to dump whatever emotions his mind was formulating. It was the first time Ishida hadn't directed him onto the fluttering bench, but it was possible that concealed devices were evaluating him in some novel way. On a deeper level, he was aware of feeling puzzled, disappointed, angry—

"Understand, this has nothing to do with your actions downside," Dakou was quick to add. "In point of fact your handling of things has been flawless. Center is duly impressed."

The woman no one had bothered to introduce continued to sit quietly in the corner with her legs crossed, keying entries into a small unit she wore Velcroed to her belt.

Remy looked at Dakou. "If Morli's data is valid, I really think I should be allowed to continue." He sniffled. "I mean, hey, I know the real estate now. I've got the scents down. I'm in touch, believe me, I'm in touch."

Ishida looked up from the deskscreen to trade glances with the counsel. "You know we can't confirm or deny the validity of the data, Santoul."

Remy waited for her to go on.

"Your apparent success aside, the fact remains that Xella's hold on the Grand Assembly is as secure now as it was six months ago. This, despite the vigor of our campaign to influence the Kwandri on a cultural level."

"You're wrong," Remy said, "or the Dazyldesk intel assessors are. The demonstrations have increased. Two days ago the offices of a Xell'em shipping concern were bombed. The underground is growing." He snorted. "Hell, the cin-dens are packed nightly, the Club Vegas was standing room only . . ."

"Yes, yes, we're aware of all this," Ishida said. "But you're talking about a relatively small percentage of the populace."

Remy showed his palms. "Give it some time to gain momentum. I mean, is someone proposing active destabilization?—arms shipments, what?"

"Any such efforts would violate NCorp's present charter."

"Then how?"

"By seeing to it that the aphrodisiac becomes widely available," Dakou said.

Remy smiled and slapped a knee, setting the leg in motion again. "I think that's a terrific idea, I mean it, I do." He paused to consider a stray thought that worked its way through the scintillating force field his mind had erected. "The Consortium's willing to sanction this, huh?"

Dakou inclined his head to one side. "Let's just say that it falls within the parameters of the charter."

Remy could feel the eyes of the tall woman appraising him and swung to face her. "We know each other, don't we?"

The woman nodded and extended a hand. "Csilla Voss, Mr. Santoul. I did some time on Enddra during the war."

"Right," Remy said, clutching Voss's slim hand. She was a highly decorated veteran; ice cold where it counted. So why then had she let her hair go gray? It bothered him. "I remember now. Good to smell you again."

Voss blushed and Dakou cleared his throat. "Ms. Voss will be working with us for a time."

Remy nodded vigorously. "I could show you around downside. Wait'll you inhale Likat, it's . . . oh, man, it's just— And you'll have to meet Morli, of course. And check out the clubs and—"

"The tour will have to wait," Ishida interrupted. "You're being relieved here, Santoul. I'll be handling Morli in your absence."

Remy swung to her. "You? But—I'm going somewhere?"

Dakou spoke to it. "We're having difficulty procuring additional shipments of the aphrodisiac. An operative has been killed."

"An NCorp operative?" Remy asked.

"Yes. Although we're not sure why or by whom. Someone has learned of our interest in the substance and put several distributors out of business. The price has been driven up. Efforts to consolidate the suppliers seem to be under way."

"Procurement?" Remy said. "Why doesn't TechSci just cook up a couple tons of the stuff?"

"Because it didn't originate in Center labs. This is a naturally occurring substance. TechSci is close to synthesizing the active ingredients, but we can't afford to wait."

"We want you to set up a network for resupply and delivery," Ishida said.

Remy scratched at the palms of his hands. "So what is it, a plant or something?"

Dakou shook his head. "Do you know what a marat is, Remy?"

"Sure, a kind of a cat, isn't it?"

"Yes, a kind of cat. The aphrodisiac is derived from the scent gland of a rare species of marat, known as Skaro's Marat."

"I've heard of it," Remy said, trying to remember where.

"In terms of the aphrodisiac, the creature is only valuable at the moment of death. Death has a curious effect on the cat's scent gland."

"Yeah, I've seen the effect it has on other life-forms," Remy interjected. "So we capture one of these marats and clone it. What's the problem?"

"Precisely what Center intends to do—eventually. But recently the marat's natural habitat has become overrun with poachers and organized marketeers. Center is disinclined to mount an operation just now. As things stand, though, the cat will be extinct in another year if the poaching continues unchecked."

"A group of militant species-rights advocates has become involved," Ishida thought to point out. "If they succeed in arousing public concern, the issue could go to the League courts and even a single specimen might prove difficult to come by."

Remy gnawed at his fingers. "We need to get to the marketeers, then."

"And arrange for sufficient shipments to finish what we started on Kwandri," Ishida said. "It won't come cheap any longer." She jabbed at the desktop screen. "I've already arranged for the transfer of several pieces of art. You'll be able to draw against their value to the amount of eight million NuYen."

"You want the stuff that badly?"

"We do."

"But I'll be able to return to Kwandri after I set up supply?" Remy asked anxiously.

"Of course," Ishida said, with a tight smile.

"Jalak's going to fight you every step of the way when he gets wind of this. It's not only a matter of cultural impact; he's worried about a population explosion."

The station chief waved a hand. "Cultural impact is to be considered desirable in this instance. There'll be ample time to address the societal issues once the possibility of a Xell'em-leaning regime is eliminated.''

"And as far as an increase in population," Dakou added, "TechSci has given us assurances that a contragestational agent can be added to the aphrodisiac without diminishing its potency."

"Jalak will be watched," Ishida said, directing her attention to Csilla Voss. "Ms. Voss is going to be keeping an eye on things while you're away."

Dakou said, "Jalak has been informed that we're sending him a personal secretary."

"Live-in," Csilla smiled, revealing slightly crooked teeth.

Concerns about Els Nanff suddenly surfaced in Remy's mind as he studied Voss's gray streaks. "I've got a favor to ask," he said. "The Kwandri kid I've been helping. His legs are healed. I promised the father I'd make sure the kid got back home safe and sound."

Ishida showed him a disapproving look. "I don't know what you expect us to do. You were aware of the risks posed by indig attachments."

"I know. But he's just a kid—"

"Think about that next time," Ishida started to say when Csilla Voss interrupted her.

"I was just thinking that I could arrange for Professor Jalak to oversee the youngster's rehabilitation." She glanced back and forth between Remy and Ishida. "It would give Jalak something to busy himself with."

The station chief gave it a moment's thought. "All right," she said at last.

Remy rubbed his hands, eager to get on with things. "So where do I find these Skaro's Marats?"

The counsel folded his arms. "Dhone," he said.

Jalak couldn't take his eyes off the bowl of fruit, centered as it was on the low table that apparently served as Colonel Gong's desk. While the rest of the room was prosaic by Xell'em standards, each piece of heavy furniture, each statue and mask, was worthy of close examination. But Jalak was fascinated by the shapes and colors of the fruit.

Two security officers in dark attire were standing silently on either side of the door behind him; Gong, seated opposite him across the table, wore white.

"I have always wanted to visit your world," Jalak said in tradespeak.

The colonel favored him with a tolerant smile. "Perhaps one day you shall." The music of wind and percussion instruments drifted in from the embassy ballroom downstairs. "Please help yourself to a sample of our native fruit in the meantime." Gong's English was thickly accented but comprehensible.

Jalak chose a spiny oval and set his bony fingers to work on the brown rind.

"Now, what urgent business takes us from the pleasures of Xell'em song and dance and aged wine, Professor Jalak? The 'sin-sational pleasures of Xella,' as I believe you termed them in your monograph."

"*Sensational*," Jalak amended.

Gong contemplated the distinction. "I see. Well, then, suppose we lay our points on the table."

Jalak refrained from playing speech instructor, and instead directed an uncertain glance over his shoulder at the pair of security men. Gong watched him, then aimed a dismissive motion at his officers. The door issued a pneumatic hissing sound as it opened, and music filled the room for a moment.

"I have information," Jalak announced weakly.

"Indeed."

"Information about NCorp's designs on Q'aantre." Jalak's mouth was bone-dry when he tried to swallow, in spite of the copious amounts of *yika* he had consumed earlier on. He sucked at the pulp of the partially peeled fruit. "A plan to disrupt Xell'em influence."

Gong touched the inch-diameter spool that distended his left earlobe. "When I learned that you had approached one of our Special Investigation advisers, I asked myself: What game could Professor Jalak be playing? Now you say you have information about a plan to counter Xell'em interests.''

The colonel rearranged himself into a posture of caution as he spoke—right hand raised to the ceiling, right elbow cradled in the left hand. "Perhaps you should begin by explaining how an academic—a 'culturist'—comes by such knowledge.''

Jalak felt hopelessly tongue-tied, but managed, "I, I've done some clandestine intelligence gathering for NCorp. In exchange for permission to carry on with my work here. My work is the most important thing to me, Colonel Gong. Can you understand that?''

"I'll let you know when we've finished.'' Gong passed a hand over a sensor-studded device on the table. "And when you say that you've done some intelligence gathering for them, what exactly does that mean?''

"I've employed agents—here, in Likat. I've passed along data. I've investigated underground activities.''

Gong raised his hairless browridge. "You're conversant with the natives' olfactory idioms?''

Jalak nodded and wiped a rivulet of fruit juice from his chin.

"I'm amazed, Professor. And would you be willing to identify any of these agents?''

"No, I—''

Gong motioned him silent, his eyes fixed on a monitor screen above the door. Jalak heard the hiss again and turned to see a handsome Xell'em woman enter the room. The colonel waved her to a chair with the same silent command he had used to dismiss the security men.

"You were saying that you wouldn't identify the agents, Professor.''

"The data they passed was of little consequence—to Terra or Xella. I can't—''

"Forgive me, Jalak, but of what use can you possibly

be to me otherwise? I thank you for advising me of the existence of this 'plan.' But really, Professor, what assurance do I have that your coming forward is not simply part of that very plan?''

Jalak squirmed, his bladder about to burst all at once. ''Because I'm willing to tell you the name of the operative who's heading it up. Expose him and you can approach the League. You can put an end to NCorp's efforts.''

''Nonsense,'' Gong said. ''No one operative can be so important. Center will simply send another.''

''Of course they will,'' Jalak argued. ''But it will take months of training to outfit a second operative. NCorp might not even be able to afford a second attempt. You'll have time to prepare.''

''So Center, too, has financial difficulties.'' Gong's expression grew serious. ''Jalak, permit me to advise you about something now: If what you say is true, it may be necessary to do more than expose this operative. I don't wish to be indelicate, but my superiors may find termination the more prudent course. Do we still understand one another?''

Jalak tried to dismiss all thoughts of Remy Santoul. Who was Santoul after all, but a facilitator of NCorp's insidious methods. ''Exposure *is* the best course,'' he told Gong. ''Xella will be able to demonstrate that the Consortium has violated the Accord.''

''That isn't for me to decide,'' Gong said. ''But I want to hear you say that you won't hold yourself to blame for this operative's death, Professor.'' He tugged at a drooping lower lip. ''I have to know that you won't suffer some crisis of conscience afterward.''

''Q'aantre is all that concerns me,'' Jalak said. ''I make no judgmental distinctions between cultures, Colonel. In the best of all possible worlds neither Xella nor Terra would involve themselves in Q'aantre's affairs.''

Gong smiled. ''But this is hardly the best of all possible worlds.''

"It isn't. But the Manifest isn't resorting to NCorp tactics. Xella isn't flooding this world with consumer goods and mind-altering flickdisks. Xella isn't out to destroy the very fabric of Q'aantre society by—" Jalak stopped himself before he went too far. He feared that mentioning the aphrodisiac would only give Gong ideas of his own.

The colonel and the woman with the luxurious black hair and reshaped chin were regarding one another. "Where is this NCorp operative now?" Gong asked.

Jalak continued to writhe in place; the pressure on his bladder unbearable. "Upside."

"On Terra station."

Jalak shook his head. "On the *Tao*. Departing for Dhone."

Gong looked puzzled. "But that's a former Raliish world. Why there?"

"I'm not sure," Jalak confessed.

"And his name?" the woman asked, speaking for the first time.

"Santoul," Jalak said, facing her. "Remy Santoul." Jalak realized that he had met her. At a Grand Assembly gathering, shortly before Santoul had been sent downside. Jalak even remembered her name now; it was Karine Mareer.

PART THREE

—UPSIDE DOWN

TWELVE—

REMY—*CLOSE TO A FULL STANDARD-WEEK*
in biostat—had aged two months by the time the *Tao*
was inserted into orbit around Dhone, a planet known
across near space as a "hot-water world."

Decades before, faced with the task of revivifying the
planet's pollutant-ravaged stratosphere and protecting
the downside populace from UV radiation, Dhone's
Enddrese rulers had rejected a Terran-designed air-
scrub program and opted instead for city smog shields.

DisneyCorp, Dow-'Bishi, Tass, and hundreds of
lesser offworld concerns had all had a hand in fashion-
ing Dhone's terminal phases. Ozone-depleted and
surface-stripped, the planet was all but used up—sucked
dry, hunted out, beyond redemption.

Emerging onto the street from one of the more flour-
ishing of Zalindi's hundreds of commercial banks,
Remy was struck first by the fetid odor of the place.
Scent-laced half dreams of Kwandri had provided background for the near week in torpor, but he had known
nothing but sterile enclosures since—the few upright
hours he had spent inboard the *Tao*, and the succession
of vehicles he had ridden ship to port, port to Zalindi
city center.

137

One could walk or ride from one end of the city to the other—from its crooked spine of arid mountains down to its brackish bay—without leaving the filtered air and polarized light of slideways, tunnels, and pedestrian bridges; but Remy had chosen the amber outdoors if only to ascertain whether his tutored nose was still operating.

The wonders of biostat had him walking and seeing straight once again, but he felt hungry for something his body had yet to identify.

He stepped out of the pedestrian traffic flow to partake of a deep, intelligent breath, and the next thing he knew he was slumped against an epoxy wall, Earthnorm gravity weighing him down, head swimming with black, amorphous shapes. What little oxygen there was to be had rode in on an acidic hydrocarbon stench. Sulfur, nitrogen oxide, and flawed fullerenes. Remy's nose staggered him with noxious combinations of plastics and petroleum; vehicular exhaust, coolant and propellant spray; insecticides, solvents, and rust.

He supported himself stiff-armed for a long moment—just another new arrival acclimating to Zalindi's soot and smog, Dhone's commitment to ecocide.

Affixed to the wall was a holo-advert depiction of the tigerlike face of a Skaro's Marat. A linear rush of LEDetails gave the time and place for an upcoming speech by species rightist, Woodruff Glasscock.

The second thing that struck Remy was the heat, which seemed to radiate as much from the nebulous sky as the ferrocrete-surfaced ground. It hardly mattered he had arrived dressed for it, shaved and shorn, since Dhone wasn't the sort of place one could prepare for.

Originally colonized by Enddrese spacefarers, it had been one of the first worlds to fall to Ralii's push for empire. The occupying armies were gone now, but tens of thousands of Raliish refugees who had fled their homeworld before the outbreak of the war had remained behind.

They were a translucent, smooth-faced race of bipeds, with teardrop torsos and spindly limbs—a sinister version of the cinematic XTs Earth had always expected to encounter out beyond the solar winds. Postwar, NCorp had secured safe passage for several dozen Raliish military officers of dubious background, who had agreed to serve as double agents in Xell'em espionage networks. One of these—a former cybereugenics researcher named L'sser—had agreed to act as liaison between Remy and Dhone's principal processor and supplier of the scent-gland aphrodisiac.

But for all their numerical presence, Remy had to walk ten blocks before he spotted his first Raliish—his first three, to be precise. The apparent owners of a juice bar adjacent to the lobby entrance to the towering Hotel Ramuhl, where DisneyCorp had arranged for a suite.

The juice bar hadn't been there during the war; but then neither had the Ramuhl, nor the ever-present holoposter warnings about sexually transmitted diseases. The city streets were barely recognizable as the ones he and Jasna had walked four years ago. The tea stalls and fragrance shops that once surrounded the central square were gone, replaced by credit unions and drug outlets. A few of the older buildings still bore the slag-scars from plasma drops, but overall the city showed small evidence of the hellish assault Earth Force had waged against the entrenched armies of the mad Raliish monarch, The *Kell*.

Diehard Enddrese were what one bumped into most, hurrying along unfazed through the heat and stinking haze. They tended to be short and stocky, but were otherwise close to human aspect, save for a slight purple cast to their leathery skin. The men favored brightly colored wraparound skirts and status-designated head-cloths; the women wore heavy metal necklaces and shawls of the sheerest weave. A look that had followed them from the islands of equatorial Enddra and was well suited to Dhone's final-days climate.

At the other extreme were the spacers and freelance riggers who had gravitated there while Terra and Xella were busy dividing up the spoils of the war. Many were habitat exiles, Earthers of mostly Hispanic and Asiatic extraction, who wore their hair long, in spiked rooster-tails or tousled eye-concealing styles, and adopted uniforms of borrowed bits and pieces from a dozen cultures: ceramic jewelry, balloon pants, web belts, and cumbersome grav boots—invariably unclasped.

Remy touched a hand to the beads of perspiration that had formed on his forehead and rubbed them into his fingertips, as though some chemical message was to be derived from their salty content. But all he experienced was apprehension.

NCorp's power had seemed unlimited in those early days on Dhone, its future secure, much like Remy's own at the time. Now here he was come full circle, Jasna here as well, anchoring him in the rough currents of his past . . .

He bought a refreshing citrus concoction from the trio of Raliish at the juice bar, and allowed a swarthy Enddrese door attendant to usher him into the cool lobby of the Hotel Ramuhl.

A Terran woman at the front desk voiced him for a door lock and informed him that his luggage had arrived and was already inroom. Several messages were waiting, which Remy said he would access from the suite terminal. She explained that the elevator voice-command units were down, and inquired whether he had any special needs for the evening—drugs, an escort, hired hands. When Remy assured her that he was fine for the time being, she saw him off with a professional, blue-lipped smile.

The suite was appointed in Enddrese fashion, with woven wall hangings and silk flowers in each of the three rooms. The spacious bedroom enjoyed a view of Banah Bay.

Remy commanded the air-conditioning off and slid

open the doors to a balcony enclosed by tinted glass. Fifty stories up, the suite was above the thickest of the smog, and Remy could see a forest of like towers piercing the ground cover in an arc that followed the broad sweep of the harbor. The sky over the water and distant hills was a frightening shade of yellow.

He had the bar fix him a drink while he called up messages on the sitting-room display. Scrolling through the hotel's welcome notes and service menu, he finally located what he was looking for among several pages of NCorp screen litter concerning DisneyCorp business.

The message read: *Remy: Welcome back to hell. And in case you are wondering, you can find her running the Newli table at the Casino Kimeli.*

Jasna, Remy thought.

The message was initialed: *L.*

"I might've known the aphrodisiac was something you cooked up," Remy was telling his Raliish liaison several hours later. "TechSci's too synth-oriented to see what's right in front of them for the taking."

L'sser's tapered cuplike hand mimicked a human gesture of dismissal. "You afford me undue credit. I was searching for some way to aromatize the cat's scent-gland secretions when I made the discovery." The translator the Raliish wore like a collar rendered the words in a whispering rasp. "But you must understand, Remy, the scent gland was valued for its aphrodisiac qualities long before I thought to investigate it."

"Known by who?"

"By Enddrese dreamtime biota-gatherers who travel the cat's habitat—the Lannsmar. Hunters spoke of spontaneous sexual orgies whenever a group chanced upon a recently killed marat."

L'sser's case officer, an NCorp operative named Mi-Jung, had set up the meeting and was with them now in the vapor room of the Ramuhl's CEO club. A lack of funds had forced NCorp to close its upside station, and Mi-Jung ran the downside show. The two Terrans were naked, seated on a tiled bench. The Raliish wore a transpirator mask and a cloth robe that left much of his translucent legs revealed.

Remy's Kwandrized nose had introduced him to the natural Raliish scent a few moments earlier, and he was thankful for the overpowering aroma of the baths' steam-fed biovapors. He ventured that the war might have ended differently had the Raliish odor been accessible to normal human olfaction.

"They're calling the gland extract 'lube,' " Mi-Jung offered, cupping her left breast and examining it for some defect Remy certainly couldn't see.

"As in what, *lubricant*, *lubricious*?"

L'sser was shaking his hairless head, almond-shaped eyes bright above the muzzle of the mask. "The word is Raliish for 'ecstasy.' There are religious connotations."

Mi-Jung laughed. "Like Santoul said, *lubricious*."

Remy tuned to regard her: She was sweet-smelling and nearly as white and hairless as the Raliish, save for a mane of brown hair that cascaded in ringlets to the middle of her muscular back. Her hands and feet were disproportionately long, her small breasts upturned and somewhat walleyed, with large, erect nipples. Remy observed that he was sweating a lot more than she was.

"Perhaps you wish to try some, Remy?" L'sser asked, following Remy's gaze.

"You do," Mi-Jung answered for him, holding his eyes for a moment.

L'sser's translator rasped a laugh.

Remy had known the Raliish during the war. L'sser had just been ordered to assume command of Ralii's torture compounds on Dhone when Remy had been assigned to oversee his defection. L'sser had always maintained that he owed Remy his life; but Remy suspected he hadn't so much saved the Raliish from his military superiors in the compounds as he had saved L'sser from some black side of his own nature.

"Narca has been informed to expect you this evening," L'sser said. Narca, Remy had learned, had become Dhone's chief supplier of the aphrodisiac. "Naturally, everyone is excited by the prospect of contracting with DisneyCorp." L'sser's tone put quotes around the corp name.

"Narca," Remy repeated, trying it out. "Terran?"

Mi-Jung shook her head. "Enddrese. Lube's become just another illicit to add to Dhone's export lists. Enjoys quite a powerbase in Zalindi. Second to prostitution right now."

Prostitution had been an Enddrese contribution. The purple-tinged XT's were raised to believe that children must repay their parents for bringing them into the world; and prostitution was viewed as a desirable form of employment.

"This Narca's your boss, I understand," Remy said, looking at L'sser.

"For the past three years."

"Any chance Narca had something to do with the murder of our operative?"

Mi-Jung's face clouded over with grief. "Fiona was killed by Glasscock's mercs during a raid on a processing plant."

"Species rights," Remy said, recalling the adverts diplayed throughout Zalindi.

"One and the same."

"What's Center's interest in lube, Remy?" L'sser asked. "Even Fiona didn't know where the shipments were ending up."

Mi-Jung threw her agent a scolding look.

The Raliish stiffened. "I only meant—"

"You've been hearing things," Remy said. "Let's have it."

"Just talk."

"About?"

"An NCorp plan to aid the habitats. By using the aphrodisiac against Earth," L'sser said. "Create a sexual frenzy among the Muslim downside as prelude to an attack."

Remy nodded noncommittally. As crazed as the rumor was, it seemed a good one to perpetuate. Neither Mi-Jung nor L'sser were privy to the op on Kwandri, and there was some benefit to keeping everyone in the dark.

Mi-Jung said, "I favor the Kwandri rumor, myself."

Remy maintained an expression of tolerant receptivity. "Kwandri?"

"Jobber circuit says there's work available in Dazyl all of a sudden. Architecting a second Terran station or something. Four crews left Dhone for Kwandri just last week."

"So it's construction," Remy said, downplaying. "Where's lube fit into it?"

L'sser raised a foot to scratch at his featureless groin. "Some say the League has considered relaxing restrictions on use of the wormhole. With Burst and Daleth accessible, there'll be an import rush. Lube could prove a major earner, unless direct stim vogues."

Remy said nothing, hoping they would read his silence as disinterest. The case officer crossed her legs, sluicing moisture from one thigh. "I still don't see why they wormed you in, Santoul," she said, without looking at him. "I could've run Fiona's follow-up. I've had dealings with Narca."

Remy shrugged. "I spent years here."

"Maybe," Mi-Jung said. "But the Dhone you knew doesn't exist anymore."

"Except that Remy's old enemies are still about," L'sser thought to point out.

The steam room grew quiet for a moment.

"The *Ambii'th* was a long time ago," Mi-Jung said.

L'sser voiced a rasping sound peculiar to his species. "Not for some," he said, watching Remy.

Welcome back to hell, Remy recalled from L'sser's short message.

L'sser entwined his arms in a demonstration of regret. "Perhaps they wouldn't even recognize Remy. He seems to have weathered the war so much better than most . . ."

Remy heard the inference and swung around, hair whiplashing moisture in L'sser's direction. The Raliish returned the look.

"Yes, I told Jasna you had arrived, Remy. Not to do so would have been unjust." L'sser rasped again. "You could visit with her before you meet Narca."

"No reason for me to go all the way out to the Kimeli," Remy said quietly, looking for some way out.

"But there is," L'sser told him. "Narca owns the casino—and Jasna."

"Still the movie star," Jasna said, pushing a stack of casino chips across the likefelt tablecloth. "Figured you'd've had yourself altered by now, Remy. Especially coming back here."

Remy positioned five chips in the rectangle in front of him. "It's the one I was born with, Jasna. What do you want from me?"

The game they were playing—Newli—was a variation on an old Earth card game called blackjack. But in Newli one not only bet against the house but played the odds against computer forecasts as well. The minimum had just been raised to five hundred NuYen and Remy and Jasna had the kidney-shaped table to themselves for the moment.

Minutes before, she had watched him approach through the curved-top doors leading from hovercraft debark, expecting him, arms folded across high breasts while the autoshuffler fed plasticized cards into the shoe. Her green eyes cruel at first, weary when Remy sat down.

"What do I want from you . . . That's crystal, Remy, truly." She slid two cards toward him, face up.

"There has to be a motive for looking you up?"

"If the helmet fits, Remy." She turned her own cards over and swept his chips into the sorter. Remy positioned five more in the rectangle.

"You like to go around pretending you're a saint, Remy. You always did." Remy asked for a card and entered a bet with the computer. "What do they have you pretending to be this time?"

He won the hand against the computer, but lost to the bank. "Too bad you're no longer a member of the club, Jasna. Maybe I could tell you."

It was just before midnight, fifteen minutes remaining before the appointment with Narca. Earlier, he'd spent almost an hour at the suite's scopescreen watching the Casino Kimeli come to life on its island in Banah Bay. Water taxis hovering in from hotels on the point, where the fog didn't roll in until midmorning.

A dozen times he had been half out the door when something pulled him back inside the suite; some bit of business he hadn't attended to, some message he'd forgotten to send. But he'd only fooled himself that first time out; then it had become a kind of game and the hours passed, allowing him just enough time to say hello to Jasna before the meet. After all the years, maybe it was the best way to play it, he kept telling himself on the hover ride out, the spray in his face, a constellation of dried salt on the tux jacket now.

Jasna wore green to highlight her eyes, a sleeveless dress of some clinging fabric. She was bone-thin and her blond hair was clipped short. Most of the other dealers and croupiers were Raliish, whose long arms lent a certain panache to the deal.

The gameroom was filled with Enddrese high rollers, their mates and lovers, there to be seen; and pale Terran roustabouts with hired hands, on downside leave and prepared to dump a month's pay on a night's entertainment. Gamblers were drawn to the place for the novelty of hands-on play and games thought archaic in corps-operated casinos. In keeping with the low-tech atmosphere, the waitresses were flesh-and-blood kids in skimpy outfits, working the floor for tips and whatever else might happen along.

"So you didn't come all the way across the stars to see me, then?" Jasna was saying, relieving Remy of another small stack of chips.

"I wasn't even sure you were onworld till yesterday. But, yeah, maybe I would have if I'd known."

"So who are you here to see, Remy?"

"Your boss."

Jasna laughed sardonically as she slid two cards from the shoe. "Talk about matches made in paradise . . . Eleven," she announced for the benefit of the pit boss.

Remy matched his opening bet with a second stack of chips and tapped a forefinger against the table. "Double down," he told her. The computer displayed a pessimistic appraisal of his chances.

Looking at her, inhaling her, made him think of Karine Mareer, who he thought he had left behind in biostat with the rest of Kwandri memories. Jasna's face had the same planes and angles, only she had come by the chin naturally and the perforations in her ears, though many, probably wouldn't accept more than thin rings.

L'sser had said she was strung out on zap, a potent narcotic that eroded memory. Everything Remy sensed about her seemed to confirm the fact. The gold flecks in her eyes weren't as bright as they used to be. Her scent was a mix of rotting lace and parched earth.

Remy was glad they hadn't shaken hands, for what he might have read from her palm. He could still hear the whisper of L'sser's translator device: *Narca owned her.*

Jasna had played a part in the op that brought L'sser out during the war, and a larger part in the *Ambii'th* Incident later on—a misfortune that bound the three of them together in a tragic web. Remy's was the name most closely associated with the incident, but it was Jasna who seemed to have suffered most . . .

He drew a three and Jasna turned over twin picture cards.

"House wins," she said. "Peripheral losses have been charged to your account."

Remy sighed and thumb-tossed his single remaining chip. "Looks like you took just about everything I had, Jaz."

Her lifeless eyes locked on his. "The difference between you and me, Remy. I know when to quit."

THIRTEEN —

No ONE HAD BOTHERED TO MENTION THAT Narca was a woman. She was a few years shy of Enddrese middle-age, long-haired and aubergine-colored. And everything about her was full: lips, breasts, thighs. Though almost twice her height, Remy ventured he was half her weight. The jocularity was false, obviously meant to put Remy at ease. He inhaled the pungent scents of the sharp marketeer beneath Narca's open displays. Whiffs of curry, cayenne, and saffron stung his nose; a trader's spice rack.

They were in the casino owner's upstairs office, a hexagon of on-off glass overlooking the Kimeli's high-roller room. A few of Narca's Terran and Enddrese lieutenants were pacing the room's one-way floor; others sat quietly at flatscreens and holo units, monitoring tableside transactions.

The office was a museum of mismatched knockoff Terrana: wall-mounted Ginsu knives and golf putters; Gut Busters and hockey sticks; Easy-Squeeze nutcrackers and diamond-studded sharpeners; garbage bag sealers, Power Press orange juice makers, and liposuction vacuum tubes. Narca had a thing for what she took to be weapons and torture devices, Remy decided.

"Narca just observing Remy at table," she was saying in the local pidgin. "Remy favoring the woman—for this evening maybe?"

Remy shook his head. "Remy knows the woman."

"Ah, Remy knows her. She's honest this one, not like some who treasure the zap. She spots a Xell'em cybercon for Narca only last week. A walking interface, that one. Can dazzle a system from across a room."

"One has to be careful," Remy said, eager to move the conversation along.

"The reason the Kimeli is hand-ons, Ter. Narca losing her trust in hardware." She gestured broadly with a plump, short-fingered hand. A Terran kid with a raised scar from ear to ear brought drinks for the two of them.

"Narca knows you from somewhere."

"Remy gets this all the time," he started to say, but the casino owner was already forging on.

"Wagering you were here during the war."

He considered denying it, but denial hadn't been paying off lately. "Short time."

"Remy Santoul at the restaurant by the hoverdocks—the one with live meat."

"Remy knows it."

"Remy remember woman standing day-day outside selling oils and amulets?"

Remy rubbed his jaw. "I think—"

"That's Narca!" she said with her huge arms wide. "You buying an amulet from Narca."

He touched the wrist on which he used to wear the thing: a bracelet of terror bird talons. "Long gone now."

"No dazzle." She beamed at him. "Narca supply another. You have to be casino guest, Remy Santoul. Kimeli finest room—twin Terran toilets."

Remy bowed slightly. "Thanks, same-same, but I'm happy with the view I have."

She made a disapproving sound. "Remuhl for tourists. Hotels overcharge.'' When Remy didn't reply, she attended to her drink. ''L'sser tells Narca Terran corp exec interested in lube.''

He sniffed a turn in her thinking; the Enddrese was guarded now.

Narca studied him. ''This personal needs, yes?''

''I'm in position to negotiate substantial purchase behalf DisneyCorp.''

Narca raised painted eyebrows. ''Narca want to hear this from you, Remy Santoul. To make sure L'sser isn't mistaken. But DisneyCorp . . . Concerns arise.''

Remy signaled his willingness to talk.

''What would Earthers want with the lube?''

''Corp exec perks.''

''To replace direct stim?''

''As an adjunct—choice-choice.''

She took a moment to digest this. ''Thinking we have important product here. New desire for natural stimulants, narcotics, aphrodisiacs.'' She motioned to the closest monitor. ''New money enjoy old games, DisneyCorp thinks execs could like-like lube . . . Even Narca fails anticipate demand. Not now.'' Her inlaid teeth reflected the office light.

Remy said, ''Now Narca control Zalindi lube-flow.''

''But she wants move slowly. L'sser fail synthesize lube. But who to say what DisneyCorp smart-smart techs can accomplish. Are we online, Santoul?''

The joviality had disappeared—along with the gutterspeak pidgin. Remy set his empty glass aside. ''DisneyCorp has no interest in synthesizing it. We simply wish to secure a supply.''

Narca laughed. ''Yes, of course you do. To stockpile. Narca earns meager NuYen transfer, while DisneyCorp makes big business in back-to-basics trade.''

''Charge whatever you want for transport,'' Remy said, sweetening the pot.

Black eyes appraised him. ''You won't be moving it yourself?''

"DisneyCorp can't afford to involve itself in an environmental scandal."

She nodded. "Narca is beginning to see more clearly. But how great is DisneyCorp's need?"

Dakou had run the calculations. "Say, four hundred liters—to start."

Narca's mouth dropped open, revealing a thick, coated tongue. "Four hundred? Not that much in all Zalindi. Even if, Narca has other customers to satisfy."

The same ones NCorp was buying from, Remy assumed. "Just how much is available?"

Narca wriggled her massive shoulders. "Perhaps one hundred. Possibly one seventy-five."

Remy shook his head. "You'll have to do better than that."

"Maybe Santoul doesn't appreciate difficulties involved. The cats grow scarce-scarce each day. Narca's teams have to use local dreamtime trackers, charge heavy for services. District supervisors, police units to appease. Good hunt bring fifty, sixty scent glands. L'sser can extract ten liters, no more, of the pure."

"Which converts to one hundred liters of lube."

Narca frowned. "We no hit ten-to-one, Santoul. Narca supply finest lube on Dhone. Seven-to-one, never more."

"At what price?"

Her eyes narrowed somewhat. "Fifty thousand each liter."

Remy feigned shock.

"Difficulties," Narca said quickly. "Santoul knows about Woodruff Glasscock?"

"Species rights," Remy said.

"Some years ago Glasscock makes a field study of the marat. He thinks he is Damir Skaro reborn—the one who named them. When he learns the cats are being hunted he returns to Dhone. And when he learns his own people are receiving monies to look away, he appeals to friends in the League and hires mercenaries to

safeguard the cats' territories.'' She shook her head in anger. "Last month Narca loses three of her best hunters to hired weapons."

"What about cloning a reserve?" Remy asked.

"Impossible. Dhone lacks technology."

"Something could be arranged," Remy mused. "But not immediately. How difficult would it be to bring in a live cat?"

"*Very* difficult. Many police, many checkpoints."

Remy mulled over the idea of countering Glasscock's mercs with a small contingent of NCorp freelancers.

"Glasscock here in Zalindi," Narca continued in an agitated voice. "Talking, bribing everyone to gain political support. This happens," the Enddrese snapped her fingers, "the market close. Narca would kill the man if she could, but he is well protected." She clenched her fists. "Narca fighting for her survival. All marketeers in danger of extinction."

Survival of the fittest, Remy thought. "Can I get out to the cats?"

"You can. Narca can see to it. But Santoul plays his own odds."

"Understood."

They discussed a plan over second and third drinks. Narca had a hunt scheduled for the end of the week.

"Santoul certain he doesn't want dealer at Newli table?" she asked as Remy was leaving. "Choice software." She showed him a phial of clear liquid. "Narca give you free taste of both—woman and lube."

"Some other time," he told her.

Back at the Hotel Remuhl, the elevator voice-command units were still down. Remy keyed his floor into the touchpad and rode what must have been the local all the way up to fifty.

He voiced himself into the suite and checked for signs of forced entry into the rooms or the computer terminal. Nothing had been disturbed.

* * *

Narca contacted him the following morning to suggest that he pay a visit to the processing lab. Some Enddrese poachers had arrived in town with a cache of freshkill scent glands, and L'sser would be available to lead Remy through the entire extraction and refinement process. Remy agreed, and a midday rendezvous was arranged. Narca said she hoped he wouldn't take offense at the precautions, but she insisted that the lab's location remain a closely guarded secret.

Remy recalled that NCorp's former operative on Dhone had been killed in a Glasscock-directed raid against a lube lab. He retrieved a stunner from his attaché, and placed the weapon with his data and credit cards.

He had breakfast sent up and nibbled at dark bread and fruit while heavy drops of rain spattered against the tinted sheets of thick glass that enclosed the balcony. He thought about calling Jasna at the Kimeli's staff condo, but never got around to it.

Woodruff Glasscock was addressing a local chapter of the Free Species Organization later that morning in the Remuhl's ninth-floor conference hall, and Remy had just enough time left to finish the meal and ultrasonic the previous night's casino smoke from his hair.

With him in the elevator he rode downstairs were three Terran women sporting holo-buttons that read: PRESERVE DIVERSITY: SAVE THE MARAT. They engaged him in conversation, asking whether he was familiar with the cats' plight. When he admitted as much, the talk turned to other species-rights matters, and by the time the four of them stepped out on nine, Remy had learned that the trio were from DuPont habitat, on a fact-finding tour organized by Free Species. The tallest among them, Chanel, had a son who worked for DisneyCorp and wondered if Remy might know him. He said he didn't, explaining that the 'Corp kept him on the move quite a bit. This seemed to arouse the woman's interest even more.

"Perhaps we could have dinner this evening," Chanel said as they were entering the conference hall. "If you don't have plans, that is."

Remy said that he was free. There was something about her he liked; a scent, he decided, lusty and self-assertive, even under the gardenia she had splashed on sometime earlier.

"Oh, by the way," she added, while her two friends were heading for reserved seats up front, "it is Warren Beatty, isn't it?"

"Several times removed," he told her.

"That's okay," she said, showing him a lascivious smile. "I've never had one of you before."

Remy lingered by the door watching the room fill up. The audience was largely Terran and Enddrese, with a scattering of Xell'em and other offworlders. It was a different crowd than the one that patronized Narca's island casino; not one to line up for lube. Although Remy had to wonder about the Terran woman. There was still that free taste of the aphrodisiac—*the lube job*—Narca had offered . . .

Woodruff Glasscock entered ten minutes late, and had the flustered look of a man who was rarely on time. The beard and the glasses reminded Remy of Jalak. Glasscock was taller, though, deeply tanned, and a good deal heavier, almost the picture of a sportsman himself, were it not for the haphazard style and edgy manner.

Perhaps unaware that he had already been fitted with an audio pickup, the species-rights advocate began yelling orders to the Enddress sound engineers.

"You mean I'm on?" Glasscock said at last, his words booming from the room's PA banks. "Well, why didn't someone tell me?" When he swung around to face front, it was as though he had just discovered the audience.

It was clear from the whispered comments and amused chuckling that everyone found the nuttiness endearing. What wasn't clear was whether these same species rightists felt the same toward the rifle-armed guards Glasscock had stationed at either end of the stage.

"You know, I'm the first one to accept that planetary life conspires to evolve an advanced life-form and move that life-form offworld," the man plunged right in. "I'll grant, on Earth for example, that humankind paid its dues during its long climb out of the swamp, that it suffered disease and geological upheaval and in some sense earned the right to utilize the lower forms for food and clothing.

"But Dhone knew no self-conscious anthropoid forms until the Enddrese arrived. Life was still evolving on this world when the wanton destruction began. Hundreds of species have already been lost. But we're in time to prevent the extermination of those that remain. First, however, we must punish and exile the ones responsible for hunting these forms to near extinction. These few—these devolved and debased few who represent Dhone's true lower forms—"

Remy left before Narca's name came up.

"They're planning to vaporize portions of the road south," L'sser was telling Remy later on. "Terminate on detection anyone found in Rambela or the Lannsmar without authorization."

Remy nodded. "Glasscock was militant from the go-to. There's little enough left of Dhone. Everyone has to fight to preserve what remains—especially those life-forms found here and nowhere else."

The translator made L'sser's laugh sound like a death rattle. "Life-forms? Did he really say that?"

Remy touched the Mickey Mouse tie clasp he wore on the pocket of his jacket. " 'On all that's sacred,' as the 'Corp teaches its execs to say."

The lab occupied the partitioned-off rear area of a single-story building Remy assumed was a plastics factory—at least his nose believed as much. Two of Narca's Terran underlings had delivered him to the place in the windowless back of a utility hover.

He supposed that someone with Zalindi's puzzle of streets, waterways, and tunnels committed to memory would have been able to decipher the route, but Remy had no such overall command of the layout. He wasn't even sure he could come within a square mile of pinpointing the factory on a map—the city had changed so since the war—but forced to guess he would have placed it in one of the dry canyons east of the shuttleport.

"The Earther is a fool," L'sser said. "The marat's time has come whether the species is hunted to extinction or left to die out on its own. Dhone itself is finished. What would Glasscock do, transport the cats to a new world?"

"He would if he could get the funding."

"This indiscriminate affection for creatures who have long outlived their usefulness . . . I have always found it curious. But then you water-world races seem to share a penchant for empathy. You view yourselves as servants to some larger evolutionary plan rather than the very architects of that plan."

"We used to," Remy said.

"Used to? Then how do you explain someone like Woodruff Glasscock?"

Remy shrugged. "Not sure I can. There's a retroprogram at work. For a while we were all sick of our homeworld, now a lot of us seem to be homeworld sick—for the beliefs and fashions of those early days, anyway. I don't know what it means."

L'sser's elastic arms were doing strange things. "Little wonder The *Kell* lost his war to Earth and Xella. There is no understanding you."

The Raliish scientist had directed Remy over to a dewarlike liquid nitro container about the size of an issue EVA helmet—an ice-olation chamber, L'sser called it. The scent gland had already been removed and was lying in an off-pink mound on a one-foot-square piece of plotting glass. It resembled an outsize human pancreas.

"Not the best specimen," L'sser commented, prodding the thing with a curved finger, "but viable, at least. Typical of what the poachers bring in. Old cats, easy to hunt."

Only the Raliish were maskless and gloveless, Remy had observed; everyone else was outfitted as he was, in respirator and arm sheaths. The Enddrese on the other side of the room were using waldos to handle the potent extract.

"What happens if I finger that thing?" Remy said.

L'sser's reaction approximated a snort. "Arousal. Concupiscence in the extreme. No self-respecting 'life-form' or piece of furniture in the immediate area would be safe for at least six hours."

"It doesn't affect you at all?"

"Not in any way you would understand. I could juggle half a dozen of them and no one would have cause for concern."

"But you discovered it, you told me."

"I discovered the extract's effects. My hands transferred it to some glassware which was quite innocently passed around . . . The next thing I knew, half the techs in the lab were copulating with one another. You've never seen such an integrated group. Those without partners were turning to less yielding apertures and far more solid protuberances."

Remy allowed it ten seconds of play in his mind's eye. Bad enough that the filtration mask wasn't protecting his doctored nose the way it should have, without feeding himself reinforcing mental images of groping hands and entangled bodies. His prick had been rock hard for twenty minutes now, and he could well imagine the sex-crazed scene L'sser and his Raliish assistants had witnessed.

"What is it, Remy?"

Remy wiggled a bit, adjusting himself for comfort. "Just an itch," he said.

He was still aching by the time Narca's men dropped him back at the Hotel Remuhl. The boner that wouldn't go away, he told himself, finger-tipping fifty into the elevator touchpad and thinking wild thoughts about Free Species militant Chanel in room 5213.

He planned to call her first thing, but had no sooner voiced himself through the door to the suite when the pain took hold.

His gut torqued and launched a searing jolt directly at his heart. Air burst from his lungs and wouldn't return. His vision tunneled, then gave way to absolute blackness. He made it halfway to the commo unit before collapsing to the floor.

FOURTEEN—

REMY ALWAYS FELT THAT L'SSER'S DEFEC-tion had gone too smoothly. It wasn't that he believed the Raliish had set them up or were feeding them a double, nothing like that; just that things almost never went by the numbers and the damned op had: one, two, three, and L'sser was out.

He had approached an Enddrese agent early on in the war and made it known that he was willing to do any-thing for a shot at freedom—freedom from his own peo-ple, who under The *Kell*'s fanatical leadership had become a race of equally fanatical warriors. The Enddrese ran him for more than two standard-years, dealing the data L'sser furnished to operatives in the Consortium's fledgling intel agency, NCorp, then turned him over to Center's care when their own homeworld was conquered and occupied. L'sser, meanwhile, had been relocated to Dhone and put in charge of Ralii's cybereugenics program. Just what The *Kell* had in mind for Dhone's Enddrese populace was never fully under-stood, but the program itself was given utmost priority and L'sser treated accordingly.

By that time Remy and Jasna were already in place on Dhone, interfacing with what remained of Enddra's spy network. Earth Force had yet to enter the war, but it would have L'sser to thank for many of its early successes. And it fell to Remy and Jasna to get him out.

The two intel officers were still basking in the afterglow of the successful defection op when they married in secret; but NCorp wasn't quite finished with the trio that operation had birthed. Earth Force needed confirmation about a shipment of plasma weapons rumored to be leaving Ralii for the Daleth system. At great personal risk L'sser finagled that confirmation from the son of a Raliish starfleet admiral, and Remy and Jasna had passed the intel on to Center without bothering to seek corroboration from secondary sources. They were so much in love . . .

Earth Force was waiting when the ship—the *Ambii'th*—emerged in Daleth and annihilated it before it had cleared the wormhole's nimbus.

Only the ship wasn't transporting weapons. It was carrying close to one hundred thousand Raliish and Enddrese women and children who had been packed into the holds like so much stuffing.

The *Kell* was eager to issue a full disclosure once the events surrounding the so-called *Ambii'th* Incident became known. Some were foolish enough to believe even at that late date that some mistake had been made; but L'sser had divined the truth and Remy was at least halfway there. Because defection ops never ran smoothly; it just didn't happen.

The Raliish admiral's son had been acting according to plan: the one hundred thousand innocent deaths were L'sser's punishment for leaving the program. And a clear message to those who had helped him. The *Kell* thought that way . . .

Remy seemed to inhale the nightmare recollection from Dhone's smog while he lay near death in the hotel suite. When his eyes opened, it was L'sser's near featureless face and marblelike eyes that greeted him.

"You've returned," the voice box whispered. "Any near-death experiences you wish to report—corridors of light, familial presences, heavenly choirs?"

"We once thought you people were angels," Remy managed, "long time ago."

An alloy medical kit was open on a nightstand beside the bed, along with bioassay and diagnostic units, an injector and several smart cartridges. Remy eased himself up against the padded headboard and tried to focus on the entertainment monitor's digital time display. Someone had undressed him and fitted the bed with med-sensor sheets and blanket. Jasna was pacing in front of the balcony sliders, her head lowered. Night had come to Zalindi.

"I can't read it. How long have I—"

"Not more than thirty standard-hours. Six hours ago you were lucid enough to inform us that you'd made some terrible mistake; then you screamed and lost consciousness."

Remy shook his head. "I can't remember . . . What's she doing here?" he asked quietly.

"I didn't know who else to contact. Our mutual friend is away on business." L'sser turned to Jasna. She caught the look and hurried from the room without glancing at Remy. "She's been here the entire time. It hasn't been easy for her."

Remy took a shuddering breath. "Yeah, but what the hell are you doing here? What happened to me?"

"*What* indeed happened to you." The Raliish looked around uncomfortably.

"The attaché," Remy said, pointing to the room's walk-in closet. "Raise the top and enter six-four-four on the touchpad." L'sser followed Remy's direction and returned to the foot of the bed.

"We can talk now?"

"Go ahead."

"An informant told me that plans had been made to dispose of a Terran exec. A new arrival."

"Who made the plans?" Remy asked, reaching for a glass of water.

"This we don't know. As I told you, Mi-Jung wasn't available, so I tried to contact you here and got no response. When this continued I asked Jasna to intercede. She enticed someone at the front desk to manual the door. I waited until the attendant left and Jasna and I found you on the floor."

"No one saw the two of you together?"

L'sser's somewhat triangular-shaped head shook. "You were as white as the walls of this room. I sent Jasna for my instruments and here we've been, just the three of us, like old times."

Remy's fingers located tender places along both sides of his rib cage and abdomen. His throat was parched and his joints ached. "So what'd I have, a cardiac?"

"No. My guess is that you were poisoned."

"Your guess."

"Yes. A novel substance." L'sser gestured to his instruments. "Something we've never seen."

Remy's first thought was the lube his supersensitized nose had inhaled in the lab. He told L'sser as much, but made no mention of the implants or his olfactory training.

"Most unlikely," the Raliish said. "There have been instances of overdose, but the damage done is neurochemical and easily corrected. Even in the case of an allergic reaction, the effect wouldn't approximate that of a toxin. No, Remy, you were poisoned. Sometime during the past thirty-six hours. By whom and by what remain to be seen."

Remy tried to assemble the details of the six hours leading up to his collapse. Breakfast in the suite, the Earthers in the elevator, Glasscock's speech to Free Species . . . "This informant of yours," he said after a moment.

"A Raliish working with the Enddrese. I've asked him to continue his efforts."

"Someone from the old network," Remy mused aloud. "Someone who hasn't forgotten the war."

"Or the *Ambii'th*," L'sser said. His arms entwined as Remy threw him a hard look. "A speculation, nothing more."

They tossed it back and forth until Jasna returned with a meal she had conjured from the suite's sampler.

"You two have things to discuss," L'sser whispered, and left the room.

Jasna cleared a space on the nightstand and set the food down. "You shit," she told Remy at the same time, "I figured you'd come here just to die on me."

"The prospect of dying on you isn't as bad as it sounds," Remy said. "From my vantage."

"Asshole," she muttered.

Remy slid over to allow her room at the edge of the bed and she eventually sat down. "It's all right for me to stand by and watch you kill yourself, is that it?"

She snorted. "I'm not killing myself, Remy."

"No, you're letting the zap do it for you."

Jasna aimed an angry glance at the sitting room. "What's he been telling you?"

"Nothing that isn't obvious, Jaz. Why'd you come back here? I heard you'd gone home."

"Earth and I don't get along anymore," she said, quieter now. "I finally realized I couldn't get away from Dhone, so I decided returning'd be easier than running away."

Remy expected her to withdraw her hand when he reached for it, but she didn't. "Nothing wrong with working it out. By why the zap?"

"Because it's therapeutic, Remy. I can forget."

"And Narca? The casino?"

She glowered at him. "Solid citizens don't keep company with people like her, huh, Remy? Then what the fuck are you here for?" Remy's silence seemed to disperse the force of her words. "Look, I didn't know what I was looking for when I got here. I found L'sser, he was working with Narca. Things assembled themselves. He's been a friend. So has Narca.''

"A friend," Remy said. "She offered me you."

Jasna laughed at him. "You're losing it, Remy. She knows about us. Narca was scanning you."

It sounded right, and Remy smiled briefly. "You shouldn't have left Dhone in the first place, Jaz."

Her face straightened. "What was I supposed to do? I couldn't look at you without thinking about the ones we sent to their deaths."

"It was a long time ago. There was a war."

She shook her head. "It was yesterday, Remy. It's always going to be. I begged you to resign, and you wouldn't."

"You wanted to blame NCorp," he told her. "You still do. But it was our goddamned fault, that's what you've got to confront."

Her look was pitying. "I live with that, every minute of every day. But at least I'm out of the game, Remy. I'm not *looking* for another oversight to happen."

"And you figure I am."

"Unless you can set me straight. Unless you tell me Center's seen the error of its former ways."

Remy fell silent again. Regardless of his altered senses, he had begun to think of Kwandri as a dream, a shadowy unreality on the far side of the Arm. And he had come to think of Narca and the scent-gland aphrodisiac as some new op, disconnected from the petty intrigues in that remote corner.

"You better get something inside you," Jasna said, getting up.

"I guess I'm ready to have something."

"Oh, one more thing," she said from the door. "A woman named Chanel stopped by asking for you. Said you two had a dinner date or something."

Remy looked up from the tray. "What d'you say?"

"I told her you were married."

* * *

Remy kept going over it after they left. He'd taken breakfast in the suite, fruit and bread and Enddrese coffee. But L'sser seemed convinced that the toxin was quick-acting, and there had been no ill effects from the meal.

Remy went over his morning rituals in the bathroom, in the ultrasonic. He recalled his conversation with the three species-rights activists, recalled Chanel's gardenia fragrance. Then the trip out to the lab in the windowless rear compartment of the hover vehicle. There had been no time to eat after Glasscock's speech, and Remy remembered being hungry. . . Everything pointed to the lab, and yet L'sser maintained that a toxic reaction was impossible.

Even for someone with a stepped-up olfactory tract. Remy had actually presented it like that: *All right, then forget about allergies and overdose. What about an infantry specialist—a sniffer?* The question had aroused suspicion, but L'sser had attempted to conceal it. "For the last time," he said, "psychosis, yes. Toxicity, no. Besides, the tests revealed that whatever crippled you could not have been airborne."

So it was either something he ingested, or something he had *absorbed*. Inadvertently or deliberately. Something perhaps lying in wait for an unsuspecting, tacitly doctored NCorp agent.

L'sser had cautioned him to stay in bed for the rest of the evening, but the way Remy saw it he'd just awakened from three days' worth of rest and there were things to be done, things that couldn't wait. His would-be assassin was bound to circle in for a second try.

He thought he would begin by retracing his steps, at least as far as the corner where Narca's men had picked him up. L'sser had promised to run a check on the utility hover itself and sweep the lab for anything suspect.

Remy took a last look around the suite before he

voiced the door open and walked down the corridor to the opposing elevator banks. A moment later inside the north bank car, Remy took for granted that the voice-command unit hadn't been repaired and simply keyed nine into the touchpad.

He had the answer before the car had descended twenty floors.

"It's got holes, Santoul," Mi-Jung was telling him the following morning. "You said yourself the security cam disks don't show anyone smearing anything on the touchpad."

"It wouldn't necessarily require an applicator," Remy argued. "Someone could've been carrying it on a fingertip."

"And risk being poisoned?"

"So whoever it was was wearing gloves or a prosthesis."

Mi-Jung gestured to the security recordings Remy had spent the entire night going through. "And does anyone on those disks fit either description?"

"It's difficult to say."

"Because the idea doesn't work, Santoul. No one's going to walk into an elevator and slather some unheard-of toxin all over the place just to dispose of a single agent."

Remy didn't like the sound of it coming back at him like that. L'sser's case officer had pulled strings to arrange access to the elevator security recordings, and here he was insisting she accept his conclusion while cognizant of only half the facts. They were in one of the security station offices just now, a windowless room on the twentieth floor, empty save for a single desk, two chairs, and a dozen or more monitors.

"There's another possibility," Remy said at last.

Mi-Jung perched her shapely rump on the edge of the desk. "I'm all ears, Santoul."

Hardly, he thought. "See, they wouldn't need a glove,

a prosthesis, or a goddamned applicator because whatever they were carrying wouldn't have an effect on them.''

Mi-Jung's mouth twisted. ''But they'd run the risk of poisoning everybody who walked into those two cars and keyed fifty? Come on, man.''

Remy blew out his breath. ''Suppose they knew I was the only one capable of absorbing the toxin.''

''A Remy Santoul–specific toxin,'' she said. ''A bit grandiose, isn't it? They'd have to access your DNA profiles, key into your personal genome . . . Too sophisticated for Dhone.''

''They wouldn't need either.''

''Then how, Santoul? How does someone figure you and you alone can absorb the stuff? I mean, I'm willing to follow you only so far. Someone takes a contract out on you, opts to use an osmotic poison, decides to hit you here, in the hotel. Your room number's no problem to come by but since the door's voiced, the elevator touchpad seems the best bet. But even if we're talking about a Raliish assassin, why aren't any of the other seven Earthers on fifty sick or dead?''

Remy sat down next to her on the desk, edging her over a bit with his hip. ''I'm going to tell you something you're not cleared to hear, which means you're not hearing it, understand?''

She nodded.

''I've been worked on,'' he said flatly.

''Don't tell me,'' she said, grinning. ''You're not Warren Beatty's clone after all.''

''Not my face. My nose, my hands.''

She looked him over uncertainly.

''I can sniff out data. I can absorb information from bodily secretions.

Mi-Jung took a moment to respond. ''All right, then, tell me what I'm thinking,'' she challenged, leading with breasts and chin.

Remy stood up and faced her, took her cool hand

between his and leaned into her candied scent. "You're thinking we should just knock off and go up to the suite."

Her face reddened slightly. "Am I that obvious?"

"Your scents are."

"But why would Center . . . This op has something to do with Kwandri, doesn't it? Why else would they fit you for a new nose?"

"You didn't hear it from me," Remy reminded her. "Important thing's someone knew to get to me through these." He examined his hands, then looked up. "Someone on Kwandri blew my cover. Xella's behind this."

"The slopes," Mi-Jung said, "the chinless wonders." She gave the cam recordings a second look. "Tell me what we're looking for."

Remy retrieved the composite he had dubbed from elevator surveillance covering the days since he'd arrived downside. "These are just the ones that touched fifty," he said, slotting the disk into a player. "No one jumps out at you we start from scratch."

He showed her the Remuhl's human guests first; then the Enddrese—including a dozen hotel staffers who apparently had something against using the service elevators—and finally the Raliish. Mi-Jung told the machine to freeze on the final subject.

"Cloud Nine," she said, tapping a black lacquered fingernail against the flatscreen. "The discolorations on his face," she explained, "they look like clouds."

The freeze frame showed only five of them. The XT's eyes and skin tone suggested old age. He was taller than L'sser, but thinner, not as well proportioned.

"Part of Ralii's old-boy network," Mi-Jung continued. "Spent most of the war running internment camps on Enddra. Recruited by the Xell'em about three years ago. He's been on Dhone since."

Remy ran his tongue over his teeth. "Was hoping

you'd say that. 'Cause I've got him in both elevators. Four trips, riding to fifty each time.''

"I think I know where to find him," Mi-Jung started to say, but Remy shook his head.

"We're going to wait for him to show up."

"It could be hours, Santoul. Days."

Remy grinned at her. "We could put our heads together, figure some way to pass the time."

L'sser was deep into the Terminal Meditation of the Summoning when the apartment's external sensors responded to a breech in the perimeter. The alert tone was of a low frequency, but intrusive enough to rouse him from the depths of the abyss he had fashioned and ladder him quickly through the Seven Incantations of Return.

A motion of his pointed hand brought visuals to life in the holo units adjacent to the conical altar. Not intruders but visitors, he noted: Mi-Jung, Santoul, and some unidentified third party under cover of an appliquéd Enddrese shawl.

Most unexpected.

He disentwined his arms and rose to clothe himself in translator and tunic—the one to make him understandable to human ears, the other to render his form palatable to human eyes.

The servant, Maash, would know enough to admit the three to the receiving room, and L'sser padded upstairs to meet them now, deactivating the altar on his way. His movements were slow and awkward, as he was still in the throes of the Summoning, but foresight compelled him to hurry the return to vigilant mind. The Earthers and their companion were waiting for him when he arrived.

Even more unexpected, Mi-Jung had a weapon in hand, aimed in a lazy fashion at the Raliish she had commanded to kneel on the smallest of the room cush-

ions, bloodied head lowered to the floor and outstretched right hand encased in a transparent plasbag.

Remy Santoul stood off to one side, back to the
carved Xell'em screen Narca had procured for the place,
hands thrust into trouser pockets, jaws working at what
was surely a stim-wafer. By the look of him, he wasn't
fully recovered from the effects of the toxin. Either that
or he was far behind in sleep.

Without waiting for invitation, L'sser took a curious
step toward the Raliish. Mi-Jung's bright eyes tracked
him, her hand weapon emitting a short series of enabling tones. The old Raliish prisoner lifted his head
and the lingering consequences of the Summoning van-
ished.

"You dare desecrate the home by bringing this one
here?" L'sser said to Mi-Jung in a tone of outrage and
disappointment.

"I apologize," the woman said. "I was against
it—"

"We needed a secure place," Remy said, with no
hint of apology.

L'sser whirled on him. "The home is *my* secure
place, Santoul." He calmed himself, if only to offset
the prisoner's hideously pleased grin. "Do you realize
who you've brought here—you of all people, Remy?"

Santoul exchanged an uncertain glance with his fellow Terran. "Cloud Nine—"

L'sser instructed the translator to amplify his disapproval. "Your tongue's most offensive terms would be
too kind still." The contempt he directed at the prisoner was answered by an expression of arrogant disre-
gard. "This is Fan'nat," he told the Earthers.
" 'Deathmaster,' the Enddrese called him, the overseer
of hundreds of internment camps. He was responsible
for more suffering—"

Than you were? Fan'nat subvocalized.

L'sser gave him a look. *Than* we *were*, he sent.

Fan'nat and L'sser as instruments of The Kell, *servants of the campaign.*

L'sser had been aware of Fan'nat's presence on Dhone these past years, but their paths had seldom crossed. And when they had the old one was always in the company of his Xell'em employers. Else—

"Why is he here?" he asked, oblique eyes remaining fixed on Fan'nat.

Santoul spoke to it, explaining how Fan'nat had poisoned him by depositing a toxin on the elevator touchpads. Mi-Jung had identified the Raliish in the security recordings, and she and Santoul had taken him into custody when he had returned to the Hotel Remuhl for a second attempt.

"Then you have a sample of the toxin?" L'sser asked. "An applicator of some sort?"

Mi-Jung bent down to seize hold of Fan'nat's right wrist.

"On the first digit," Remy said. "You're safe," he added, noting L'sser's reluctance to step closer. "It's a discriminating toxin."

The NCorp man disclosed that his olfactory and tactile senses had been Center-augmented as part of his current op. But Fan'nat's knowledge of the enhancements established that Remy's cover had been compromised.

L'sser experienced a moment of humiliation. He had not perceived his friend's alterations; but worse was that Remy had withheld all mention of them. L'sser accepted that secrecy was the climate of the landscape they continued to inhabit, but for the first time he could see clearly the Remy Santoul Jasna's despair had defined all these intervening years.

"So why exactly did you bring him to me?" L'sser asked at last.

Santoul stood over Fan'nat, legs apart, glaring down at him. "I want you to talk to him, L'sser. In a language he'll understand." Grinning once more, Fan'nat flicked the tainted digit at Santoul. Remy squatted eye level with him, one foot weighing down the would-be offending hand. "I want to know where he came by his information about me. And I want to know who he's working for."

Fan'nat's vocalizer issued strangling sounds as Remy brought more of his weight to bear on the wrist. "That isn't necessary," L'sser told him.

Fan'nat subvocalized a comment that L'sser decided to leave untranslated. Santoul would only be tempted to inflict further physical suffering, and such emotional displays merely slowed the task at hand.

L'sser hooked a cushion with his foot and slid it into a position opposite Fan'nat's. *We were destined to have this talk, you and I,* he subvocalized as he lowered himself into an encountering posture. He wondered what Remy would make of the fact that it was Fan'nat who had masterminded the *Ambii'th* Incident.

More to fuel an outburst, L'sser decided. *But perhaps you'd enjoy such a beginning,* he sent to Fan'nat. *An entertainment before we commence . . .*

You will never break me, Fan'nat answered through eyes that had gazed on more horror than L'sser could possibly summon against him. *Not the way I broke you.*

L'sser conceded the point; the one hundred thousand deaths Fan'nat heaped about him had indeed broken him for a time. But since then he had surrendered to that torment and emerged from under its curse. He pained for life now, while Fan'nat, Fan'nat continued to live for pain. And only by negating the fulfillment of that all-consuming need could L'sser inflict a punishment befitting the crime.

He had known from the moment Fan'nat lifted his face from the floor that this was the one course open to him.

Fan'nat was staring at him, beckoning a beginning, urging the hurt, willing a test of strengths.

"Take his arms," L'sser said to Mi-Jung. "Behind

his back, please. Tightly.'' The case officer passed the
hand weapon to Remy and scissored Fan'nat's thin,
fragile limbs backward.

*Yes, yes, L'sser, you are as drawn to it as I am,
murderers the both of us, one in spirit living only for
the contest of wills, the wonderful play of give and take,
the easement of release . . .*

But instead of pain L'sser sent him a mental recon-
struct of the horrid cybereugenic experiments he had
once been ordered to perform on Dhone's wartime cap-
tives. A hands-on adept's approach to the problem of
psychic redesign. Or so it was meant to be.

He reached out and took Fan'nat's face between his
hands in the grip they had once called *the vise of death.*
Fan'nat suddenly realized his intentions and screamed,
through mind and translator both.

L'sserl'sserl'sserl'sserl'sserl'sser . . .

''Shit,'' Santoul said, bringing a hand to his ear.
''Take that damned voice box—''

L'sser withdrew his hands and Fan'nat tipped forward, head striking the wooden floor with a hollow
crack.

''Better go easier next time,'' Mi-Jung cautioned,
Fan'nat's hands in hers.

''It's finished,'' L'sser said over his shoulder to Santoul.

''You got it already?''

''There is no breaking this one.''

Remy and Mi-Jung traded looks of concern.

''Yes, Remy,'' L'sser said. ''I've killed him.''

Karine Mareer regarded the chalk-white body of the
dead Raliish with an unsettling mix of rage and relief.
She had never found Fan'nat an especially admirable
creature, but to see him like this—naked, wide-eyed,
trussed up like some plucked and parboiled fowl—was
more than she had bargained for.

Beings unknown—but presumably Santoul and his

downside NCorp cohort—had delivered the rigid body an hour ago, rolling Fan'nat out of the back of a speeding hover as it shot past the Xell'em safehouse a block west of Nafouri Station.

Karine refused to take blame for the setback, but it was unlikely Colonel Gong would see things her way. Although she'd urged all along that they employ a human or Enddrese asset. If only Fan'nat hadn't been so persistent with the local overseer, Major Imix. It was as though the assassination of Santoul had been more personal vendetta than job; some unfinished piece of past business.

"So what's to be done with it?" Kin asked, striding scavenger circles around the bloated corpse.

"Sit down," the major told Karine's partner harshly. "You expect us to think with your boots shaking the whole room. Over there," he added, gesturing to a seat. "I don't want to look at you. And get something to throw over this thing first. It's leaking all over the mat."

Karine couldn't resist a look, and instantly regretted it.

"And you," Imix said, turning his wrath on the stocky Kwandri SPECVES lieutenant who had accompanied Karine and Kin to Dhone. "You told us your . . . secretions were powerful enough to kill him."

Els Matut gulped and hacked a dry cough. "Santoul's tolerance is greater than I suspected, Major Imix."

"Obviously greater, Lieutenant. Or perhaps you're simply in poor condition."

Matut stifled a reply, and Karine felt for him. Anyone could see what Dhone's heat, humidity, and smog had done to him. The cough had commenced the first day downside, and now his flesh was pale, his silver coat dull and matted. Outdoors, he smelled almost as bad as the dead Raliish.

"Let's not blame Matut," Karine said. "It's our own fault for favoring subtlety over boldness, Major."

Imix sighed resignedly. "But it had just the right touch of irony, Mareer. To succumb as a direct result of the talents for which he'd been prepared . . . The *message* Santoul's death would have sent Center!"

Karine scowled. Not to be argued that the Terran's termination by Kwandri toxin would have earned both of them a promotion; but as things stood, a demotion was more in order. It was time to set aside finesse and go straight for the kill.

Exactly as she told herself on Kwandri when Gong had tasked her for the assignment. There was something about Santoul that begged caution. She remembered him from the feast at Norak Baj's, the speech he had given in the name of DisneyCorp. And she thought she remembered him from several other occasions, which she couldn't bring to mind. At times, it almost seemed that he had stalked her in dreams, insinuated himself into her midst.

"Rather pleasant-looking for an Earther, isn't he?" Imix was saying, studying a surveillance shot of Santoul.

"A pervert," Kin muttered from across the room while he was draping a tarp over the leaking body of the Raliish.

Karine had learned that Kin and Santoul had thrown fists during a SPECVES raid on one of Likat's notorious nightspots. She feigned disinterest in the surveillance holo, but secretly agreed with the major's assessment. Santoul was handsome—for an Earther—but about as far as one could be from the Xell'em ideal. Well, maybe the hair and skin coloring were all right, she decided, but he was far too tall and thin-lipped, his hair was much too curly, his forehead much too straight. No, she preferred the altered good looks of her own kind, of someone like Kin, she thought, regarding him out of the corner of her eye.

"This Professor Jalak, your informant on Kwandri,"

Imix said, turning to her. "Do you think he was merely pretending ignorance of Santoul's mission to Dhone?"

"It's possible he knows something. But NCorp is careful about how much they divulge to their operatives."

Imix tapped a finger against his protruding lower lip. "Then we must assume this has something to do with the casino owner, this Narca."

Karine nodded, wondering where the major was headed.

"And we know that Narca is involved in drugs as well as gambling. Especially with this scent-gland extract—"

"Lube," Karine said.

Imix regarded the covered corpse for a moment, contemplating something. "Santoul's guard will be raised now. It will prove difficult to get close to him." He grinned at Karine. "But perhaps we've overlooked the most willing assets we could find."

"More willing than Fan'nat?" Karine asked, gesturing.

"Of greater number if not single-minded purpose."

"Enddrese descendants of the *Ambii'th* casualties," Kin said, pleased with himself. But Imix only waved him off.

"Nothing so crude."

Karine was smiling now. "Woodruff Glasscock's mercenaries," she said. "It's only right we inform them that a new marat hunter has arrived on Dhone."

FIFTEEN —

BONES WERE ALL THAT WERE LEFT OF THE cats, eleven in number by skull count, the bleached remains scattered across a rock-strewn depression in the parched Lannsmar grasslands. Leafless broadtrees, home to a group of noisy carrion birds, sheltered the basin on one side.

"Guess they lucked on a healthy feed," Narca's current field expert grunted, hurling a small stone at the trees. The birds stirred from lofty perches of flayed bark, lifting off on great wings into Dhone's dome of white sky. Remy's shielded eyes tracked them against a smear of orange sun, as they circled overhead squawking indignation.

The hunter was a Terran named Ryder, ex–combat soldier and specimen collector for AmWay. He was Remy's height, layered in force-fed muscle, bullet-shaped shaved head inked with depictions of jungle foliage. He wore ear and nose rings; goggles pushed up on his forehead just now; one foot planted champion-style atop a hole-shot cat skull.

Ryder's all-terrain was parked a hundred feet away, four Enddrese hunkered down in a narrow wedge of shade.

"You extract the glands through the anus," he said. "Then gut the things for hearts and livers, skin 'em for pelts. Slip the gland into a licknite container, chow down on the internals, sell the skins off in 'bela. Animals take care of the rest."

Two bare-breasted Enddrese women in Rambela had offered Remy a marat pelt when he'd stepped away from the truck to relieve himself. The town was the closest settlement of any consequence, about a day west by all-terrain; a supply town for the regional troops who manned the Lannsmar checkpoints. Ryder's file in Rambela listed him as a licensed guide, a hard-earned cover that entitled him to unrestricted access to the territory and allowed him to organize legitimate hunts using standard projectile weapons.

The Enddrese drivers and camphands worked for Narca as well.

Remy Santoul, DisneyCorp exec, was Ryder's client.

"Yeah, these poachers made out," the hunter was saying, surveying the hollow with an appraising eye.

"Came across a pride, is that it?" Remy asked.

"No. The marat's a solitary cat—like an Earth tiger, you hear of those? Erect ears, striped coat. Very territorial. Whoever killed these cats had a lucky week, got one here, one there, used this place for the finish work."

The cat's pelt was dun-colored but fine. Fingering the one the Enddrese had warily displayed, Remy found himself thinking about Morli, Baj, a dozen other Kwandri. But one day soon half of Kwandri would take to the stars, where Skaro's Marat would survive only as floor-mats and lube.

"Probably took the scent glands on site," Ryder said, raising dust with his boots. "You can't be wasting too much time gutting or skinning with troops cruising the area."

"Unless they've got a hand in."

"Used to be. Thing now is Glasscock's paying them

more for an arrest than any cut a cat poacher can afford.
Before that, Glasscock was the biggest prize. Narca'd
up the amount every week, but the man's not void.
Convinced Zalindi's politicos to let him bring his own
people and weapons in.'' Ryder laughed, flicking sweat
from his nose. ''For cats.''

Remy's own laugh sounded shrill, prompted as it was
by sheer agoraphobic terror. On Kwandri's high plateau, he at least had the confining security of the vehicle; but Ryder was hinting that they might be spending
a night or two in the Lannsmar—in pup tents, for chrissake. Eating out of shape-memory bowls, sleeping in
warmsacks . . .

If anything was in phase transition, it was Remy. Visiting the field was a bad idea. If NCorp wanted a marat
donor-clone, they could send in some downsider like
Ryder to collect the damn thing. The whole op was
making less and less sense to him. The liters of lube
Narca had already shipped off would be more than sufficient to keep Kwandri's spy business running for a
couple of years. So what were another score of scent
glands going to contribute, except putrefying flesh for
a treeful of sick-looking black birds?

Ryder seemed to be sizing up one of the marat skulls
as a potential trophy.

Being hunted was what had spun him around, Remy
decided, recalling his collapse in the Hotel Remuhl and
the events the attempt on his life had set in motion.
Fan'nat hadn't confessed to being run—not that L'sser
had given him much of an opportunity—but the unidentified fingerborne toxin itself was proof enough of a
dirtied op and a Xell'em thirst for Santoul blood. Remy
had used the body of the executed Raliish to convey his
understanding of the new rules of Xella's downside operations chief, but hadn't received a response.

Just how his own death was going to contribute to
the deadly game Xella and Terra were playing with ga-

lactic peace he couldn't say. He was like the marat and perhaps the Kwandri in that: ultimately expendable.

It was graveyard thinking, Remy told himself as his booted toe disturbed the lay of a shattered leg bone.

Ryder had worked his way to the rim of the basin and was gesturing to him to hurry along.

The Enddrese trackers had returned from a brief recon of the sparsely forested landscape. All three had attached themselves some months ago to a group of dreamtime medicine gatherers who lived on the fringe of the grasslands, subsisting on foodstuffs bartered in Rambela for dried strips of hallucinogenic bark and sundry alkaloid botanicals.

"They've got a fresh scent," Ryder explained as Remy came alongside, glad for species companionship in the vastness of the plain.

The woman tracker was down on one knee sniffing at cat spoor. She had located the bone-splintered droppings half a click east of the basin in a cluster of dry brush and tall trees, whose limbs reached like dendrites into the colorless sky.

"About six hours old," Ryder said. "There's older spoor from a second cat nearby—probably one of the poachers' kills. My guess, this one was drawn by the butchering. Maybe signposting some new territory."

Remy joined a second tracker who was busy sniffing out the brush for scent markings. "She's in heat," the Enddrese told him.

Remy's nose twitched as he leaned in for a closer whiff. The odor had the sting of sharp cheese, but wasn't as pungent as the refined extract he'd inhaled in L'sser's lab.

Ryder said, "That's the raw lube you're smelling. The spray from the anal gland." He waved a hand at the trackers. " 'Course these people don't put much stock in the stuff—even though they've seen the kind of party it can whip up among the gatherers."

· "Why not?" Remy said.

"They go for the male cat's penis, the spines anyway. Say that's where the magic is."

Remy snorted. Tiger's penis, rhino horn, black bear gall bladder, blowfish kidneys, pink dolphin oil, meloid "Spanish fly" beetles. He wondered what kept the myths alive—

"Damn male cats can fuck *fifty times* a day if they have to," Ryder said, as though plucking Remy's thought from Dhone's superheated air.

Remy duckwalked a bit farther into the bush, waving away insects but attuned to the scent now, the trackers laughing at him and slapping one another on the arms.

"Santoul," Ryder said, "they say you're going in the wrong direction. They're calling you 'dung-tied.' "

Remy's fingers inspected a series of grooves the cat's claws had left in a fallen tree branch. The scent signature of the paw pads gave him what amounted to an olfactory portrait.

"Santoul," Ryder shouted, impatience in his voice.

"Over here," Remy said.

The hunter came storming through the brush muttering to himself. Remy cut the reprimand short by indicating the claw marks.

"Rape a Raliish. How the fuck d'you do that, Santoul?" He turned his back to call the trackers. "Phatt, Ina, get your purple butts over here."

"The cat headed south," Remy said, "through here. The scent from its muzzle glands is all over these bushes."

Ryder scratched in a puzzled manner at the tattoos above his goggles. The trackers, along with a few curious bark gatherers, were coming into view now, wearing like expressions of amusement and surprise.

"They say you're right, Santoul."

Remy stood up, sniffing at his hands. "How far can it travel in six hours?"

"Depends on how hungry it is. But we'll get it now. I'll have the AT brought around."

Remy nodded and began to follow him out of the
brush, hands parting the tangle. But the trackers
weren't moving. "What's wrong with them?" he asked
Ryder.

The hunter swung around to exchange a few brief
phrases with Phatt, the woman; then he laughed, slapping a hand on Remy's shoulder. "Congrats, Santoul.
They want you to lead."

"The trackers have locked on to the scent," one of
the mercenaries reported, cupping a hand around the
small receiver plug in his ear. "They're moving toward
the rift now. One truck, Ryder and four staff. The trackers are on foot about a quarter of a kilometer forward,
the newcomer holding point."

Woodruff Glasscock glanced at the Xell'em woman
seated beside him in the vehicle's front seat. "Your information was apparently correct, Ms. Mareer. This
man, Santoul, appears to be leading Narca's trackers."

"I'm sure she paid well for his talents," Mareer said.
"Santoul's senses were augmented by some people who
worked for your government at one time."

Glasscock bridled at the woman's presumption. "I
am God's subject, Ms. Mareer, no one else's. Certainly
not the Consortium's or NCorp's."

"Sorry, Mr. Glasscock."

The woman's calm voice belied the controlled fury
Glasscock read in her eyes. "I know what you meant,"
he said in a gentler tone. "But you must understand, I
have broken ties with all of them. I respect natural law,
Ms. Mareer, the laws of cosmic order. I have no use
for the rest."

"I admire that, Woodruff."

She is dangerous, Glasscock thought. More dangerous than a dozen Narcas. "Where are the gatherers?"
he directed to the radioman. "I don't want them caught
in the middle of this."

"They won't be. They've separated from Ryder's

party. It's just the three trackers, the Terran, and Ryder's four. We'll take them the usual way, unless you've got something special in mind.''

"Keep it simple,'' Mareer said, instinctively. "Santoul's a dangerous quarry,'' she added, subservient all at once, the actress again.

"By all means keep it simple,'' Glasscock instructed the merc. "Lead them into the rift. But make certain your people don't overuse the marking scent. These are experienced trackers we're dealing with.''

"Don't worry yourself, Glasscock. They're not going anywhere.''

He waved the radio off and threw up his hands. '' 'Don't worry,' they tell me. Do you see how deplorable this situation has become? They were supposed to *capture* Narca's poachers last time. Instead, they killed them. I'm forced to employ rogues and murderers because brainless drones fill the seats in Dhone's council.''

Mareer patted his forearm. "You're doing the right thing, Woodruff.''

Her touch raised the hairs on the back of his neck. Was there nothing she wouldn't do to see Santoul killed? It was just the sort of manipulative, *civilized* behavior that had propelled him into wildlife studies to begin with.

Back in Zalindi, where Mareer had sought him out, she had described Santoul as a professional hunter, hired by Narca to bring new life to the traffic in marat extract. *Lube*—how he detested the word! But it had taken only a few minutes to see through the Xell'em's lies. Oh, Santoul was unquestionably altered, but he was no more a professional hunter than Mareer was the concerned Free Species advocate she claimed to be. No, Glasscock supposed it had to do with some insane power play designed by NCorp or its Xell'em counterpart.

That the two victors of the war should now be close

to engagement was further vindication of his hatred for all systems of government. An ally one moment was an enemy the next; it had been so for tens of thousands of years and was likely to remain so for tens of thousands to come.

Earth's on and off relationship with Xella—allied when the Heregep had inadvertently spread jumpdrive technology through the Arm, then opponents for the planetary systems the drive brought within reach; allies again during the Vega Conflict, enemies in its wake— suggested parallels with humankind's historical attitudes toward cats in general: revered in the ancient world only to be associated with witchcraft and black magic a millennia later; then embraced as allies during the Black Death and domesticated since.

So what might a tomorrow ten years from now bring for enemies Karine Mareer and Remy Santoul—were he to live that long? Bedfellowship? Marriage? What then was he to think in allowing himself to be used as an instrument of political assassination? And what was he to make of the Q'aantre, Els Matut, whom Mareer and her gladiatorial "husband" treated like some pet or mascot? . . .

The Q'aantre summoned thoughts of Professor Simon Jalak, whose work Glasscock had read, and who had been Damir Skaro's contemporary on Dhone.

Skaro . . . the object of Glasscock's worship and undying love. The one who had taught him the value of asceticism and sexual abstinence; who had shown him how to redirect his base desires; who had helped him find God.

Saving the marat was the least he could do in return. Even if men like Santoul had to die as a result.

Glasscock could only pray that Dhone's Council would eventually close the territory, or that Free Species would raise the funds necessary to transport the few remaining cats offworld. Or that the new trend in

back-to-basics naturalism would put an end to the craving for sensual excess and *aphrodisiacs*!

Until such time it was up to him.

"Weathers," he said, reactivating the MV radio.
"Tell your people to make certain Ryder's group is well
within range before they open fire. I don't want any of
them to escape."

Remy sent the trackers on ahead and hauled himself
up into the lower branches of a lifeless tree, just high
enough to clear the crest of the stiff grass that had already exacted a blood toll from his hands and face. The
all-terrain was several hundred yards to the rear at the
leading edge of a sinuous swath of flattened grass. Remy
secured both feet in a notch of limbs and leaned out
from the tree, hanging on with one hand while he commenced waving the other.

Taking the point had been the latest in a series of bad
calls. Not that he hadn't fully impressed the trackers
with his olfactory skills; it was just that the rest of his
talents didn't measure up. Twice he'd stepped dead center into hostile currents of red soldier ants, some of
which scurried as high up as his ears before he'd managed to pluck them off—somewhat imperfectly, so that
their pincer-equipped heads were even now attached to
his flesh like costume gems.

The seven-foot-tall grass had actually provided a
sense of comforting, operative claustrophobia, but there
were sharp ends and jagged edges to contend with; and
the more Remy thought of Ryder sitting pretty in his
armored mobile, the more frustrated he grew at the
arrangement. Why not stick one of the trackers on the
sloped prow of the AT and let the vehicle do the bush-
whacking? Why not a goddamned robo-sniffer for that
matter?

Then, just when he was ready to abandon the hunt
altogether, or at least trade places with Narca's number

one man, his nose had alerted him to a scent that shouldn't have been there.

Ryder jumped from the cab of the idling vehicle and met Remy halfway, plainly entertained by his client's somber expression and disheveled state. "Grass giving you a bit of problem, huh?"

"And other things," Remy told him, tugging a disembodied ant head from the underside of his wrist. "How much real estate did you say these marats call home, Ryder?"

"Thirty square, give or take. Why—you thinking we've gone to far?"

"Phatt read the spoor as six hours old. So I'm figuring we're either following a different scent or this cat's on a marathon run."

"Different scent, you say."

Remy felt around in the empty space the hunter left. "All right, *foul*, then. Ina picked up on it, too. We've got paw and muzzle marking scents, but something else—humanoid by the smell of it."

Ryder stroked his stubbled chin. "Could be poachers following the same cat, what d'you think?"

"That you're supposed to be the goddamned expert, is what I think."

The hunter grinned and picked an ant from Remy's nose. "Let's climb up top the toy and have a look around."

The four Enddrese who had been riding inside the all-terrain were standing in the grass fanning themselves and flicking fly whisks about. Up top, Ryder cupped his hands to his mouth and shouted a contact call to the trackers. A patch of grass stirred half a mile along, and Remy trained field glasses on the spot. Ina's head came into view a moment later, but Remy couldn't tell whose shoulders she was standing on. In the far distance, the flatness of the Lannsmar was broken by a steep-sided rift. Dhone's sun was a tear of color in the western sky.

"I don't like it," Ryder said. "I'm calling them back in."

Remy was relieved, but only for a minute. Back on the ground Ryder ordered two of the Enddrese to belly under the vehicle. Remy heard bolts being turned, compartments being opened, and at just about the same time the trackers showed up, the XTs reemerged with half a dozen directed-energy rifles.

"You know how to use one of these?" Ryder asked while passing the weapons around. He gave one an upright toss to Remy.

Remy snatched it, wide-eyed, and immediately checked the rifle's safety and standby code.

"Don't bother looking for a laser marking, Santoul. They're manufactured right here on Dhone. Earth Force knockoffs, but better tooled than most."

Remy was too busy inspecting the weapon to hear him. "Have these fucking things been test-fired, Ryder? I mean, I'd rather take my chances with rival poachers than end up with half my face vaporized."

"They'll do the trick—just aim high. Besides, I don't figure them for poachers." Ryder thumbed the charging switch and the weapon whined to life. The trackers and camphands followed suit. "Love that tune," he said, grinning.

"Glasscock," Remy said.

Ryder handed Phatt a radio set and directed a short burst of commands to the team. The seven Enddrese nodded, grim-faced, and snaked off single file into the grass. "Climb aboard," Ryder told Remy from the door to the cab.

"What the hell, you're gonna confront them?" Remy asked, strapping himself into the right-side bucket.

Ryder glanced at him, tight-lipped, scarred hands gripped on the AT's control sticks. "Narca tell you she lost three of her best? Well, she's been waiting for this. We all have."

Remy bit back a reply. He had lost track of the

Enddrese in the grass, but it was obvious they were headed for the rift.

"Glasscock probably laid down a false scent trail. That's the foul you smelled—one of his sickshit mercs. Figure to lure us into the rift."

"So we turn around," Remy said. "Where's the loss?"

Ryder laughed and flipped a series of console toggles. Blast shields rose to cover all but the vehicle's front windows.

"It's part of the fun, Santoul."

Remy rapped his knuckles against the metal plating that wasn't there a moment ago. "This, too, I suppose."

"All strictly legit," Ryder said. "Protection from the big game's what it is." He pulled a radio handset from its mount alongside the driver's seat. "You can start your run," Remy heard him say after a female voice responded at the other end of the freq.

"Put us ten miles south of Ranak's Knoll on the east side of the crack." The woman signed off and Ryder howled, slamming a hand against the ceiling. "Stay tuned for bigger and better surprises, Santoul."

They were a half a mile from the edge of the rift, well north of the trackers, when Phatt's voice piped from the console monitors. Ryder listened and responded in clipped sentences. "I told them to hold up on the lip," he said, braking the all-terrain.

Remy assisted him in initiating a thermal sweep of the opposite face of the rift. "There's your big game," he said as onscreen signatures of petro-driven vehicles began to register.

"They're reading our scan," Ryder said, "Prepare to take fire—"

The first blast struck even as the words were leaving the hunter's mouth—a conventional round that cratered the ground not fifty feet in front of them. Reports echoed in the rift as several more explosions set fire to the grasslands behind.

Phatt reported that the trackers were taking fire from two scoutcars on the west rim and troops positioned above the fractured clay riverbed. Ryder told them to return fire but to stay in motion and gradually work their way back to the vehicle.

Ryder commanded the AT forward through the firestorm, angling down into the nearest blast crater and bounding back out into the grass. A directed beam slagged a good portion of the rear doors, filling the interior with acrid heat, which exhaust fans did their best to disperse.

Remy's tear and mucus ducts were running riot. Ryder wiped his face with his shirtsleeves and turned Remy a maniacal look. The hunter seemed to be enjoying himself thoroughly.

Glasscock's mercs were showing themselves, running odd and even crisscrosses down into the rift in pursuit of the trackers. The AT's forward scope revealed most of them to be Earthers.

Remy estimated they had covered some two miles by now, and he was beginning to wonder where the trackers might turn up when he saw Phatt and three others running through the grass off to the left of the AT. Ryder noticed them and brought the vehicle to a boneshuddering stop, leaning out of the driver's door to encourage them with frantic hand gestures. Conventional rounds continued to impact the area, raining dirt and stones against the blast shields.

"Nip and tuck, Santoul," he said, swinging himself back inside, "it's gonna be a close call—"

The secondary radio emitted a crackling sound, and Ryder made a grab for the handset as what remained of the Enddrese contingent threw themselves into the AT's rear space through the side doors. One of the camphands was short an arm.

"Give us five and ground-zero the ball a mile west

of the main burn," Ryder was shouting into the mike, working the foot pedal controls at the same time.

"Ground-zero what?" Remy said above agonized cries from the rear.

"Like I told you: Narca's been expecting this."

The AT had been maintaining a northerly traverse, but Ryder suddenly swung the vehicle away from the rift. "There!" he said with an upraised forefinger pressed to the windshield.

Leaning as far forward as the confining harness allowed, Remy could just make out a small, supersonic air-breather streaking in from the northeast.

"Yeaaah, kiss me where it counts, lover!" Ryder screamed to the sky, launching a loud smack with his fingertips.

"The hell's going on?" Remy said.

"BFD," the hunter said. "A little 'neuter' for Glasscock's grunts."

Remy stiffened in the seat, all the blood drained from his face, as Ryder maxed the accelerator and raised the last of the AT's blast shields.

Just a BFD. A bit of dark outlaw humor leftover from the worst of the war. A battlefield fusion device . . .

Ryder was cackling like a madman, oblivious to the ground-pounding explosions rocking the AT side to side. The Enddrese sat huddled in the rear in an inward-facing circle, heads between knees. Praying.

Remy watched mesmerized as the thermal screen flared to blinding intensity. The radios screeched, the AT lurched as though it had been kicked in the ass, and the sudden heat sucked the life from his lungs . . .

The device had altered the terrain, leaving a mile-wide blast crater west of the rift. It would have made little sense to go down into it even if they could, so they skirted the hot edge searching for signs of life.

Phat found evidence of a vehicle far enough removed from the epicenter to have survived the explosion. It had apparently left under its own power. The rest were memories, fused now to the rock strata underlying the Lannsmar's grasslands.

As for Glasscock's hired troops, well, Remy thought, who could say for sure where they were.

They did come across a few bodies in the fire-ravaged grass that surrounded the glass-sand crater.

One of these turned out to be the Xell'em heavy hitter Remy had tangled with in the back hallways of the Club Terrana. Kin—Karine Mareer's escort on the night of Baj's dinner party.

Lying on the blackened ground nearby was what Remy first took to be a dead marat. Except that Ryder was circling the thing, face twisted up behind the clearmask of the antirad suit, shouting things like: "What d'you make of this, Santoul?" and "How the hell did this get here?"

That was when one of the Enddrese had rolled the creature over on its back and Remy found himself looking down into the irradiated face of SPECVES Lieutenant Els Matut.

Remy thought about Fan'nat's fingerborne toxin—Els Matut's poison secretions—and got sick all over the burnt ground.

PART FOUR

—DOWNSIDE UP

SIXTEEN—

DAZYL WAS JUST RISING WHEN REMY LEFT the hotel. Kwandri's morning air felt especially chilled after three weeks of Dhone's heat and the stale womb-warmth of torpor. A spring was back in his step, but it was the planet's subnormal gravity that had put it there.

Dakou told him he could expect to find some changes downside; but nothing the counsel said had prepared him for Likat's utter transformation.

Outside the envelope, some eight vessels from as far away as Valis Prime were parked in stationary orbit. Remy thought they carried construction crews for a recently begun station, but frenetic activity aboard the Terran wheel suggested something more nefarious at work. No one was saying just what that might be.

At the expanded shuttleport Remy had noticed dozens of shadowy figures in exec tech suits, hurrying about toting unusual-looking alloy carrycases.

Hints of Kwandri's new face ran clear back to the first meet with L'sser and Mi-Jung—the rumors that shipping restrictions imposed on Dazyl's wormhole were soon to be lifted; that the Burst system was about to be opened up to colonists and corps. And later, on the return jump from Dhone, there was the Enddrese rig-

ger, Ntendo, who'd whispered from the torpor drawer
adjacent to Remy's of the sensual delights awaiting visitors to Kwandri.

Sensual delights? Remy recalled thinking, unable to
piece together images of hedonistic pursuits and cold,
mountain-high Likat mornings. But that was a real-time
month ago, and now the evidence was right in front of
his eyes.

Cin-dens and paraphernalia shops could be found on
almost every block. Storefronts were boarded up; pro-
and anti-offworlder slogans scrawled on splattered
walls. Refuse fluttered in the cobbled streets. Indigs lay
sprawled sleeping or intoxed on sidewalks, in doorways
and alleyways . . .

The effect was numbing—enough to launder his mind
of some of Dhone's psychic debris. The planet's nightmare mix of pulse-pounding moments and evil endings
had him casting suspicious glances at every person he
passed.

Woodruff Glasscock had been on-site for the BFD
detonation—apparently in the vehicle Phatt surmised
was at the outer edge of the killzone. Glasscock appeared on live vid in Zalindi with the radiation burns
to prove it. Calling for a death sentence for Remy Santoul, Dhone's ace marat hunter.

With Mi-Jung's help, Remy had already gone into
hiding by then; but Narca, Ryder, and the woman pilot
who'd dropped the device barely escaped Dhone in time.
Government troops raided and razed both the Casino
Kimeli and the warehouse lube lab. L'sser and Jasna
ultimately became Remy's outlaw mates in two rooms
Mi-Jung secured high up in one of Zalindi's hillside
ghettos.

A touch of the old days for the three of them, living
the fugitive's life, drawing the curtains, and only ven-
turing out under cover of night. Together, L'sser and
Remy had managed to keep Jasna away from the zap;
and Jaz, in turn, had filled Remy's head with dreams of

possible futures—providing, that was, he was willing to resign from NCorp.

But with Glasscock demanding Remy's head every night on the evening news and wanted holos decorating half of Zalindi, plans for resignation seemed poorly timed; and in the end it was only with Center's assist that Remy succeeded in eluding his pursuers and wormholing back to Kwandri.

Ironically, Narca's retaliatory airstrike had actually worked to Free Species' advantage not only by providing Glasscock with the political ammo he'd been seeking all along, but by discouraging would-be poachers from returning to the Lannsmar's irradiated grasslands for some time to come. There was even talk of rounding up the surviving marats and transporting them to a custom-designed wildlife habitat on Moad'dzin.

Audjo Ishida had sat passively through much of Remy's debriefing. She concurred with his assessment that the DisneyCorp cover was blown, probably by Simon Jalak, whose authorization to remain onworld was no longer subject to the good graces of Center but Kwandri's own Ministry of ExtraPlanetary Affairs. But the revelation of Remy's identity was of minor consequence, the station chief had asserted—despite the fact that it had nearly gotten him killed—because the overall operation had been such a resounding success. Narca's initial aphrodisiac shipments had reached Kwandri, and Center had gathered the intelligence needed to present its case to the Consortium regarding Xella's designs in Burst.

Ishida and Gong had even reached an accommodation.

Envoy Densign and Ambassador Xu were soon to be instated by the Grand Assembly, and the operation on Kwandri was effectively concluded.

Simple as that.

So why then, Remy asked himself as he walked Likat's sour-smelling streets, did Kwandri feel like a world on the way to becoming another Dhone? And why wasn't he feeling pleased with the contributions he'd made?

The marat had escaped, but Kwandri hadn't.

Females in tight-fitting attire, eye makeup, and bleached or colored manes sauntered by him, trailing musky odors and making purring sounds. Others leaned seductively against lampposts, wafting enticements to passersby. A few had their wedgelike feet dyed to resemble high heels.

Remy quickened his pace through an olfactory onslaught of pheromones, rounding a corner only to have a male youth accost him from the flashing front of a sex club.

GIRLS! GIRLS! GIRLS! an LED-screen advertised. BOYS! BOYS! BOYS! DUOS, TRIOS, COMBOS! ALL REQUESTS ENTERTAINED!

"Kwandri open soda bottle," the youth announced in English, shoving a holocard in Remy's face. Remy glanced down his nose at a depiction of a Kwandri female and a designer seltzer bottle engaged in an obscene stage act.

"Kwandri make drawing," the youth read from the back of the card as the scene in front shifted and showed the same naked female squatting over the blunt end of a wandwriter.

"Kwandri blow out candle. Kwandri pick up ball bearings. Kwandri drink through straw. Kwandri shoot long fruit."

The eager hustler showed a second card, a male depicted on this one, nine inches erect. "Kwandri catch hoops," the kid recited, "Kwandri play keyboards. Kwandri put out fire. Kwandri blow up condom. Kwandri punch hole in trash bag! You come club next street. No cover. Much girls, much boys, too too much fun!"

When Remy pushed past him, the youth began to follow him down the block. "You, Ter, like boys or girls? Both, maybe, huh? You lika lube job, too? Vanna, maybe?''

Remy stopped short and whirled on him. "Lube? You have lube—here?''

The boy grinned, adopting a streetsmart pose. "Sure thing, boss. We got lube. But," he leaned closer, "but Vanna better, you know. Which you want—Vanna black, Vanna red, Vanna white, we got all type for you.''

"Vanna?" Remy said.

"Sure, you know. Kwandri pure, boss, no lie. Pure Vanna, all kind." The boy slipped a card into the breast pocket of Remy's jacket.

Remy yanked himself away once more and hurried down the sidewalk past clique after clique of streetpeople and Kwandri hired hands of both genders and all ages.

Not everyone was friendly, however. Shopkeepers stood fast in doorways belching and farting auras of anger and discontent.

"Earther go home," someone snarled at him.

Remy stopped at the mouth of an alley to upend one of the trash containers. Farther along he left three parallel ink marks knee-high on the door to a commo booth.

At the intersection he turned right, away from the river, and began to head back toward the hotel. But all the wind went out of him as he neared a cin-den in the middle of the block.

There in full color, beneath a tradeslang translation of the title, *Bonnie and Clyde*, was a bigger than life holo-portrait of his donor-clone. Warren Beatty.

A crowd of young females spied him as he was staring at the poster, screamed wildly, and pursued him down the street.

"I rushed over as soon as I heard you were back," Baj said, coming through the door to the hotel suite.

Remy had stepped to one side to motion him into the front room when Baj turned without warning and took hold of his testicles. "Oh, Remy," he went on, giving a firm *Tegganon* tug, "it's so good to sense you again! But why didn't you tell us? We've all been asking what your motive could have been?"

"Tell you," Remy said, working on it. "Actually I only just arrived. I didn't have a chance to transmit a downside reserva—"

"Not that. About who you are! What you had accomplished before DisneyCorp recruited you!"

Remy spent a long moment regarding Baj's electrically heated gloves and Goosh-ball pendant necklace, his bellbottom trousers and sheathed three-speed epilator.

"Remy?"

"Yeah."

"Why didn't you tell us?"

He thought about the small mob of scent seekers that had chased him all the way from the cin-den only hours ago. "Because that . . . that *guy* you see on those posters isn't me, is why."

Baj's lightened brow furrowed. "Remy, there's no reason to—"

"Look, Norak, what's my name?"

"Remy . . . Santoul," Baj said uncertainly.

"Right. And what's that, that guy's name, the actor?"

The Kwandri smiled. "Warren Beatty. But I see what you mean, Remy. That was just a—how do you call it?—a screen name, is that it? You don't want any of us to refer to you by your screen name."

"No, no, no," Remy said, stomping around the room. He let out an exasperated sigh. "I'm a . . . clone," he added wondering what had suddenly compelled him to lower his voice so. "I mean, I am a *clone*." More forceful now, proud of it. "That Beatty guy was my donor."

Baj was fingering the hennaed hair under his chin. "Clone. Like a father."

Remy raised a finger. "Not a bioparental."

"A father but not a bioparental."

"You got it."

But Baj didn't. "Like an adopted father, then. What you became to Els Nanff for a time."

Nanff, Remy thought. He'd scarcely had time to think about the boy. "Suppose we save the story of my life for another occasion," Remy said, taking Baj by the elbow and directing him to the couch. "I want you to sit down and tell me what's been going on while I've been away."

The Kwandri appeared flattered. "To me?"

"To you, to Likat, to Kwandri."

Baj took a deep breath. "Well. Just so much, Remy. More than I could do justice to with a brief summary."

"Try. You can start by telling me about the General Assembly."

Baj explained how the Assembly membership had recently voted to invite a joint panel of Terran and Xell'em representatives to act in an advisory capacity on matters pertaining to civil conduct, comportment, and all internal concerns of a sociopolitical nature.

Baj reeked of evasive scents. "What exactly does 'concerns of a sociopolitical nature' cover?" Remy asked him.

"Laws governing the use of force, of search and seizure, that sort of thing," Baj said offhandedly.

"Rights, trials, punishments."

"Yes."

"But not everyone's happy with this new arrangement, Norak. I've smelled, er, seen the signs."

"A dissident few. But it's normal to experience some discontent during a transitional phase. You said as much the night of my party. You were quite eloquent, in fact."

Remy pried the sex-club holocard from his pocket

and slid it across the table. "Part of the transition, right?"

Baj's face darkened; his coat emitted a defensive scent. "Q'anntre is in search of its identity. If some of the old ways are left behind, so be it." A hint of impatience in his voice. "Why should this surprise you? You encouraged it."

Remy looked away, deeply aware of his own confused exhalations. "I was making a point, not trying to start a social revolution."

Baj shrugged. "It seems you succeeded in both."

"But, but these sex clubs and cin-dens," Remy said after a pause, "all these young people on the street. The closed shops, the slogans . . . when did it start?"

"Almost immediately after you left. Just about the time your vids began to appear." Baj smiled at him.

"Tell me, Norak, you've been to some of these clubs?"

Baj shuddered. "Ah, that's not for me. I have a family to think of." He took hold of the Goosh-ball pendant. "You know I have a fondness for the things of your world, Remy, but I'm a traditional man. I burn incense to Moki Jo."

Remy worked his jaw. The words sounded right, but the scents were all wrong. Baj was omitting something. "What's going to happen to those traditions, Norak? What about the *Tegganon*? What happens to that?"

"Those who are advising the Grand Assembly will think of something." He sighed. "Most of Q'aantre has accepted the fact that you offworlders are more intelligent than we. Earth knows best, as we have been saying."

Remy ran a hand down his face, contorting his features. "What's Vanna?" he asked, looking up and locking eyes with Baj.

The Kwandri's myopic gaze grew even more narrowed. "Vanna? I'm not sure I know the term."

"Just like you don't know what's going on inside the

clubs, right?'' Remy shot to his feet. ''Come on, Norak, red Vanna, white Vanna, black Vanna . . . The
whole street's whispering it.''

Baj shook his head in a mournful way. ''You're the
intelligent one, Remy. You tell me.''

Remy waited until dark to check the drops, when
there was less likelihood of his being recognized and
hounded by aroma fanatics. Likat's walkways were more
crowded than he had ever seen them, cin-dens and
clubs, hired hands on the street corners, all doing a
brisk business.

By midnight Morli still hadn't responded to any of
the cues, but early the following morning, Remy discovered that the parallel lines he'd left on the commo
booth door had been crossed in kind by a series of
intersecting marks. Properly read, the resultant grid
supplied the time and place for the meet.

Noon that same day Remy was seated on the bench
Jalak had used for quick drops with his principal agent,
Glans. Empty food and drink containers and Frisbee
plates littered the meager lawn. The climbing apparatus
where Remy had watched schoolchildren at play a few
months back had become the haunt of overeager lunch-
time lovers. Were it not for the all-clear scent, Remy
might not have recognized the Kwandri in matted coat
and filthy clothes who shuffled into the park half an
hour late for the meet.

''Res,'' Remy said, standing up and purposely offering his hand. There was nothing to decipher from Morli's dry palm that Remy's eyes hadn't already told him.

''I told myself I wasn't going to answer you,'' Morli
said, sitting down and staring at the ground between his
furred feet. ''But wherever I walked I saw your messages.'' He quarter turned with bitter breath. ''I didn't
want you to see me like this.''

''What's happened?'' Remy asked, all sincerity and
concern, gritting his teeth.

Morli nearly smiled. "Your sudden departure gave us no chance for farewells, Remy. But I trust your travels were enjoyable. Profitable. Whichever DisneyCorp requires they be."

"Yeah, I had a terrific time, Res. You couldn't ask for more from a business trip."

"Ah, is that what it was? Your, uh, replacements weren't specific on that point. But they did tell me that you would be back and, well, here you are."

"What else did they tell you?"

Drunken laughter drew Morli's attention to the playground for a moment; his eyes were shut tight when he swung around. "Only that they wanted to thank me for the intelligence I'd provided. And reassure me that my 'secrets' were safe with them."

"How'd they say thank you, Res? With toilet seat covers and Nerf football pillows? A set of matching electric toothbrushes?"

Morli puzzled over Remy's expression, then laughed sardonically. "No, Remy, not with Terrana. Surely you recall the gift your superiors urged you to give me before you left."

"The . . . motion lotion," Remy said, swallowing the word *lube*. "The aphrodisiac."

"Yes." Morli paused to collect himself. "The sad truth is that I didn't wait until the *Tegganon* to try it." He turned to Remy. "And it worked, Remy, just like you promised it would. It worked so well that I encouraged my friends to try it." Morli's mouth twitched. "You have to understand: it allowed us to be ourselves. For the first time."

"Is that so bad, Res?"

He laughed again. "At first I didn't believe so. How could I when it seemed a gift from the gods, Remy? That's why I agreed to share the wafers Ms. Ishida gave me with *all* my friends. Not just with a select few, no, but with everyone I could. I exhaled its praises, Remy.

I convinced friends and acquaintances that the lotion was Kwandri's path to self-realization.''

Remy's eyes widened. ''You said Kwandri.''

''Yes?''

''You said Kwandri, Res. No Q'aantre.''

Morli shrugged. ''Q'aantre was.'' When Remy didn't reply, he added, ''Aren't you curious to know the results of my campaign of liberation?''

Remy let his eyes answer for him.

''That's right. All you need to do is gaze and sniff about you. Pay a visit to Likat's nightclubs, or talk to our new breed of lube dealers. Lube, Remy, that's what they're calling it.'' He gestured in a broad manner. ''Take a walk past our theaters and flesh markets and see the *wonders* Morli and his magic substance have given shape to.

''But don't misread my scent, Remy: all this is *beneficial* to Kwandri. All this releases us from the bonds of our traditions and elevates us. Why, Kwandri is almost worthy of joining ranks with the Consortium or the Manifest—''

Remy took hold of Morli's arms and spun him around on the bench. ''Stop using it. Tell everyone you made a mistake.''

Morli shook him off and snorted. ''You think they'd listen now? I resigned my position with the ministry to get them to listen. But now everyone looks to our offworlder 'advisers' for leadership.'' He made a mournful sound. ''The stars aren't for me, they never were. Besides, the ways of your kind are too habit-forming to dispense with overnight, Remy.''

''You mean—''

''No, the lotion itself isn't addictive. But what the lotion has loosed is. Especially among our young. Do you really think they would heed the advice of an old man—the one who started the trend?''

Remy cursed. ''Shut down the lube outlets, arrest the dealers. Prevent anyone from buying it.''

"Buying it?" Morli laughed and stood up, preparing to leave. "Who said anything about *buying*, Remy? You forget that fair trade has always been Kwandri's way. Barter, Remy, barter."

"Barter for what, Res? What's Kwandri giving in return?"

Morli glanced about. "I have to go, Remy. We shouldn't be seen together."

Remy put a hand out. "But there has to be a way to stop it, Res."

Morli sniffed in Remy's direction. "Perhaps. Perhaps a time will come."

An Enddrese band provided live music for the patrons and onstage caged dancers at Club Wet Spot. The beat was incessant, primal, and the Kwandri performers gyrated to it with abandon.

The females wore sheer bras and bustiers; midnight black boxer-style panties and red lace teddies; single-snap camisoles, minislips, and sheer peignoirs. Some, Remy noted, had had reductive alterations and color impregnation jobs done to their wedgelike feet so that they now resembled spiked heels.

Faces, breasts, and bellies were fully depilated, and coats were buzzcut or coiffed into outrageous styles. Coloring ran from jet-black to rainbow. The males affected lip gloss and eye shadow, and wore little more than G-strings or codpieces.

On a second stage at the other end of the long room, a Terran male in garter belt and stockings presided over an amateur wet fur contest, where Kwandri of both genders were being hosed down with water-soluble dyes.

Still other Kwandri, identified by numbered pendants, rocked in swings suspended from the rafters or displayed their talents on the dance floor. Remy waved off approaches from numbers six, fourteen, and sixty-six as he sidled through the mixed crowd of indigs and offworlders and found a seat at the bar.

Light strobed from the ceiling and pulsed from the walls. The live sex shows and genital stunts were restricted to the back rooms, but a small price could buy anyone admittance.

Remy surveyed the table action on the raised tiers above the dance floor, where a noisy, dangerous lot of offworlders in dark glasses sat hunched over drinks, pounding hands and feet in time to the music. A few of the exec techs Remy had observed at the shuttleport were up there as well, circulating table to table with their alloy carrycases, arms draped around the shoulders of Kwandri teens.

These same suits could occasionally be seen entering or emerging from a doorway left of the bar. The matte-black door was flanked by prime specimens of armed human beef.

Remy had tried to talk his way through a similar portal in the first club he visited that night, only to be told the room was members-only. *And how did one go about applying for membership?* he'd asked. *You have to be sponsored, sport,* a seven-footer informed him.

Remy turned to order a drink when a familiar voice behind him said, "Santoul! Thought some worm ate ya!" Vegas, wearing a synthsilk suit and looking every bit the happening club owner, extended a hand. "Where you been, spacer?"

Remy shook hands, absorbing the success. "Yesterday and tomorrow."

Vegas waved one of his bartenders over. "Give the man whatever he wants."

Glans was waiting behind the bar. "An AI, straight up," Remy said, staring into the Kwandri's smug grin. "Better make it a double."

"Key, man, what chew say," Glans answered in English.

Vegas clapped him on the back. "So what d'ya think of the new place? That's two for yours true. Not bad

for a vet, huh?'' The big man was rocking back and
forth on his feet, a bundle of raw energy.

Remy gave an approving nod. "Looks like you fell
into some good shit.''

"And came out smelling sweet, Santoul, 'bout as
sweet as it can get before you oh-dee, know what I'm
saying? Kind of deal where the front credit doesn't care
about the overhead and nobody steps on your toes. And
it's only the beginning, man. I'm working on a third
opening 'cross the river, maybe a place with twice the
real estate . . . ''

Glans brought the drink while Vegas droned on, talking directly into Remy's ear. The club owner was a sea
of scents, but beneath it all, Remy caught a familiar
fragrance . . . a Kwandri scent he couldn't quite place.

On the far stage, the wet fur contest was fast becoming an exhibitionist's dream. Some of the contestants
were already peeling off their clothes to enthusiastic
applause from a growing crowd of onlookers.

"Check this out, Santoul,'' Vegas said, placing a
holoviewer on the bar. Remy zapped through a sequence of calendar screens, each month crowned by a
different bikini-clad Kwandri female.

Vegas grinned. "Primate of the Month. The swim-
suit edition. 'Course I've got a more revealing version
for the hardcore, but this one alone'll probably hang in
every shop in Likat.''

Wild cheers from the far stage filled the room. Many
of the contestants were down to the bare essentials now.
Males and females were helping the stragglers out of
what few items of clothing remained, while others were
caressing one another in a provocative, teasing fashion.
The professionals Vegas had obviously placed among
them were striking alluring poses and simulating various sexual techniques. The audience members below
were pressing toward the stage, grinding against who-
or whatever was nearby. Video monitors carried close-
ups for those elsewhere in the club.

"You don't do something, you're gonna have an orgy on your hands," Remy said.

"I should be so lucky," Vegas said, scratching at his palms.

Offworlders seated at tables on the first tier were shouting out numbers, rushing off into back hallways and rest rooms with their chosen Kwandri partners. Humans were joining the stage show, half the audience down on the floor now, writhing.

Remy reached for his drink and saw a plump Kwandri hand come down on his own. A young female pressed soft breasts against his shoulder and purred, "Hello, big Ter."

Remy looked over his shoulder. "Kitti?" he said in astonishment as she slipped onto his lap.

At the same time Vegas tapped him on the forearm to show him a plastic bottle about the size of an old lipstick dispenser. The club owner squeezed a couple drops of red liquid into one cupped hand, then began to rub his hands together vigorously.

"Help yourself, Santoul," he said, proferring the bottle.

"What is it?" Remy asked, inspecting it.

"Vanna," Vegas said, with a quaking, ecstatic breath.

SEVENTEEN—

CSILLA VOSS'S LAUGH PRECEDED HER
through the door. She had someone with her, but it
wasn't Jalak. The front door swung back and two figures stepped into the darkness of the room. Csilla was
still laughing when the lights came up, a knee raised
under a precariously balanced package. Her companion
was Els Nanff.

Spying Remy in the armchair, the youth let out a
spirited sound and rushed over to embrace him. Remy
stood up to return the hug, lost in scents, watching
Csilla all the while, her expression concerned as she
glanced between Remy and the short walkway to Jalak's
front door.

"Remy, Remy!" Nanff was enthusing, tattooing
blows against the small of Remy's back. "What you
bring me?" The boy was dressed in baggy knee-length
shorts, fingerless gloves, and a poncho much like the
one Csilla was wearing.

"Uh, it's back at the hotel, Els," Remy covered up.
"I'll drop it by tomorrow, how'd that be?"

"What it is?"

" A surprise, Els."

"By what kind surprise?"

210

"Now, Els," Csilla said, putting the packages down, "it won't be a surprise if Remy tells you." Nanff turned to show disappointment. "Why don't you go make all of us some tea," she continued through the false smile, "while Remy and I talk."

"Tomorrow?" Nanff said to Remy.

"My pledge," Remy said, offering a Kwandri hand-sign. Els hurried off. "I let myself in," he told Csilla once the boy had left the room. "Too cold to lurk around outside."

Csilla took a seat opposite him near the door to Jalak's office. "The weather was better last week," she said in a neighborly way. "When did you get back?"

"Few days ago. I asked Ishida to keep it quiet."

"You're full of surprises, Santoul."

"You could say that."

Csilla sighed and looked around the room. "Back door?"

"Kitchen window," Remy said. "I'll pay Jalak for the damage. When's he due?"

She glanced at her wristwatch. "Soon. He had in-formants all afternoon. Said he'd be home by dark."

"Sounds cozy, be home by dark. You do the shop-ping and look after the kid, is that it? What's he doing here, anyway?" Remy added before she could respond, motioning with his chin. "You were supposed to see he got back to Tsegg Tsirran."

"I did, Santoul, but . . . Look, it's a long story."

Remy shrugged. "I'm free."

Csilla made her lips a thin line. "We've sort of adopted Els, Santoul."

"He has parents. I know, I met them."

"Not adopted exactly. We've extended the *bal*. Els wants to be schooled in Likat. So we've been appointed his legal custodians while he's here."

Remy shook his head in a theatrical way. "I keep hearing this 'we.' "

"Simon and I," Csilla said quietly.

"Simon and you," Remy sneered. "You were assigned to watch him, Voss, not den mother his informants." He stood up and went to the window, peered through heavy drapes at the darkening street. "Wounded in service," he said with his back to Voss, "twice cited for meritorious service, recommended for Department Five by the deputy director himself . . ." He swung around. "What is it, Voss? Kwandri's air too thin for your blood?"

"You're one to talk," she said. Her nostrils were flared. "I don't need you to tell me how to run an op, Santoul. It's just that things have become . . . complicated since you left."

Remy positioned himself behind her. "It's what happens when agents go over, Voss." She turned in her chair to regard him. "Don't look at me like I'm virused. Jalak's gone over. I don't need to hear how or why, I just want to know what made it all right with you."

Csilla was silent for a moment. "I love him, Santoul."

Remy might have been able to think of a reply if the door tone hadn't sounded. Jalak stepped in, dropping his attaché and reaching for his pocket as the front room scene registered; but Remy's weapon was already out and raised to Jalak's face.

"And I got a hug from Els," he said, backing away until he had both of them in view. Jalak's beard and glasses were back. "Take it out slowly and lay it down on the floor, Jalak. Or'd the Manifest title you by now?"

"It's not what you think," Jalak told him, stooping to set the stunner down. He nudged it toward Remy with a foot.

"But then you don't know what I'm thinking, do you, Professor?" Remy said, pocketing the weapon along with his own.

Els returned from the kitchen a moment later with the tea. He placed the tray on the table and smiled at everyone. "Did you bring a wedding present, too?" he asked Remy.

Remy looked at the Kwandri, then back to Jalak and Csilla, whose hands reached for one another.

"That's right, Remy," Jalak said. "We're married."

Jalak went on to explain how the elder Els had performed the ceremony over a month ago in Tsegg Tsirran.

"It was wonderful," Csilla said, with a loving gaze for her husband. "Villagers from all over the plateau attended. Scent-summoners, artisans, divinators, so much incredible food . . . You should have seen it, Santoul."

The three of them were in Jalak's office by then, recorders switched off and noisemakers activated. Els was studying English in his room in the rear of the house.

"I know it runs contrary to everything in my file," Csilla continued. "But I knew from the moment I set foot downside that Q'aantre was the place I'd been dreaming of. After I got to know Simon, I realized I couldn't do what Ishida was asking. Not to someone who had Q'aantre's best interests in mind."

She read the disbelief in Remy's eyes. "You still don't understand, do you? I've wanted out for a long time, Santoul. I just didn't know how to go about it. But once Simon told me about NCorp's plan, I had all the justification I needed. I don't care what Center tries to do to me, I won't go back." She looked to Jalak. "Even after Simon confessed that he'd met with Colonel Gong, that he'd dirtied the operation, I couldn't bring myself to inform."

Never trust a gray-haired woman, Remy thought.

"It was the aphrodisiac, Remy," Jalak started to say.

"Simon," Csilla said, shaking her head in warning.

Jalak gave Csilla's hand a squeeze. "Why, what's he going to do—kill us?" He regarded Remy. "I don't think he will."

"The aphrodisiac," Remy said.

The culturist nodded. "I told you last time we were together in this office that you were asking me to violate the most basic of my principles. What's more, I could see you had no idea what NCorp meant to accomplish by introducing lube to Q'aantre. Are you familiar with the term?"

Remy said, "I've heard it tossed about, yeah."

"I'll admit I didn't even understand the full scope of the operation then, but I grasped enough to know that this world's very future was imperiled." Jalak's gray eyes met Remy's. "The Xell'em were my only hope. I thought if they could stop you from accomplishing whatever Center sent you to Dhone to initiate, that Q'aantre might be able to buy time." He shook his head. "In retrospect, I see how naive I was."

Remy snorted. "Your shortsightedness almost cost me my ass, Professor."

"I never meant for you to come to any harm, Remy. I mean, I suppose I knew they would take the most expedient course, but I forced the thought from my mind. It wasn't you, Remy. It was simply that you were the one sent to do the job."

Remy ran a hand through his hair. "So you told Gong we'd found a way to interface with the Kwandri on a biochemical level."

"I did. The colonel was quite impressed."

"How many times did you meet with him?"

"Three," Jalak said. "I'll swear to it, for what it's worth. They asked for the names of our agents, but I wouldn't furnish them with anything."

"Just mine."

"Yes," Jalak said quietly.

"And you didn't mention the aphrodisiac, the lube?"

"I told Gong that NCorp was mounting an operation to destabilize Xell'em influence with the Grand Assembly."

"Who else was present at the debriefings?"

"With the exception of the meet at the embassy, Gong and I met alone. That first time there was a woman officer named Mareer present. I haven't seen her since."

It sunk in like a smart secretion. *Mareer!* Remy thought, remembering the flayed remains of Kin and the Kwandri SPECVES lieutenant, Els Matut. Remy ventured that where they went Mareer had followed—including into that big hunting ground at the edge of the known cosmos . . .

"But none of this matters," Jalak was saying, "now that Ishida and Gong here have worked out the details of the transaction."

Remy watched him. "The full scope, as you say."

"Yes," Jalak said, returning the look.

"For Vanna, you mean," Remy said, deciding to take a chance.

Jalak and Voss traded glances. "Then you know."

"I know it's become the object of the game. But I'm still not clear what it is."

Jalak grew watchful again, then snorted. "Of course you do, Remy. It's possible you're subject zero when it comes to Vanna."

Remy waited.

"Remember when you first ordered me to spread the aphrodisiac around my network? You'd been making smart secretion pickups from Morli for what, two, three weeks already? And you were flying on the effects of those pickups. I can still recall your voice and the way you looked—wired, squint-eyed, hunched over. Strung out, as it was once called—*addicted*. Why? Because of what your lube had done to Morli's physiology. What the lube handed out by the operatives who have come in your wake has done to all the hapless people who've fallen under its so-called liberating intoxication."

"The secretions," Remy managed.

Jalak nodded grimly. "Lube is *enhanced* by its passage through a Q'aantre's system. It's empowered, if you will. And it's certainly the most addicting sexual euphorant to be unleashed on the Arm since direct stim. That's Vanna, Remy, in but one of its countless guises. It's like the vaginal libations that were so prized in old Earth magic, but *it works*.''

Remy felt his jaw drop.

''You were duped,'' Csilla said from across the room. ''We all were.'' She adopted the position Remy had taken with her earlier on, her voice behind his chair like an oracle's.

''The scent-gland extract was supposed to be used to secure intel data from Morli and his subs about Xella's activities in the Burst system. But in fact Xella *has* no operations planned for Burst. It never did. Densign has practically admitted as much. The scare was a fabrication, spread by Center itself and backed up by rumors about the system going accessible to the corps and private speculators. A way to misdirect everyone's attention from what was really going down on Q'aantre.''

Jalak left his desk to join Voss behind Remy's chair. ''NCorp must have known about the extract's effect on Q'aantre metabolism long before they had you run it on Morli. But maybe they weren't sure just how well those altered secretions were going to work on humans and God knows who else. That's where you came in. When they debriefed you upside and ran their scans, your own scrambled metabolism told them everything they wanted to know.

''But your body must have also alerted them to the fact that you couldn't be trusted to continue serving as a conduit for the extract. They were worried you were becoming a second Simon Jalak, and they saw themselves losing yet another of their officers to this world. You showed up on-station with a Q'aantre teenager; you talked about Morli as though he were a friend, not some agent you were running.''

''So they shipped you off to Dhone,'' Csilla said, ''and shuttled down a network of distributors and collectors.''

"The exec tech suits I've been seeing all over town," Remy said.

"That's them," Jalak affirmed. "They set up banks, complete with deposit and withdrawal accounts. All a Q'aantre has to do in exchange for lube is put in a quick stop at one of the Vanna banks and make a smart-secretion deposit."

Remy thought of the sentried back room at the Club Wet Spot. "There's no shortage of the extract, then. It was all a lie."

Jalak shrugged as he stepped into view. "Who knows? Maybe there was. Maybe TechSci has synthesized it by now."

Things were coalescing in Remy's mind with all the subtlety of a star system whirling itself into creation. Vanna white, Vanna red, Vanna black . . . The varieties were near countless because each and every Kwandri was a separate biochemical laboratory. It made him think of Earth's oyster-slurping bars of generations back.

He thought too about Lieutenant Els Matut's self-generated toxin, and what SPECVES-secreted Vanna must be like. It bogged the glands!

"No wonder Ishida wasn't concerned that you'd gone over," he said to Jalak. "I figured her estrogen level was depressed." He looked over his shoulder at Voss. "And she was probably thinking of herself as match-maker when it came to the two of you." He laughed. "I come up out of Dhone's well in one piece, so they have me returned here. But I'm not only compromised, but a goddamned cin-den idol in Likat."

Jalak cleared his throat. "Yes, we've, uh, seen some of the adverts. Ishida must have decided to compromise you further."

Remy stood up to pace the room, turning the revelations over in his mind. "But why?" he asked after a moment. "Just for some new addiction they could dump on the Arm? What's in it for Xu and the rest of the Xell'em downside?"

"Funds," Jalak said flatly. "And power. Think about NCorp, Remy. You're looking at an agency that can barely sustain itself on what the Consortium allocates to operations. You yourself said so. And I suspect the same holds true for Center's Xell'em equivalent. The war's over. There's no dire need for intelligence right now. But that doesn't mean Ishida and every NCorp officer like her is going to sit still while the agency is dismantled underneath them.

"No, with funding there are always ops to run and intrigues to fashion. And on Q'aantre—in Vanna— Ishida and Gong have found a well they can tap for the funds required to finance projects in a dozen other systems. They could go public with the NuYen Vanna will bring in."

"It isn't just Q'aantre anymore," Csilla interjected. "It's about secret alliances and unsanctioned penetrations. It's about destroying a culture just to keep yourself employed."

Remy tried to recall what he'd learned about Earth history's odd paring of governments and drugs: about heroin being introduced to offset morphine addiction after World War I; about the use of LSD for mind control; the smuggling of cocaine to fund covert operations . . .

He took a long hard look at Jalak and Voss. "You two are talking like this thing's already accomplished. But I'm not hearing it in your voices."

Csilla relaxed some. "Lube's secondary purpose was to quash the rebellion," Jalak began. "By keeping everyone in the movement so busy discovering their sexuality there'd be no time, no motivation, to stage a revolt. At the same time, Envoy Densign and Ambassador Xu quietly slip into positions of power.

"But there is an opposition. The same one that's been trying to minimize offworlder influence from the beginning, and the membership is increasing every day. They're searching for some way to present Q'aantre's case to the League. But first the Grand Assembly has to be convinced to rid itself of Densign, Xu, and the rest of these so-called advisers who have assumed control of Q'aantre's internal affairs.''

"How do we get to this group?" Remy asked.

Jalak swallowed and found his voice. "Most of them are my informants. Morli included.''

Remy laughed. "So you've finally learned how to run a network, Professor.''

Jalak blushed. "With Csilla's help.''

"Right now the Consortium is too pleased with NCorp's apparent success here to wonder how it came about,'' Csilla said. "But if the opposition can find a voice with the League . . . ''

"They will,'' Remy said, sure of himself. "Only it's up to us to show them how.''

Karine Mareer slid a hand into the hair at the nape of her neck and blanched as a huge tuft came loose between her quivering fingers. She removed her hand as delicately as she could, but the once-luxuriant clump continued to loosen of its own accord and dropped from the shoulder of her uniform to her lap, where it lay there like the tail of some small animal. Colonel Gong's slope of hairless brow furrowed as he regarded it, but he went right on speaking as though nothing had happened.

Karine wanted to scream.

And kill in ten thousand lingering ways the man who had brought the sudden hair loss about. The man responsible for the deaths of Kin and Els Matut, and the burn treatments she and Glasscock had undergone in Zalindi. The man who would surely have left the two of them to die of fluid loss or radiation poisoning if the fusion device hadn't killed them outright.

How well she could recall the flash, the evil wind, the hell she had inhaled that afternoon on the Lannsmar. The retreat to the city in the near-crippled land crawler, the smell of vomit in the front seat, the smell of illness and death clinging to all else. Glasscock at the controls, vacant-eyed, navigating by rote . . .

"And while I appreciate your desire for revenge," Gong was saying, "I cannot sanction what you ask at this time. We wish no problems with NCorp or Kwandri, and a political assassination of the sort you propose would only undo our hardwon alliance." He stared at the strands of hair in Karine's lap for a moment, and added, "I'm sorry, Major. For everything."

Major, she thought; her promotion, her reward. She tried to speak but coughed instead, feeling as though some fluid-filled sac had burst in her lungs. "But, Kin," she managed to say.

Gong was leaning as far from the desk as his chair would permit, certain she was about to launch a second blood-speckled spray in his direction.

"Major Kin afforded his life a noble end," he said finally. "His account has been credited and his name logged in our files. At any rate, Major, it is my understanding that Narca and her smugglers are more to blame for his death than the Terran."

Karine brushed the strands of hair from her lap as though they were hateful insects. "I can always attend to them later, Colonel. But Santoul is here, now, and who can say where he'll be reassigned tomorrow. And even if you choose to credit the Enddrese with the kills, there remains the matter of the Raliish double agent who was abducted by Santoul and tortured."

Gong made a dismissive motion with his left hand. "Fan'nat was a nuisance. Santoul did everyone a favor."

Karine fought to remain seated. She was tempted to fling a handful of her irradiated scalp across the desk into Gong's fatuous face. A *favor* indeed! "I want Santoul," she said firmly.

"And I repeat: You have no authorization." Gong glared at her with slightly crossed eyes, then softened his expression. "Are you aware, by the way, that Santoul is quite well known in the entertainment world? His filmworks are playing in quite a few theaters in Likat—''

''I want his balls!'' Karine screamed, making two upraised cups of her talon-fingernailed hands.

Gong showed her a disapproving look. ''Forget your grievances, Major. Regard your mission as an unqualified success: in your own small way you and Santoul have contributed to a much needed rapproachement between the Consortium and the Manifest.''

''But surely this isn't to be desired, Colonel.'' Her voice was pleading now, desperate.

''Perhaps not in the long run,'' he was willing to concede. ''But for a time, yes—for reasons I'm not at liberty to discuss. Favor me by attending the Grand Assembly meeting as my guest. It's still two weeks off and by then perhaps your, er, hair will have grown in.'' Gong cleared his throat. ''You'll see for yourself how wonderfully we're all getting along.''

Karine thought she could take out both of Gong's eyes if she lunged just then, but again she restrained herself. ''Can you at least promise me that the Terran murderer will attend?''

The colonel rubbed his nub of jaw. ''I can't promise, of course, but I could certainly arrange for an invitation to be forwarded through Santoul's superiors. Would that be enough?''

Karine resisted an urge to scratch her scalp and kept the grin limited to a tight smile. ''Yes, Colonel,'' she said after a moment. ''I just want to see him one last time. To thank him for helping to mend the wounds that have kept our worlds divided.''

EIGHTEEN—

Remy spent the next two weeks deciding where best to place the charges that would bring down the house NCorp had built on Kwandri. Ishida had him fluttered to gauge his reaction to the downside transformation, and while Remy initially believed he'd been successful in dazzling the neurometric instruments, the station chief was suddenly hinting that reassignment might be in order.

His countersuggestion was that he at least be allowed to serve out the role as DisneyCorp exec, if for no other reason than to keep his cover intact for future ops. Ishida saw no harm to it, but Phajol Dakou's suspicions had been aroused. Each evening when Remy returned to the hotel suite, he would find a message from the counsel waiting onscreen. Dakou's dark eyes narrowed, something sly about the set of his mouth as he asked, "Why those particular vid requisitions, Remy? Am I to take it you've grown self-infatuated, or is there perhaps some more righteous method to your madness?"

And each morning Remy would transmit the same message to the station: "It's true, Phajol, I can't seem to get enough of myself. There's something thrilling about being chased down the street by an adoring mob of scent seekers. Besides, what better way to keep in shape. As ever, Remy.''

He had begun by having the disk of *Bonnie and Clyde* dubbed. Copies of the flick were now showing in five different cin-dens in and around Likat.

Then he'd requested DisneyCorp to send down several other works featuring his donor-clone, under the pretext of studying the effectiveness of a vid festival to stimulate point-of-sale purchases of ersatz Terrana. He cited in particular the Beatty film *Shampoo*, which—what with its emphasis on haircare and personal adornment—might create a downside market for creme rinses, conditioners, fixatives, and the like. He offered up examples to reinforce the pitch—the current trend in coat coloring and laser-combing, for one—and as a result not only received the requested disks but an employment placement offer from a visiting DisneyCorp veep.

Within days Likat's cin-dens and odor theaters were inundated with his handpicked selection. In addition to little known classics like *The Parallax View* and *McCabe and Mrs. Miller*, there was *Splendor in the Grass* (retitled "A Q'aantre Tragedy"), *Reds* ("The Smell of Beets"), *Heaven Can Wait* ("*Tegganon* Can Wait"), and *Ishtar* ("Zaniness on Dry Land")—which audiences failed time and time again to comprehend.

Concurrently, without Ishida's knowledge, Remy began to make personal appearances.

As Warren Beatty.

Since the Kwandri were inclined to believe that vids showed life as it was really lived outside their small circle of cosmic space, Remy had an easy time convincing his audiences the flicks were more in the way of biographical pieces than works of art. So he would use a film like *Splendor in the Grass* to illustrate a point about the pitfalls of youth, or the dangers of wandering too far from tradition. Or he might use *McCabe* to discuss drug addiction, or *Shampoo* to discuss the problems associated with multiple sex partnerships. But he would always lead up to *Parallax View* to show how easily a being could be manipulated by evil forces, and *Reds* to demonstrate how even those evil forces could be overthrown.

Hardly what the Kwandri came expecting to hear. But they listened, and they sniffed, and they exhaled olfactory whisperings to one another while Remy delivered his messages from makeshift rostrums and hand-painted lecterns with built-in fans that wafted his NCorp-enhanced emanations into the crowd.

To drive home the point, he closed every appearance with a dimensionalized version of *King Kong*, hoping some would get the message that a fall from the tower was too great a price to pay for bright lights, big city.

By the end of the first week of the Warren Beatty festival and lecture series, incidents of Kwandri attacks on offworlder consulates, banks, and corp concerns had tripled and appreciated in strength.

And by the end of the second week, Simon Jalak's growing band of dissidents was ready to hear Remy out. Sort of.

"Please, quiet down!" Morli was shouting at the audience, backing the words up with stinging aromas Remy and a stage-frightened Els Nanff could smell from centerstage. "At least let him make his point."

"Why should we?" someone near the front returned. Remy recognized her as a former staff officer from SPECVES, many of whom had joined the rebel movement after the unexplained disappearance of Els Matut. "DisneyCorp is as responsible as any for this crisis!"

Remy winced. He realized now that it was probably a mistake to have had Morli introduce him as a rep from the 'Corp. NCorp was unknown to most Kwandri and DisneyCorp had apparently come to symbolize a primary source of the world's woes. Still, there were a few shouts of encouragement from the audience.

Billed as an ethnological forum hosted by Professor

Simon Jalak, the meeting was being held in a spacious but cold riverside theater. Jalak and Csilla Voss were also on stage, but well off to one side—where Remy wanted to be.

"It's true!" a second staffer echoed from the back. "Down with Disney Corp!" Several more were on their feet, overpowering Morli's exhalations with nidorous fumes of their own.

"We were told this would be a strategic meeting, Res Morli, not some excuse for further propagandizing!"

Morli turned a hopeless look Remy's way before attempting to answer the charge. "We *are* here to discuss strategies. If you'd only silence and deodorize yourself."

A dozen more stood up, raising fists in unison and directing some mordant scent toward the stage.

Morli adopted an imploring stance. "He isn't here to speak on DisneyCorp's behalf but Q'aantre's." He gestured to young Els Nanff. "He has one of our own with him."

"We can speak for ourselves, Res Morli!"

"We've nothing to learn from a country boy!"

Remy worked his jaw as he glanced around the room. The turnout was better than expected, but it suddenly seemed unlikely any good would come of it. Perhaps it had been a mistake as well to count on Els helping things along.

A burly male near the door aimed a finger center-stage. "I've already heard this Terran speak."

"Then you know I stand with you." Remy said into the antique mike before anyone could offer a follow-up.

"I know you speak in riddles," the Kwandri said, turning to those nearby. "He's a product of the system they've sent to ruin us. He wears the face of our enemies. He subverts our youth!"

"Lube is your enemy," Remy answered him. "Lube and what some of you have been donating in return."

"No one here!" a female said.

"Listen to him, then," Morli chimed in, "if you wish your world returned to you."

Gradually the crowd quieted. Remy's nasal passages began to dilate; he took a deep breath and inhaled aromatic scents of wariness commingled with receptivity. He exchanged smiles with Els.

"The way I smell it," he began, "the only way to stop the flow of lube and Vanna is to get rid of the advisers the Grand Assembly has placed in control in Q'aantre's affairs. But you're not going to accomplish that by continuing to single out banks and consulates with your stinkbombs."

"You'd have us silence our only voice, Terran?" someone asked.

"No. But your attacks are only giving the Assembly cause to entrust offworlders with the power to regulate civil law. The Assembly has become too frightened to listen to you any longer. Your government hears the stirrings of discontent, and it interprets these as the rumblings of revolt. Their next step will be to call for offworlder troops to protect the peace."

Remy paused. "You'll have no recourse but to resign yourself to the end of Q'aantre culture as you know it. One by one your traditions will crumble and fall. Your world will grow overpopulated, polluted, crime-ridden. The Consortium and the Manifest will offer you salvation in the form of League membership, but with that will come absorption into the homogeneous whole and a loss of the things you hold sacred." Remy gestured to his young friend. "Think of your future. Your children."

The crowd was growing restless. Remy picked up traces of the violent odors his previous public appearances had given rise to.

"To whom do we vent our anger if not to your embassies?" the burly Kwandri wanted to know. Others voiced similar demands.

"To the Assembly members themselves," Remy said.

"They must be convinced to order Xella and Terra off-world. They must be convinced of the fact that we off-worlders are no different than you are. That we don't have all the answers, and that we certainly have no rights to impose our culture on your world."

"But the membership looks up to you," a female thought to point out. "Half of Q'aantre would willingly surrender itself to Xella's or Terra's control. We are your . . . lessers."

The basement filled with sullen scents and no one spoke for a long while.

"Give us weapons we can hold to the Assembly members' heads," someone said at last. "We'll convince them." There were shouts and smells for and against the idea.

"There's a better way," Remy said, holding his hands aloft in a gesture of pacification. When everyone was quiet again, he added, "But the plan requires some of you to use lube one final time."

Karine Mareer's plan was a simple one: she meant to kill Remy Santoul. It was just the where and how she had yet to work out. She already had the when—during the Grand Assembly session slated for the day after next. Kwandri's top officials were expected to surrender control of the planet to a joint Xell'em/Terran council headed by Ambassador Xu and Envoy Densign. The day Remy Santoul would be surrendering his life to the woman he had nearly killed.

The *bald* woman, Karine thought as she regarded her image in the vanity screen.

She ran a hand back to front over her smooth scalp and let it pass down over her face to her mouth, where it became a white-knuckled fist muffling the scream lodged in her throat. No, her hair had not grown back as Colonel Gong suggested it might. In fact, it had begun to fall out in larger and larger clumps—collecting around her feet in the water shower like some undone bird's nest—until there was nothing left to do but shave it off entirely.

She leaned closer to the mirror's optical pickup, then upped the magnification so that she might inspect the tissue grafts on her face. Thankfully, these were hardly discernible now, except for a fingernail-size patch of slightly crinkled tissue over her left cheekbone, which cosmetics would conceal. But her lips looked as plump and perfect as they always had; her earlobes fell to just the right length on both sides; her nose retained its graceful outward curve. And her body looked fit, she decided, turning to admire the flat of her belly, the firm round swell of her breasts and buttocks, the power inherent in the smooth muscles of her long limbs.

With a wig, who would be the wiser? But even as she bent to scoop the hairpiece from its lifesize mannequin bust, she felt the fire return to her blood, and instead of donning the raven thing she hurled it across the room, where it struck the corridor door and slid noiselessly to the carpeted floor like some dead creature from Dhone's nuked grasslands.

Which Karine felt herself to be.

The embassy cosmetologist had promised that given a week's time he would be able to seed her scalp and return her hair; but she understood that this would mean nothing unless done in celebration of Santoul's death.

Despite Colonel Gong's beliefs to the contrary, Karine was convinced that Santoul had been apprised of her mission long before he had lured her and Glasscock and the rest to the circular grave his fusion device had carved out for them in the Lannsmar. At the very least, the Terran had tortured the truth from the Raliish agent, Fan'nat. She was more inclined to think that Simon Jalak had delivered false information from the start. But what could she have done to Santoul that had aroused such venomous designs against her?

Karine was certain now that she had seen him on several occasions before Dhone. Sessions with the hypnotherapist onstation revealed that Santoul had actually been *following her* for at least a standard-week prior to his departure. So why hadn't he made an attempt on her life then? Why arrange for such a tedious journey and hideous death unless deep in Santoul's mind there festered some wound from long ago.

And from just how long ago? she had been asking herself. She didn't think they had crossed paths during the war; but then could she really be sure of anything anymore?

She found it a comforting thought, though, that Santoul had experienced for perhaps years what she had come to feel these past weeks. It gave them something profound in common; more than the tenuous bond Gong had held forth as a kind of rationale for the sufferings she had endured at Santoul's hands.

But as much as she desired to nurse a sadomasochistic delight from imaginings of Santoul's unknown wound, the compulsion to avenge herself was overpowering. And, with this in mind, she had begun to case the Assembly hall for potential kill zones as soon as sources assured her that Santoul would be attending the occasion.

As a DisneyCorp rep.

On this historic occasion.

And she had decided in the end to take him out in the very fashion that had failed on Dhone—using the literally hand-held Kwandri-exuded toxin. Only this time she planned to wear it herself . . . To approach tactile-enhanced Remy Santoul boldly in the welcome line, extend a broad smile and a poison-smeared gloved hand to him, and say in her best English: *How wonderful to see you again, Mr. Santoul.*

NINETEEN —

"How wonderful to see you again, Remy," Norak Baj said, emerging from the crowd on the Assembly hall steps with his arms open.

Remy eliminated all possibilities of a ritual testicle grasp by stepping into Baj's embrace, bending way over to exchange claps on the back with the Kwandri.

"I haven't seen much of you these past two weeks," Baj said, stepping back, but keeping Remy within reach. "Up close, that is. But word has it that you've been seen all over Likat promoting your, uh, your donor's films." He showed a paternal grin. "So you enjoy being the idol."

"Stardom has it privileges," Remy said.

"Assuredly so." Baj scanned the noisy thousands pressed behind police cordons at the foot of the stairs. "Who would have dreamed that so many would attend. And to demonstrate *support* for the Grand Assembly's decision . . . Well, it's certainly more than I expected."

"And what was that, Norak?"

Baj sniffed. "Billowings of disapproval, at the very least. Rage, violence, explosive displays. Note the number of police units in attendance. It's apparent the Assembly members had similar misgivings."

Remy tugged at the sleeves of his tunic jacket while he searched for familiar faces. He caught sight of Morli and a dozen other dissidents about midway down the staircase, positioned either side of the carpet that ran from the hall's columned entryway to the street.

"Even Res Morli is here," Baj said in a private voice. "Are you aware that he resigned the ministry? Imagine abandoning a post that took one into space—up the well, as you say. What I would give for such an opportunity." He paused for a moment of reverie. "But you know, Remy, I'm doubly surprised to see him here. What with all the rumors."

Baj was conspiratorial now, leaning into Remy's space. Remy said, "About the rebel movement, you mean."

"Exactly. And yet, here, around me are some twenty faces I thought would be the last to welcome offworlders into the Assembly." Baj sighed and exhaled wonderment. "I am twenty times surprised—and somewhat confused, I'll admit."

"Maybe it's just the good weather that brought them out."

"That might well be," Baj said, indulging in a deep breath. "It seems that spring has come early this year."

Remy excused himself when he saw the first of the Terran Mission limos complete its wide swing into the square and motor slowly through the crowd, answering all the cheering, the hand and flag waving with short bursts of horn and siren.

The crowd parted to accommodate the limo as it neared the base of the hall's broad staircase, but hundreds of hands continued to stroke and pat it on all sides. Mothers held their children in outstretched arms; old men raised canes and crutches; everyone proffered exhalations of exuberance and enthusiasm.

Three other vehicles followed the lead limo into the

square, and even as these were discharging their resplendent passengers, the Xell'em motorcade was arriving from the opposite direction. Kwandri leaned from the windows of buildings across the square to wave or dust the convoy with confetti and scraps of paper.

Densign's staffers were beginning to ascend the steps, the men offering fixed smiles and noble gestures to the onlookers, the high-heeled women bunching long gowns to one side, concerned more about remaining upright for the duration of the climb than anything else.

But the envoy himself was lingering behind, probably waiting for Ambassador Xu to arrive, Remy decided. He pictured the two of them walking up the stairs together arm in arm, proud of the separate peace they had forged. Disregarding that it had been achieved at Kwandri's expense.

Remy edged forward through the crowd to get a better look at his fellow planetmates as they filed into the hall.

Morli and his people were offering their hands. And the unwitting Terrans were accepting them.

Morli realized that he was bouncing up and down on his feet, but he couldn't help himself. The lube was coursing through him like a hot river and it was all he could do to stay rooted to one spot on the steps. Ayyum Matut—younger sister of the disappeared SPECVES lieutenant—was alongside him, under the lube as well; and every so often their elbows, hips, shoulders, or knees would make contact and Morli would go rigid from sheer physical charge.

Not that parts of him weren't already rigid. And from the way Ayyum Matut was looking at him, it was plain that the sexual circuit wasn't operating unidirectionally.

Morli observed the same look on the faces of his male and female colleagues on both sides of the plush runner someone in the Assembly had ordered pulled from storage for the occasion. Directly across from him on the steps, Norak Kaz was actually grinding himself against Els Seff's backside as he reached over his shoulders to stroke the face of one of the Terran Mission staffers.

Well, maybe it was Els Seff who was rubbing himself against Norak Kaz, Morli thought. Heaven knew he was more than ready to tear off his clothes and let the tall and shapely Ayyum have her way with him right where they stood.

Fortunately, the people around them—the ones willing to give Q'aantre away for a lube job—were too engrossed in the task of scenting, flag waving, and well wishing to pay much mind to the inexplicable writhings of a few individuals; although Morli was certain that the *Tegganon*-laden atmosphere was going to get to everyone soon enough.

Perhaps just about the time the Vanna would kick in for the offworlders.

Not a Terran staffer had escaped the curious gauntlet Morli and the rest had set in their path. The women had been stroked on hands and bare arms, on faces and slim necks exposed under upswept hairstyles; and while the men's dress jackets had provided the Q'aantre with fewer surface target areas, there were still hands to grab, depilated cheeks and jaws to touch, ample zones for contact.

The Xell'em climbing the stairs now presented a different set of problems, because of the cumbersome costumes they affected. The Xell'em weren't as comfortable about being touched as the Terrans were. Morli, nevertheless, had already managed to lay a hand on more than his share of Manifest legation flesh, squeezing a thigh here, a breast there.

Vanna Res, Vanna Norak, Vanna Els, Vanna Ayyum . . . the offworlders were getting a taste of the range of flavors and colors.

Q'aantre's last stand, Morli had time to think. And should the day end in victory, the world would have

Remy Santoul to thank for a large part of it. He had
glimpsed the Earther earlier on the top of the staircase,
but Remy had since moved off. Morli still didn't know
what to make of the man; it was as though he had decided to make Q'aantre a personal crusade.

But better enigmatic Terrans like Remy Santoul than
the Envoy Densign, who was coming up the stairs arm
in arm with the Xell'em Xu. Densign, this strange-
looking human Santoul said was modeled after an Earth
leader of generations ago. It was difficult for even Morli
to understand how one like Densign could rise to power.
But then who could comprehend the bizarre nature of
human culture. A mere brush pass with it and Q'aantre
had been nearly tipped out of orbit.

With this in mind, Morli reached over the cordon of
uniformed arms that contained the stairway crowd and
extended a quavering hand to the envoy.

"Mr. Densign, Mr. Densign," he shouted, mimicking the almost craving tone of his neighbors.

The Terran, head lowered and close-set eyes peering
from beneath beetled brows, was busy fending off a
dozen hands; but Morli knew he had him as soon as
their eyes met. Densign collapsed the upraised V-
formation he had made of his right hand and offered it
to the insistent Q'aantre straining at the cordon.

Morli held on to the clammy hand for a good six
steps, while someone did the same with Ambassador
Xu.

There were only the last-minute arrivals to attend to,
he saw as he backed himself into the crowd, military
officials like Colonel Gong and the statuesque woman
officer Morli recognized as Karine Mareer.

Karine had had no trouble picking him out from the
crowd at the top of the stairs—the full head of brown
waves, the wide mouth, the handsome symmetrical features, the straight teeth that near glinted in the afternoon light. But now she had lost him. And fallen in

behind Densign and Xu, who were taking their own
sweet time about entering the hall.

To add to the frustration, it seemed that every Kwandri she passed was dying to lay hands on her. Already
she'd been nudged, squeezed, fondled, kissed, embraced, poked, and prodded, and she was beginning to
wonder whether she would even make it to the top with
her costume of wristlets, pectorals, and belts intact.
Fearing that someone was going to make a grab for her
hair, she had planted one hand firmly atop the wig; but
that of course had only given the Kwandri free access
to her underarm and the whole of her left breast.

Karine could well understand how the creatures were
overjoyed at the prospect of surrendering their petty
planet to offworlder rule; but the Kwandri were display-
ing something more than simple *enthusiasm*. Especially
those pressed against each other midway along the steps,
leaning in at her from both sides with hungry expressions and cloying breath. Had she not known better,
she would have sworn there was a *sexual* component to
all the crazed gesticulations and desperate lungings.

The one part of her she couldn't offer them, however,
was the gloved hand at her corseted breast, the one
impregnated with toxin and reserved for Remy Santoul.

She knew she would find him inside the hall, and
could see him there: standing at the rear of the gallery
while the members of both legations settled themselves
behind the curve of tables the Kwandri had erected.

As she rehearsed the planned greeting line a smile
played about her lips, which the spectators read as a
sign to resume their pawings.

Her bare skin was tingling strangely by the time she
reached the hall's columned entrance.

Remy checked his watch. Ten minutes had passed
since the first of the handshakes; that left no more than
five before the Vanna came on. The gallery was still
filling, but most of the offworlder legation seats were

occupied. Remy calculated that with a bit of old-fashioned luck the onset of the sexual euphorant would coincide with Envoy Densign's introductory remarks.

He and Xu were at the center of the table, with Xu's wife seated between them. On either side of the trio sat a mix of Xell'em, Terran, and Kwandri.

Remy and Morli stood in the rear of the hall among a group of rebels who could barely keep their hands off one another, and were receiving a slew of disapproving stares and angry remarks as a result.

"Show some respect for our guests," one indignant Assembly member directed to the group as he was entering the hall. Laughter and a dozen invitations to join the fun sent him hurrying off to his seat.

"How long, Remy?" Morli asked in an anxious voice.

"Three minutes, Res."

Down front, the Assembly speaker was calling for quiet. Densign gave it a moment and rose slowly to his feet, milking the applause. He wedged a finger into the collar of his shirt, took a sip of water, and cleared his throat.

Somewhere in the balcony above, Csilla Voss had her camera running.

"First," the envoy began, "let me just say how proud I am to be a part of this historic occasion." Densign radiated sincerity, jowls quivering as he shook his head for emphasis. "You know, when I was a boy—and I *was* a boy once upon a time—I always believed that our society would reach a point where it would be able to offer only its breast, er, its best to the emerging worlds of the near group. And now it's time to come—uh, now the time has come to join glands—*hands!*—with the Xell'em to lick the Kwandrian shaft—to speak in Kwandri's behalf!"

Remy fought back a grin and studied his hands. When he looked up, Densign was reaching for the water again. A confused murmuring swept through the gallery as the membership tried to make some sense of the envoy's translated statement.

"What I mean to say," Densign began again, "is that Ambassador Xu and I would like to get it on, would like to get on with it, would like to get this mating under way, this meeting under way with a few words from Madame Xu—who, may I say, has *about the nicest set of melons I've ever seen.*"

The gallery went dead still.

But instead of raking a hand across Densign's face, Xu's wife tittered. She playfully wiggled her ample bosom in the envoy's face as she stood up, sniffling, narrow-eyed, and hunched over.

"I want to thank Mr. Densign for the compliment," she told the audience. "And I'd like to say in return that I have long been an admirer of the envoy . . . and of his staff as well."

"And what a stiff staff it is!" someone said, eliciting laughs from the rest of the legation table.

Ambassador Xu, meanwhile, was whispering to the Earther beside him, whose hands were busy doing something beneath the table. Farther down the line couples were beginning to explore one another. A few were already lip-locked in passionate embraces; others were tossing items of clothing into the gallery.

The Kwandri speaker was trying to call for order.

Madame Xu shrugged out of her top and lifted a bent leg to the tabletop. A wary-eyed Densign fumbled with the fasteners that secured her shoe and commenced going down on her painted toes.

"This is an outrage!" the voice of a rebel rang out above all the others raised in protest and outright disgust. "Is this what we want to become?"

The offworlders were too preoccupied to notice. Portions of the table had been swept clean of monitors, mikes, and hardcopy to accommodate the more horizontally inclined. Some squirmed face to face or front to back in chairs and on the hall's cool floor. Densign was slavering over Madame Xu's knee, both hands raised in victory signs.

"Get them out of here!" someone screamed.

"They're animals, *animals*!" said another.

"We're better than this!" from a third.

"Animals!"

"Hose 'em down!" Remy added from the rear, hiding his mouth with a hand.

Morli took hold of Remy's upper arm. "We've done it, Remy, we've done it," he rasped.

Remy smiled down at his friend, even as his flesh began to tingle.

Several police units had burst into the hall, but were making no attempt to approach the writhing piles of bodies on the floor and tabletops. A dozen uniformed Kwandri stood a safe distance away, studying the various entanglements with perplexed and lopsided expressions. Moans and exclamations of deep-seated pleasure issued from the PA systems as the legation strived for a collective orgasm.

The musky redolence was simply more than most of the audience could absorb and many were heading for the streets. Remy, figuring his work was done, was just about to join the mass exodus when he spotted a Xell'em woman staggering toward him, one gloved hand raised in a kind of claw as she fought her way through a rush of Kwandri moving in a perpendicular direction.

It took Remy a few seconds to recognize her because the hair was all wrong—in fact, it appeared *askew*—but there was no mistaking Karine Mareer's cheekbones, even under the snarl she wore, nor the purpose of that upraised clawhand.

He didn't have time to marvel that she was alive.

Principally because Mareer was suddenly on him like a storm and driving him back into an unyielding throng of Assembly members bottlenecked at one of the doorways. Remy had had the presence of mind to grab hold of the wrist of the lethal hand, but Mareer was lightning fast with the other.

They performed a kind of ragged ballroom dance, careening from bottleneck to wall and back again, right hands uplifted in mutual salute while their lefts flailed for purchase.

Karine's lips were curled back from filed teeth, her hot breath was in Remy's face; but there was something besides bloodlust in her speckled eyes. Remy realized what it was and grinned, feeling a sudden sexual charge from Morli's inadvertent caress.

Mareer was Vannaed.

"I want you," he said to her in his best bedroom voice, the back of his left hand pressed against her breast. "I want you more than any woman I've ever known."

He felt a shudder pass through her, saw her eyelids flutter and almost close. But just as quickly the murderous intent reasserted itself and the gloved hand swung down past his face.

They were crossarmed now, like square-dance partners who had somehow missed a follow-up call. Remy pitted all his strength against her and leaned in to nuzzle her neck. She went slack for a moment, then snapped at his ear and drove her knee into his groin.

He sucked in the pain and trapped her knee between his thighs, sent her crashing down to the floor amid a group of panicked Kwandri, Remy on top, arms still between them.

Remy leaned in once again only to find that Mareer's hair had somehow *slipped down over her face!* He pulled away, but the wig was snared on his teeth and came with him.

Desperate, he let go of the Xell'em's left hand, providing Mareer with all the leverage she needed. She reversed the hold and sat up, straddling him groin to groin, her bent knees tight against his sides.

Remy whipped his arms over his head and she came

down on him, breasts flattening against his chest. He heaved his hips and she followed him, again and again.

And before long their thrusting movements found some unsought cadence. Mareer was panting in his ear: ''I want you, I hate you, I want you, I hate you . . .''

A moan that began way down inside her was gradually working its way into her throat. Remy's balls had something of their own to contribute. Mareer's moan emerged a minute later as a stuttering scream of ecstasy.

Remy joined her.

They were looking into each other's eyes when they came.

Remy felt all the strength pump out of him, and barely sensed the gloved hand as it came down square on his face.

He had a fleeting image of a bald-headed woman scurrying off into the Kwandri crowd on hands and knees before his body surrendered to the poison and darkness prevailed.

TWENTY—

FACES ORBITED IN THE BLACKNESS—JALAK,
Csilla, Els Nanff, and Res Morli—each a separate station, circling, circling . . . Kwandri pursuing him in
sleep. Remy thought he might be dreaming until scents
of concern and expectation began to excite his nose.

He closed his eyes, fell back into darkness for an
indeterminate time, then awoke: sore and out of sorts,
but focused. He didn't recognize the room.

"Drink this," Jalak said, forcing a glass of bitter-
tasting liquid on him.

Els Nanff edged closer to the hard bed to stroke his
shoulder. He was wearing the Citi ring Remy had given
him.

"Remy," he murmured, emanating relief. Csilla
urged the boy away after a moment and sent him out of
the room.

"I've been here before," Remy said, raising himself
on elbows.

Jalak shook his head. "No you haven't. We're across
the river—"

"No, I mean I know what happened to me."

Jalak traded looks with his wife and Morli. "You
do?"

241

"A SPECVES agent-generated toxin."

"That's right," Jalak said, astonished. "But how—"

Remy held up a hand. "Just tell me how long I've been out this time."

Csilla said, "Two days. We took you directly from the Assembly hall to the clinic, but no one knew what to make of your condition." She indicated Morli. "Then when Res learned about the attempt on your life, he brought over an ex-SPECVES lieutenant, who conjured a smart-secretion antidote."

Jalak noted Remy's puzzled expression, and added, "You don't want to know how he administered it, Remy."

"What about Mareer?" Remy asked after a moment.

Csilla tightened her lips. "No word on where she ended up. Ishida and Colonel Gong have people scouring Likat for her, but the rumor is she shipped out of Dazyl on an Enddrese freighter bound for Daleth."

She must have been with Glasscock when the BFD blew, Remy surmised. He shuddered, remembering their few minutes of near-death sexplay on the Assembly hall floor. Morli was regarding him curiously.

"Inasmuch as you assisted us, I can understand why the Manifest might sanction your assassination, Remy," the Kwandri said. "But Karine Mareer's sudden disappearance is most mysterious. Could there have been some personal motivation?"

Remy managed a shrug. "Maybe she doesn't like Warren Beatty flicks."

Jalak quirked a smile. "I only wish you could have witnessed the look on Densign's face when the Vanna wore off. He and Madame Xu . . ." The culturist blushed. "Well, let's just say they were rather uniquely positioned."

"Along with Xu and the rest of them." Csilla laughed into her hand. "I don't think I've ever seen a thirty-person coupling before. You'll have to view the recordings when you're feeling up to it."

Jalak showed Csilla a disapproving look. "The Grand Assembly appealed to the Enddrese consulate to put Q'aantre in communication with the League. Then Densign, Xu, and their staffers were ordered offworld. The Assembly threatened to display Csilla's recordings to the League if there was any argument. As it is, an investigative team is due to arrive any day. Until they render their decision, Q'aantre has been designated off-limits to all but a few private corps."

"The Vanna banks have been closed," Morli said. "The cin-dens also."

"Must be a lot of disappointed people around," Remy said, thinking of Norak Baj and others. Morli fingered the fur at his neck. Remy could smell his ambivalence.

"The vid closings are only temporary," the Kwandri explained. "The Grand Assembly needs to come to some decision about DisneyCorp's continued presence downside."

"Trade will eventually resume," Jalak added confidently. "But the mistake won't be repeated." He looked over at Morli. "Especially under the enlightened leadership of the Assembly's new president."

Remy's eyes sparkled. "Res—"

Morli made a dismissive, humbling gesture. "It's only a possibility. There has to be a vote, a referendum . . ."

"He's a shoe-in," Csilla whispered theatrically.

Everyone laughed.

"Any, uh, word from my boss?" Remy asked Csilla. The former NCorp operative's smile faded.

"That's one of the reasons we're across the river and not at Simon's house, Remy. Seems your supervisors have been putting two and two together. They know about the flickdisk requisitions and the personal appearances."

"You mean I'm going to be fired."

Csilla held his gaze. "*Terminated*, yes. And I don't figure Xella's going to forgive and forget, either."

Remy comprehended the meaning. "Fuck," he said softly.

"There's no need for you to return to DisneyCorp's employ, Remy," Morli said quickly. "Q'aantre would be honored to afford you citizen status."

"Thanks, Res," Remy said absently. "Any chance I can get offworld," he asked Jalak, "if I decide not to take Res up on his kind offer?"

The culturist nodded. "I've done some asking around. I believe you know a man named Vegas."

"I know him."

"He tells me that arrangements can be made to have you smuggled out of system. The cost is somewhat staggering, but I think we can manage it. Though you'll have to be content with returning to Dhone."

Remy hung his head and uttered a sardonic laugh. This is your work, Jaz, he told himself. I know you're behind it. "What the hell," he said, looking up. "I've got unfinished business there, anyway."

"That's a yes, then?" Jalak asked.

Remy nodded. Back to basics.

Morli looked disappointed. "I'll be sorry to see you leave again, Remy. And I won't be alone."

Remy gripped the Kwandri's furred forearm. "I'll be sorry to go."

"Well," Jalak announced in a determined voice, "Csilla and I better see to those arrangements." Voss leaned in with a kiss on the cheek before she followed her husband out.

"I'll be going, too," Morli said, twitching his nose, "but I'll stop back to see you this evening."

"Take care, Res," Remy told him.

Morli turned around at the door. "I meant to mention, Remy, that I've been familiarizing myself with old Earth history. I have a question about two of your homeworld's life-forms, if you'll indulge me."

"Go to," Remy said.

Morli stroked his chin. "Let me see if I can remember . . . Oh, yes, that's it. What's the difference between a human being and a gorilla?"

"A hu-" Remy narrowed his eyes. "You tell me, Res, what's the difference."

Morli exhaled a proud fragrance. "The ape's the one with the finer coat."

Remy was still laughing when the door closed.

About the Author

JAMES LUCENO has made ends meet as a rock musician, general contractor, astrologer, travel consultant, scriptwriter, and pseudonymous coauthor of a bestselling mega-space opera series.

His first novel, *Headhunters*, was published in 1980; followed after a long hiatus by *Rio Pasión* and *Rainchaser* (both published by Ivy Books) and *A Fearful Symmetry* (published by Del Rey Books).

He resides, with his two children, in New York.

DONALD MOFFITT'S
SCIENCE FICTION

IS OUT OF THIS
WORLD